PRAISE FOR PAMELA CHRISTIE AND
DEATH AND THE COURTESAN

"What a delicious and delightful tale! The Regency world is turned upside down—and much refreshed—by a decidedly unorthodox heroine. Pamela Christie writes with wit and verve, gifting readers with a vision of the period at once marvelously scandalous and oh-so tempting. I adore clever, spunky Arabella and look forward to her future adventures."
—Sara Poole, author of *The Borgia Mistress*

"Channel your inner Jane Austen and mix with a dash of the Happy Hooker (wink, wink) for a pleasingly witty and light debut. It's leisurely paced, laced with narrator asides, and plot-assisted by diary entries. All in all, very PG and what romance readers might call 'sweet.' "
—*Library Journal*

"A clever, funny, engaging read reminiscent of Fidelis Morgan's *Unnatural Fire*. Pamela Christie deftly combines the conventions of the Regency-era novel with the fast pace and careful attention to characterization found in the best modern historical mysteries."
—Kate Emerson, author of *The King's Damsel*

"Historical mystery gets a sexy twist in Pamela Christie's *Death and the Courtesan*. This is a quirky, tongue-in-cheek story of a 'scandalous' courtesan and would-be detective that will make you laugh, and the twists will keep you guessing."
—*The Parkersburg News and Sentinel*

Please turn the page for more rave reviews!

DEATH AMONG
THE RUINS

Books by Pamela Christie

DEATH AND THE COURTESAN

DEATH AMONG THE RUINS

Published by Kensington Publishing Corporation

Death Among the Ruins

Pamela Christie

KENSINGTON BOOKS are published by

Kensington Publishing Corp.
119 West 40th Street
New York, NY 10018

All Kensington titles, imprints, and distributed lines are available at special quantity discounts for bulk purchases for sales promotion, premiums, fund-raising, educational, or institutional use.

Special book excerpts or customized printings can also be created to fit specific needs. For details, write or phone the office of the Kensington Special Sales Manager: Kensington Publishing Corp., 119 West 40th Street, New York, NY 10018. Attn. Special Sales Department. Phone: 1-800-221-2647.

Kensington and the K logo Reg. U.S. Pat. & TM Off.

ISBN-13: 978-0-7582-8642-0
ISBN-10: 0-7582-8642-2
First Kensington Trade Paperback Printing: March 2014

eISBN-13: 978-0-7582-8643-7
eISBN-10: 0-7582-8643-0
First Kensington Electronic Edition: March 2014

10 9 8 7 6 5 4 3 2 1

Printed in the United States of America

To VANESSA PEPOY,

for technological acumen
and for friendship beyond value,
this book is warmly dedicated.

DEATH AMONG THE RUINS

ONE GOD; TWO HORNS

"Well," said Belinda, "you have not sought my opinion, but I think he would look remarkably fearsome emerging from the shrubbery, all hard and excited. From that vantage point, anyone sitting in the pergola might imagine herself about to be ravished."

"Perhaps," replied Arabella, pensively. "All the same, I believe I shall place him on a pedestal, in the center of the reflecting pool."

The Beaumont sisters were poring over a letter, and admiring the sender's enclosed sketch of an ancient bronze. This, the letter asserted modestly, was only a crude portrait of the magnificent statue that had been recently discovered in the bowels of Herculaneum, an Italian city buried centuries earlier in a volcanic eruption. The author of the letter and the artist of the sketch were one and the same: a dealer in plundered antiquities who gratefully acknowledged receipt of the full purchase price.

"The workmen will have to tunnel in and bring it out, you see," Arabella explained. "And the removal will be extremely dangerous, because of cave-ins and poisonous gas pockets. I expect that is why I was charged so much for it."

"Well, for that," said Belinda, "and for the extra bit."

They studied the picture again. Arabella, who always liked to examine certain features in the best possible light, was using the magnifier.

"Yes," she said. "I have seen hundreds, if not thousands of statues depicting naked manhood, Bunny, but this is the first I have ever beheld with *two* manhoods."

"Hmm . . ." mused Belinda. "That short, slender one on top, and then the longer, thicker one beneath it . . . whatever must the sculptor have been thinking?"

"Oh, come now; you know very well what he was thinking! And once I install this piece in my garden, everyone else will be thinking it, too. Yes," she said with a sigh, "you are probably right; I expect I *have* been charged more for the extra bit. And because the piece is so old," she added, "and extremely beautiful."

". . . And because you are rich," finished Belinda. "All the same, something about this does not feel quite right. Oughtn't the statue to stay in the ground, with its dead owner? I mean, it is a kind of memorial now, is it not?"

Arabella put down the magnifier. "I wish you would not be so morbid, Bunny. The owner may very well have escaped the cataclysm, you know, and died years later, in Tarraconensis or someplace. Besides, this is *Pan!* Pan, in an amorous attitude! A *doubly* amorous attitude! Even if the owner *did* suffocate at home, what sort of memorial would that be?"

"I don't know—a memorial to the perpetually stiff, perhaps."

Peals of girlish laughter flowed out through the library door and along the passage, where the peerless Doyle was headed upstairs with an armful of freshly ironed flannel nightgowns, and the incomparable Fielding was toting a load of wood to the drawing room fireplace. It was autumn, and the nights were chilly now. So were the days, for the matter of that, and the one currently drawing to its close had pulled a thick mist over Brompton Park like a new shroud; all of a piece, without any holes, yet fitting so closely as to reveal the sharper angles of the trees and houses beneath it.

Arabella loved this season. The rich smell of the woods in Regent's Park gladdened her heart when she took her walks there, the flame-colored leaves bringing out the deep auburn tones of her hair. She enjoyed reading by the fire, with a quilt thrown over her legs, and few events could so reliably elevate her spirits like donning a fur-lined, fur-trimmed pelisse before stepping into her carriage on her way to the theater. Most of all, though, she loved what autumn did to men—the way it made them want to snuggle up next to some warm female body and reward the owner of said body for favors bestowed. Gentlemen of her acquaintance were apt to be especially generous in the autumn.

The Duke of Glen*deen,* for example, her own particular protector when he wasn't off fighting naval battles, had just presented her with six magnificent horses of a most unusual color. Hides like golden toast they had, with black manes and tails. Three of them, anyway. The other three were cream-colored, but they, too, had the dark manes and tails. Arabella had started a regular trend in carriage horses with these beauties: three each of two complementary colors, as opposed to the more traditional, perfectly matched sets. The idea was very new and widely imitated. And all she had done was to murmur one morning, as she and the duke lay together after a particularly vigorous quarter of an hour, that her carriage horses were tiring more easily, now that they were older. Puddles was always a generous patron—Arabella never wanted for anything—but *six* horses! And it wasn't even her birthday! Yes, she adored the autumn.

Belinda did, too. But then, Belinda loved all the seasons, as she loved the whole world, being by nature a happy, tender, appreciative creature. The poor child was a trifle morose this evening, however, for the capricious princess regent had abruptly terminated their friendship without giving a reason, and Arabella had shewn her sister the sketch of the naughty statue to cheer her up. It had worked for a few minutes, but now that Belinda had seen it, enjoyed a laugh over it, and offered her opinion on where to put it, she was wistful again.

"I should be glad this has happened, I know; the woman is selfish and vulgar, and I am well rid of her."

"Yes, you are! Only consider," said Arabella. "What was the princess wearing, the last time that you saw her?"

"Oh! A profusion of colors, which jumped and clashed together like I do not know what, covered by an ill-fitting spencer of lilac satin! Her gown was cut so low that the tops of her nipples were exposed! I cannot recall the rest."

"Not even her shoes?"

"Oh, yes! Half boots! Primrose-yellow ones, with the flesh of her fat legs hanging over the tops, and a cap like a pudding bag—with the pudding still in it!"

"Wait a bit," cried Arabella. "Shakespeare has described that very thing!"

She opened *The Taming of the Shrew*, which she was reading for the fourth or fifth time, and leafed through it till she found Petrucchio's scene with the haberdasher.

"A custard coffin!" she said triumphantly. "One would think the bard was describing modern apparel! How ever does he *do* that?"

But Belinda, briefly revived by the amusing memory, had grown listless again. "I was hoping that the princess would introduce me to someone I might marry—I do so hate being a burden on you, Bell!"

"You could not possibly be a burden, dear! You are a wonderful, darling companion, and the longer you stay with me, the better I shall be pleased."

"Truly? Oh, I am glad *somebody* wants my company. Because it *is* humiliating to be dropped, even by a person as horrid as the Wolfen Buttock!" (This was the Beaumonts' private nickname for the princess, whose title before her marriage was Caroline of Brunswick-Wolfenbüttel.)

"Of course it is humiliating, Bunny. But you must try to forget about it. Because Lord Carrington is on the brink of proposing to you, and you need to look as pink-cheeked and sparkling-eyed as you possibly can, for him."

Belinda smiled at this, and there stole across her countenance such an expression of dreamy contentment that it did her sister's heart good to see it. But Bunny's heavenward gaze was interrupted in its journey up the library wall by the portrait of Oliver Wedge that hung there, and her smile faded.

"Bell," she said. "I own I do not understand why you keep that thing!"

Arabella regarded the picture with wistful affection.

"For three good reasons and one foolish one: as the last bequest of a condemned man, as a warning not to trust in surface appearances, and as a reminder to believe in myself—to recall that I may, with application, accomplish miracles."

"With application . . . and *my* assistance, d'you mean?"

"Of course, Bunny! I should never have tried to save myself from the gallows, but for your urging!"

"And the fourth reason?"

Arabella rose and began to pace the room. "You have just had the three good ones. Can you not be satisfied with those?"

"No! I want the foolish one, as well!"

Arabella sighed with feigned reluctance—for really, she was all eagerness to tell it. "Because," said she, stopping beneath the portrait, and gazing up at it, "he was the best lover I have ever had, or am ever likely to have."

"Oh, Bell; how can you say so? With only one encounter, on an untidy desktop? It was probably just the danger that somebody might walk in upon you."

"Pooh! I should not have cared if they had! But there is something in what you say: the danger." She glanced out her window at the misty garden. "When . . . he was strangling me, I was certain I should die. But when he stopped, just for a moment, I felt . . . as though . . . I wanted to have his child."

Belinda was shocked to the core. "That is the most perverted statement I have ever heard you utter!"

"I know. As I said, it was only for a moment. The feeling passed. But the memory of the feeling haunts me still."

"Some people are addicted to danger," said Belinda. "They seek it out, because it gives them a kind of thrill not otherwise obtainable. I truly hope that you are not one of those people—they have a tendency to die years before their time."

"Me? Heavens, Bunny; what nonsense! I am perfectly happy as I am. Home at Lustings, with my library and my cook, my trout stream, my parchment ponies, and my aviatory. What more could I possibly want?"

"I'm sure *I* could not say, if *you* could not," said Belinda with an injured air.

"I shall tell you, then," said Arabella, pulling her sister up from the chair and enfolding her in her arms. "The love and constant support of the best, the dearest little sister in all the world!"

Belinda, mollified, returned her embrace, glancing down over Arabella's shoulder at the sketch of the statue.

"Perhaps we should place him in the aviatory."

"Oh, no, dear; he would be coated with droppings inside of a week!"

"Birds fly over the garden, too."

"Yes, but he stands more of a chance outside." Arabella picked up the letter and gazed at the little sketch with fond affection. "Now, why could not *this* have been the deity who created man in His own image?"

"Because," said Belinda gravely. "Life is not fair."

A Bad Business

It was too late in the year for crickets, even in Italy. But a threatening storm lent the proper atmospherics as a knot of men stood waiting beside an excavation in the cold wind. Around them, the ghostly ruins of a dead city bore mute witness to their activities, and one of the company gave a nervous start as a palm frond rattled in the night air. All eyes were fixed upon the tunnel entrance.

"Here they come," said one of the men.

"Quiet!" hissed another.

(The reader may wonder at anyone hissing that word, since it contains no sibilants in English, but these men were speaking Italian, in which language I presume the word has an *S* in it.)

Dark lanterns were lifted as four members of the company emerged from the mouth of the tunnel, struggling and grunting with the effort of a heavy burden, wrapped in rough sacking, borne amongst them. One of the men stumbled.

"Careful with that!" growled the fellow who seemed to be in charge. This might have been deduced from the thin piece of pressboard he carried, to which a large metal clip was attached and firmly clamped over a tablet of paper. For it is well established that no other accessory conveys more authority to the mind of civilized man, except a row of medals on the breast of a uniform, or possibly, a crown.

Having set their bundle upright upon the ground, the men proceeded to pad it with more sacking, followed by a layer of canvas and a girdle of ropes. Then they wrestled it onto a small donkey cart standing ready nearby, to which other similarly wrapped items had already been consigned.

"That's the last of them," said the fellow with the clipboard. "Now, let's get clear of this place before—"

But the man's remark, like his life, was suddenly cut short by a shovel, the assailant coming down from behind with such force that the back of the victim's skull was cleft nearly in twain. At the same moment, an earsplitting thunderclap broke directly overhead, followed immediately by a downpour that drenched the men to the skin. Seizing the reins, one of their number leapt into the cart and drove it off, whilst the others grabbed up the tools and melted into the darkness, leaving only their dead companion behind.

TEA AND SYMPATHY

Dear Miss Beaumont,

I write not knowing whether you can have heard the news, but there has been a shocking contretemps involving our Herculaneum pieces! The person in whom we have entrusted all our hopes has got himself murdered, poor chap, in the very act of procuring those treasures for which you and I had paid him so handsomely. I very much fear that your bronze and my marbles have gone missing.

Yours in haste,

J. Soane

P.S. If I may be of any assistance to you in this sad business, I pray that you will call on me at No. 13, Lincoln's Inn Fields, this afternoon at half-past three. Please pardon the chaos—I am remodeling the exterior—but I think that you will find all within quite orderly and pleasant.

John Soane, the brilliant classical architect, was an ethical man. And, as he had been the one to acquaint Arabella with the opportunity of purchasing the statue, he felt personally responsible for her loss.

She was touched by his concern, and read his letter aloud to Belinda, who, owing to her sister's obvious dismay, attempted to repress the smile that rose unbidden to her lips. But Arabella saw it, just the same.

"May I ask what it is that you apparently find so amusing?" she asked severely. "I have just lost a good deal of money, you know; money which might have gone towards your dowry!"

This made no sense, for after all, the sum had been spent upon a statue. But Belinda knew better than to argue. It really was not fair, though; she had been happily constructing a miniature moon garden in a dish, when Arabella had found her on the glass-walled gardening porch adjoining the aviatory. Now, in addition to sculpting deep green recesses from baby's tears and minuscule mosses, Belinda had also to negotiate the tightrope of Arabella's volatile temper.

"I was not smiling at your situation, dear," she said soothingly, "which is distressing, to be sure; but only at Mr. Soane's curious way of expressing himself. Unless, of course, he really *has* lost his marbles."

"He *has*. And I have lost my statue! At this moment, you and I are closer to financial ruin than at any other juncture of our lives, except for that time when Charles lost the house to Mr. Branscomb!"

This statement was not even remotely accurate, but Arabella was possessed of rather a peculiar attitude toward wealth, owing to her occupation and an inborn ability to plan ahead. In this she was most fortunate, for it is in the nature of courtesans to live lavishly, spend copiously, and die in ignominy. Miss Beaumont's peers—or compatriots, rather; for Arabella *had* no peers—frequently spent all they had and considerably more, supporting lifestyles that rivaled the eastern potentates'. Our heroine, on the other hand, contented herself with a modest little manor house in a quiet corner of Brompton Park, which was nice enough, as neighborhoods go, but not so exclusive as Mayfair. She kept only six horses (though she did have rather a lot of coaches), hosted small but brilliant intellectual salons, ate and drank well, but not extravagantly. And whilst her counterparts were known to reserve entire wings in their enormous residences for the exclusive storage of ball gowns, Arabella contented herself with a single very large dressing room, and quickly disposed of any items therein that seemed duplicative.

She was keeping an eye to the future. And although she was presently rich, young, and desirable, she realized, rather sooner than most, that youth and allure would not *always* be hers. With careful planning, though, she might at least enjoy a comfortable living to the end of her days. So Arabella wisely avoided risky schemes that promised and often failed to deliver gigantic dividends, and kept her money safely tucked away in the Bank of England, with herself the sole signatory on the account. She was touchy concerning financial setbacks.

"I don't imagine you are actually planning to call upon Mr. Soane," said Belinda, who was so accustomed to her sister's articulated poverty fears that she scarcely heard them anymore. "He only seems to be suggesting it as a courtesy. Besides, I do not imagine there can be much to say upon the subject."

Belinda had stated the case with her usual accuracy. There really was nothing more to be said: The dealer was dead and the statue was gone. But Arabella had long wished to see the inside of John Soane's house, which she had often heard described, and a visit thither would soothe, somewhat, the sting of her disappointment.

*   *   *

The front wall at No. 13, Lincoln's Inn Fields, stood out—
literally—from the structures surrounding it, for three pick-
a-back loggias were being appended to its façade. The
pavement was littered with tools, scaffolding, and large slabs
of Portland stone, and Arabella had to pick up her skirts to
make her way through the mess, showing off her shapely
calves to a gang of vocally appreciative workmen.

Soane himself came to the door to bid her welcome, wearing a kind expression and a regrettable auburn wig. "How
d'ye do, Miss Beaumont?" cried he, warmly pressing her
hands. "I am glad to see you! Come, we'll have tea in the
plaister room. This is such a bad business. Oh, not the tea, I
mean the art theft, of course."

John Soane's house was so curiously and densely decorated with plaster casts, framed drawings and paintings,
models of antique buildings, and Neoclassical sculpture that
it more closely approximated an art gallery than a dwelling.
Any architect worth his salt collected such things, but in
most cases the collections were confined to a room or two at
the top of the house. In fact, Soane did keep a workshop for
his apprentices upstairs, and generously supplied it with reference materials of this type, but his collection went considerably beyond mere professional interest: He lived, breathed,
and dreamt architecture, and the house was a physical mani-
festation of the inner workings of his exceptional mind.

Fortunately, Mrs. Soane was not the sort of wife who says,
"Take all this truck out of here, John! The Ladies' Society for
the Promotion of Cleaner Homes will be meeting in the parlor in three quarters of an hour!" She bore the same love of
these odd bits and pieces as he did, and was all in favor of his
peculiar notions regarding their placement.

The tour of the premises took the better part of an hour, for,
in addition to escorting his guest round the half-constructed
rooms and explaining exactly what he planned on doing with
them, Soane had shewn Arabella the sketches for his breakfast

parlor, with its handkerchief ceiling and central oculus, and read aloud from his construction journal. But at last a paint sample for the new library (Pompeian Red) reminded him why she had come, and he quickly ushered her into the plaister room.

This was not so much a room as a three-story alcove, with small balconies on either side at the second-story level. On one of them, Arabella espied a little tea table all set and ready for use.

"Oh, my!" she exclaimed, gazing about her in rapturous delight. And for some time, that was all she *could* say.

The four walls, each of which bore the impress of a soaring arch, were completely covered in medallions, urns, Greek key friezes, nautiloid spirals, cornices, plaques, molded lions' heads, and other architectural fragments. One of the busts bore an uncanny likeness to Arabella's brother, Charles, and without thinking, she asked, "How is your son, George?"

"I have no idea," her host replied stiffly. "Nor do I care."

George Soane, a chum of Charles Beaumont's, was a notorious reprobate and his father was ashamed of him. For the great architect was a man of high moral character and impeccable standards, this private meeting with Arabella notwithstanding: Mrs. Soane was absent from home, you see.

A careless sort of man would not have minded whether his wife were present or not. Arabella was there on business, after all, and there was nothing sexual between them. But persons of refined sensibilities know that proper and improper ladies must always be kept apart, one from the other, lest their simultaneous occupation of a room, or even a building, impart a stain upon the person of unsullied reputation, which no amount of prayer, good works, or blameless conduct might ever eradicate. It was most regrettable; Martha Soane and Arabella might have been great friends, if only the latter had submitted to starvation rather than take up a life of ill repute.

At the mention of George, an awkward silence settled over the table for a few moments. But then Arabella asked whether she should pour, and everything was all right again.

"I am so relieved that you have come," said Soane.

"Relieved?"

"Quite. Having been the cause of your losing so much money, I feared that you might not wish to continue the friendship."

"You must have a poor opinion of me, then," she replied, "to assume that I would terminate our acquaintance over something that was not your fault and which could not have been foreseen! Besides, you warned me there would be risks."

"That's right, I did, didn't I? Still, when a sensible person takes a chance on a risky proposition, it must be because she has judged any risk to herself unlikely. Obviously, she does not expect the worst to happen, else she would have kept her purse strings firmly tied in the first place."

"Well," said Arabella, "I fully intend to recover it."

"Your money?"

"Heavens, no! That has surely been dispersed to the seven winds by now! I meant the bronze! The thieves may still have it. Or they may have sold it to someone else. If I can discover the statue's whereabouts, I shall offer its present custodian an extremely generous price for it. I have always wanted to see Italy, and this unfortunate circumstance affords the perfect opportunity."

"But surely," said Soane, biting into a watercress sandwich with great care, lest his false teeth should come out, "the Italian authorities are already dealing with the situation."

"Yes," she replied, "and I only hope that *I* may find my statue before *they* do!"

"To be frank, I should not go near Naples just now, if I were you. A general insurrection has long been expected, and the situation might erupt at any time."

Arabella found politics dull, and always avoided reading about it or listening to it, so she had not the slightest idea what her host was talking about.

"Well, nobody is mad at *us,* are they?"

"No; Britain is sympathetic to the partisan cause."

"Then I have nothing to fear."

Soane regarded his visitor with the affable indulgence typically shewn by educated men toward charming, silly women. Yet, in the present instance, his attitude was tinged with a faint consternation. For though one must naturally expect to encounter simplicity when discussing politics with ladies, *this* lady was willfully proposing to put herself in harm's way *because* of her simplicity. One didn't expect *that.* And Arabella wasn't just any lady. Well, she wasn't a lady at all. She was *demimonde,* and a frequent hostess to the sharpest minds in the nation. One might have expected to encounter, in her case, a more sophisticated grasp of world affairs.

"I doubt that you would be singled out for attack from any patriotic cause," said Soane, judiciously considering, "but the Continent is swarming with thieves and knaves of every description, who will be bound to see you as an easy mark. As for politics, you might find yourself swept up in something in a general way, you know. Much of the country is controlled by the French, with whom we are currently at war. And the Austro-Hungarians are also making a nuisance of themselves there. The Italians resent these invasions, with good reason, and on that account, they are fomenting rebellion."

"Then I shall look out my window every morning," said Arabella, "and if I should see waves of angry fomenters washing over the town, I promise to remain indoors and find something pleasant to read until they have passed through."

"Even setting the political situation aside, though," he persisted, "Naples is now purported to be *the* most dangerous city in the civilized world."

"And have you been there yourself, Mr. Soane?"

"Oh, not for many years," he said, stirring his tea. "Let's see ... when was it? '78? Yes; '78 to '79. I went over with the Bishop of Derry. Saw Pompeii, and the Portici Palace ... I met Piranesi, you know. Dear me! All those *P*s! I'm afraid I must answer a call of nature, now! Power of suggestion, I suppose. If you don't mind waiting a moment, I shall shew you something of interest when I return. . . ."

He was gone for some little time, and came back with a fragment of painted plaster.

"This comes from a Pompeian wall fresco! I liberated it when no one was looking," he said, handing it to her.

Arabella admired the scrap, which shewed the tip of a green branch against a pale yellow wall, and a blue smear, which might have been the sea in the distance.

"Have you been to Herculaneum, as well?" she asked.

"No. There wasn't time, and the roads were very bad. Still are, I understand. But Miss Beaumont, I must protest this! You are proposing to go to a foreign country, where you do not speak the language, in quest of a thing you have not seen, removed by persons unknown to you from a place you have never been! It is a wild, mad scheme!"

"Not so bad as that, surely! I prefer to call it . . . a caprice."

"And are you really in earnest?"

"Perfectly, Mr. Soane."

"Then I pray you will permit me to write and apprise a friend of mine of your coming. Teofilo Bergamini is a professor of ancient history at the University of Naples, a most august and trustworthy fellow. He frowns upon foreigners plundering the ruins for personal gain or gratification, but perhaps he might be persuaded to make himself useful to you, if he sees a chance of recovering the rest of the lost artifacts for his museum's collection."

"Write to him, by all means," said Arabella, "but please make it clear that if I succeed in locating the cache, the Pan statue is coming home with me."

Chapter 4

FEELING OUT BELINDA

As the new parchment ponies bore her homeward (two cream-colored in front, two golden behind, one of each in the middle), Arabella lay back against the cushions, mulling over her sudden decision. She had not known she was going to Italy until she heard herself telling Soane that she was, and now her mind returned to the subject again, as one's tongue seeks an oral cavern produced by the recent loss of a tooth. Because far from soothing her disappointment, having tea in the midst of Soane's exciting collection had only sharpened her sense of loss. He had made a good point, though; the idea of traveling abroad during war-torn times was not a sound one, and it would be sheer madness to attempt the crossing alone, ignorant as she was concerning continental politics. Companionship was essential, and in the event it should prove impossible to secure anyone, she should have the perfect excuse to reverse her decision, without loss of face.

Belinda was out when Arabella got home, having gone for a drive with Lord Carrington. Quite a long drive, as things transpired, for she did not come back again till the following day. The moment she returned, however, Belinda went in search of Arabella, to hear the final pronouncement on a newly purchased reticule. Somewhat to her consternation, she found the door to her sister's bedroom closed.

A few readers may be surprised to learn that privacy is as highly prized a commodity in a courtesan's house as it is in their own. That being the case, however, it will be readily understood that Belinda, standing outside Arabella's room and hearing the unmistakable sounds of a woman in the final stages of ultimate transport within, made ready to tiptoe quietly away again, after listening for only a *very* few moments.

"Who is it?" called Arabella sharply.

Belinda tiptoed back to the door, again. "*C'est moi,* Bell," she whispered into the keyhole. "I am sorry! But I did not know that you had company."

"I haven't. I am quite alone. Pray, come in, Bunny. I wish to speak to you."

Belinda found her sister seated at the dressing table, fully clothed, each hair of her coiffure neatly in its place. But the wings of her triptych looking glass were folded about her, for she had been engaged in closely observing her face from every possible angle.

"Practicing my vocals," she explained. "Sir Birdwood-Fizzer will be dropping by later this evening, to pay his disrespects. Which look do you think better? This . . . ?" She threw her head back, opened her mouth, and half-closed her eyes. "Or this . . . ?" She opened her eyes wide, with a look of a fey woodland creature suddenly exposed to a bonfire in the dead of night.

"They are both fetching," said Belinda, with professional interest. "I suppose it really depends upon the particular tastes of Birdwood-Fizzer. You might try both of them on him, and see which he favors."

"Bunny," said Arabella, abruptly changing the subject and spreading open the mirror panels, "how should you like to go to Italy?"

"To search for your missing statue, do you mean?" asked Belinda.

"Yes. I have made up my mind to see what can be done. But you know, I probably won't go if you . . ."

"When are we leaving?"

"Ah! You take my point quite readily, dear! But I must warn you that the current climates, both natural and political, are unfavorable for continental travel just now. We shall be two women alone. And winter is nigh upon us—the crossing is apt to be rough. If you think the risks too high, I shall honor your fears and abandon the plan."

Belinda made a dismissive noise, akin to a spurt of steam escaping from under the lid of a pot in which Brussels sprouts are fulminating. "I shall be ready to go whenever you want me."

That was that, then. They would be risking their safety, nay, their very *lives,* in pursuit of a chunk of metal that Arabella had not actually seen.

"Bell, what do you think of this reticule?" asked Belinda, holding up the item in question. "I think it may have looked prettier in the shop window than it does now I've brought it home."

"Not at all! It is quite the thing," said Arabella. But she was actually thinking about her statue, and of all that lay ahead. "Have you reflected, sister mine," she asked, "on the peculiar notion that the history of mankind is not, in fact, a record of our actual *selves* so much as it is a chronicle of our unappeasable desire for possessions?"

"Oh, yes. Frequently," Belinda replied, working out a snarl that had formed in the tassel of her latest acquisition. "Wars are nearly always fought in order to seize someone else's territory or material wealth, aren't they? Explorations are launched in search of shortcuts to overseas markets, or the discovery and exploitation of unknown resources, and monarchs are chiefly judged by the riches they bring to their respective nations."

"Even so," said Arabella, beyond words irritated that her sister had pre-empted her plan for an impromptu history lesson, "the story of mankind, which sounds so noble, is really just the story of our stuffs."

"I should have said it was the story of our *interactions* with stuffs, rather than of the stuffs themselves. Inert as they are, they can scarcely be expected to generate a history on their own."

Arabella stood up. She was really annoyed now, for Belinda had actually *corrected* her. "I am going out," she snapped. "To buy something frivolous!"

"That hardly seems like a noble endeavor!"

"No, indeed! It fairly smacks of the commercial! And, pray, do not ask to accompany me—I crave solitude, just now!" So saying, she swept from the room, shutting the door behind her rather emphatically.

Despite recitations elsewhere in this narrative of autumn's distinctive charms, it must also be admitted that the season possesses some serious drawbacks. There are the rivers, for one thing. London is full of rivers, and the rivers are full of all kinds of unpleasant things, being little more than foul repositories for those substances that man flings away from him in disgust. Thus, when the mist rises off the water, collecting to itself all the available moisture, this filthy residue is condensed and distilled into poison. And while most Londoners are hardy enough to survive such miasmas, even the fittest are often subject to chronic coughs and sick headaches in the autumn.

The season also presents major problems for the traveler, owing to its close temporal proximity to winter, and long journeys begun in the autumn are best begun early. Napoleon would come to realize this in a couple of weeks, during his invasion of Russia, but Arabella knew it already. And so, the elder Beaumont sister, who, like the younger, was reckless on the surface yet sensible deep down, ordered their trunks brought in from the stables and cleaned of hay and cobwebs that very evening.

BROTHERLY LOVE

"I can think of few situations less likely to inspire lustful passions than being raised in a household with sisters," said Charles, perusing the racing results. "Watching them grow through their gangly or dumpy stages, observing their pimple eruptions, fighting with them and enduring their endless sulks at the dinner table . . . but that is the idea, I suppose: If brothers always had first crack at their sisters, as it were, humanity would dwindle away, its bloodlines contaminated with disease and deformity. Look at what happened to the pharaohs."

Charles was sitting and smoking in the bow window of his club, occasionally glancing out at the street, frequently returning to the newspaper, and addressing, with a semi-distracted air, the odd remark to Lord Carrington. Or, in this case, the more-than-odd remark.

"And yet, in these modern times, when men of our station have the leisure to look upon sex as recreation rather than procreation, I ask myself, why not? Though I didn't ask at the time; I simply followed my inclinations. You look shocked, but remember, Carrington, I grew up in a bad family."

"Bad, did you say?"

"Oh, not in a social sense. Pater was a baronet, and we always lived as though we had plenty of money, but my parents were decadent, and much given to vice. So it is not terribly surprising that Arabella and little Belinda caught the fraternal eye one day whilst at their dancing lesson . . ."

His audience jumped to its feet.

"Spare me the details, Beaumont! I am a friend to both ladies, sir, and I'm damned if I'll listen to these foul confessions!"

". . . And then he left in rather a huff," Charles explained. "Probably to go off and brood over what I'd told him."

"It was very wrong of you, Charles!" cried Belinda.

"Indeed, it was!" agreed Arabella. "Lord Carrington was on the brink of proposing to Bunny!"

"I *know*, Bell. That is precisely why I invented the story: Carrington has not a bean in the world."

"Hasn't he?"

"Not anymore. I have saved our Bunny from an ignominious marriage. You are welcome. Please feel free to demonstrate your gratitude in the usual way, by showering me generously with monetary appreciations."

One of the advantages in being a courtesan was that one's income was always in flux, so that the public had no very clear idea of one's actual financial situation. Members of the peerage, on the other hand, might just as well have had their net worth stamped upon their foreheads in violet ink: *Their* livings were as familiar to all and sundry as their surnames. And Lord Carrington, as everybody knew, was possessed of twenty thousand pounds per annum. Or had been. But the world was soon to hear of a certain game of Loo which had taken place the previous evening, in the course of which the wretched fellow had gambled away his entire fortune. His clubmen knew it already, of course.

"That's why I lied to him," Charles explained. "The poor devil hasn't two farthings to rub together. He mustn't marry Bunny, and now it's fairly certain that he won't."

"But have you given any thought," said Arabella, making an effort to govern her temper, "any at all, to the damage your story will do to our demi-reputations?"

"Rubbish! You're courtesans! My colorful tale will merely enhance your already potent mystique."

"No," she said. "A lot of people who are otherwise broad-minded draw the line at incest. None of our wealthy clients will have us with *that* taint on our records! And if *we* fail, dear brother, *you* fail, as well."

Charles went as white and as crumbly as a good Caer-philly.

"Oh," he said faintly. "I hadn't quite thought of it in that light, you know. Um . . . what shall we do now?"

"I have no idea what *you* will do," Arabella retorted. "A good brother would go out and explain to the world that he was only having his little joke."

"But I am not a good brother."

"Precisely, *Toby*."

Arabella had coined this cognomen when they were children, because her brother's ears stuck out from his head like the handles on a Toby mug. The defect having happily resolved itself with time, the nickname proved indelible, as nicknames often will, and resurfaced whenever Charles had occasion to vex his sisters. Hence, the air at Lustings fairly rang with "Toby!" for I am sorry to say that the fellow fretted them constantly.

On this particular evening, Belinda and Arabella had been seated before the fire in the drawing room, their slippered feet propped on footstools, where, until Charles's entry and electrifying anecdote, Belinda had been engaged in making a needlepoint of Europa consummating her affair with the bull, and Arabella had been copying a sketch of Rowland-son's, depicting a trio of decrepit old men examining the business end of a happy, naked young woman.

"Bunny and I will shortly be leaving for the Continent, in connection with a private matter," said Arabella, "and now that you have seen fit to blacken our reputations, I propose to remain abroad unless and until this thing shall have run its course. Whilst we are gone, I shall write to every important friend of our acquaintance, explaining your conduct, reviling you, and begging assistance in clearing our names. You may stew in your own juices until we return—I do not mind what you do—but you will have to find somewhere else to live, for you cannot stay at Lustings."

"No, indeed," Belinda chimed in. "If we left you here alone, we should come back to find the house empty of fur-niture, and yourself skinned and on the point of gambling away the doorknobs."

An ordinary person, confronted with such an uncomfort-able truth, would have hung his head for shame. But this bothered Charles not a whit. For he had spoken truly: He was not a good brother.

"Bell," Belinda continued, "do you not think we should call at Ackermann's in a few days, in order to assess the ac-tual damage?"

"Indubitably. It is impossible that this 'revelation' will es-cape the notice of the gossip hounds. Charles, get your things together and get out."

"But . . . I've nowhere to go!" he protested. "No one will have me to stay with them, if what you say is true!"

"You will just have to find some way to cope, then, won't you?"

"I won't, Bell. You know I could not survive without you and my friends, which, according to you, I no longer possess. How will you feel when you return to find me dead and buried in Potter's Field? For the rest of your own life, which I hope may be long and wretched, you will suffer from the knowledge that I died because of your neglect."

"Oh, shut up, Charles."

Belinda was beginning to waver. "The nights *are* awfully cold just now, Bell," she said, with a beseeching sort of look at her sister.

"I realize that. Which is why he needn't be buried until we come home. They can preserve him quite nicely for us in a block of ice."

"But we cannot just leave him! After all, he is the only brother we have."

"That is a circumstance," said Arabella, "for which I daily thank Providence."

Charles has been mentioned at length, and rather pointedly, too, in a previous volume of Arabella's adventures, but the reader has not actually *met* him. Therefore, picture if you will a tall, dark, attractive man, almost pretty, a few years older than Arabella. Although he shared her forthright self-assurance, and had dark hair, like Belinda, Charles possessed a certain want of character, an absence of inner resolve, and a weakness about the mouth that were entirely his own. In fact, there was no very striking family resemblance amongst the siblings, and Arabella had sometimes reflected that the three of them might, in actuality, only be *half* siblings. (Their mother, as Charles had said, had been much given to vice.) Still, he *was* the only brother they had.

"Oh, all right!" cried Arabella, disgusted by the others' facial expressions of mute appeal. "Though I am quite certain that I shall have cause to regret it, you had better come along to Italy with Bunny and me, Charles. Perhaps a month or two with all of us out of the public eye will give things here a chance to settle down."

"You know I shall be of no help at all, either physically, financially, or emotionally," he said, plucking a bit of fluff from his sleeve.

"That is not entirely true," Arabella replied. "The presence of a male family member will lend a certain outward respectability to our party, which may well prove useful abroad. The Italians, you know, are rather old-fashioned in their attitudes, and apt to take a dim view of females roaming about on their own."

After Charles had gone, Belinda allowed herself the luxury of sniffling into her hanky.

"You're well out of that, Bunny," said Arabella, patting her shoulder. "Just think what would have happened if you had married Carrington! An insufferable bore is bearable, if not actually charming, when he is also rich. But an insufferably boring *pauper* might tempt one to murder!"

"Yes, you are right," Belinda agreed, wiping away a tear. "When it comes to gambling, Carrington is as bad as Charles. And ending up with someone like Charles is the last thing I should want!"

"Well," said Arabella, with a rueful smile. "Not according to gossip."

Rudolph Ackermann kept a print shop on the Strand, in whose front window he was wont to display the latest social and political commentary, translated into captioned cartoons by artists like George Cruikshank, James Gillray, and Thomas Rowlandson. The plethora of London newspapers and magazines notwithstanding, Ackermann's window was where one went for a quick overview of the burning topics of the day.

Shortly after Charles Beaumont had made his famous remark to Lord Carrington, Arabella discovered a print in the famous window, depicting her siblings and herself in bed together, and bearing the caption: "Brotherly Love."

"So much for befriending 'the most dangerous man in London,'" said Belinda, when Arabella told her. She was sitting in the library, having attempted to create a scrimshaw scene on a walrus tusk that Glen*deen* had once given Arabella. But Belinda had botched it, and was now carving it into a dildo, instead.

"The work was Cruikshank's," said Arabella, untying the ribbons that secured her bonnet beneath her chin, "not Rowlandson's. Tom would never do such a thing to an old friend."

"No? Last year, if you recall, he made that humiliating sketch of me!"

"That was different, Bunny. Anyone may fall down and have her frock fly up, although you would not risk exposure quite so often if your skirts were not quite so full. Besides, a narrower skirt shews off the figure to greater advantage."

"You are free to attract attention in any way you see fit," said Belinda. "However, I am determined to hold fast to my own methods."

"Hmm," replied her sister skeptically. "At any rate, Tom Rowlandson might poke gentle fun at you, but he would never dream of insulting *me*."

"I did not look upon that as gentle fun."

"Oh, surely you're not holding a grudge against him!"

"Nothing of the sort," Belinda replied. "I merely said I did not look upon it as gentle fun."

"Well, then, what did you regard it as?"

"Free advertising."

Chapter 6

THE BILLY-BOX BRIBE

The day following saw no wind, and the city cautiously awakened to brittle sunlight. It was cold, though. Walking their horses through Green Park after a good ride, Belinda and Arabella passed that farm that was so amusing to visit in the summer, when one had a mind to play the dairymaid and milk a cow.

"Are you certain you wouldn't like to curl your fingers around a nice, warm cow teat?" asked Arabella.

"Yes, I am certain," Belinda replied, stooping to pick up a brilliantly colored leaf. "My gloves are *not* coming off until we reach home. The mere thought of exposing my hands at these temperatures makes me want to shriek!"

The fall foliage was particularly fine that year, and Arabella marked, with pleasurable surprise, just how the trees were effecting their seasonal adjustments. Some turned red or gold or flaming orange on the bottom first, the colors gradually creeping upward, like a blush. Others began their transformation at the top, and the change seeped down from there. Still others altered their outer leaves first, and she even found some that were changing in random clumps.

Belinda was not bothered with the "how" of the leaves, as

all her attention was for the moment focused upon collecting the prettiest.

"Are these for your album?" Arabella enquired.

"No," said her sister. "I am making a billy-box."

Belinda was in the habit of decorating small receptacles at the end of her love affairs. Named for the first man ever to inspire their construction, they were packed with memorabilia from the lately beloved, and might contain anything from billets-doux to withered apple cores, including sketches not good enough for her album, miscellaneous locks of hair, nail parings, and tobacco pipe dottle, tapped out and left on a saucer. These collections, once complete, were duly buried in the garden, and Arabella had once made the observation that future history buffs, digging in the area of Brompton Park, would get the thrill of their lives when they uncovered Belinda's beautiful memory coffins, and then feel so disappointed upon opening them and discovering the unfailingly mundane, and occasionally disgusting contents, that for the sake of their mental health they would be obliged to take up some other hobby without the attendant risks of extreme emotional fluctuations.

But Belinda had not had a serious affair for some time, unless one counted Lord Carrington. And one *couldn't* count him, after all, as he had feet that splayed out like a duck's, and cut a ridiculous figure on the dance floor.

"I don't require one just now," she explained, with reference to her boxes. "But I like to stock them up, so that I need not feel pressured to make a billy-box when I am prostrate with grief. This one will be useful should I ever have occasion to terminate a romance in the autumn."

"How many have you at present?" Arabella inquired.

"Five or six."

"Would you let me have one?"

"Why? You think they're silly!"

"I think they are beautiful," said Arabella gravely. "I

merely deplore the waste of burying such beautiful things in the ground, crammed with, if you'll pardon me, nothing but trash. However, in the event that you will vouchsafe to give me one, I promise to fill it with lovely items and take it to Mr. Kendrick. He has a cold just now, and wants cheering up."

"Oh! By all means! He shall have the box I am currently working on! It is to be covered in autumn leaves, with gilded acorns, silver pinecones, and yards and yards of copper-colored ribbon! How very thoughtful you are, Bell!"

The horses blew air through their noses, as though to contradict Belinda's estimation of her sister's noble motives.

The young women walked on for a time, until at last, Arabella said, "No. It is rather selfish, actually. You see, I have just decided that the rector shall accompany us to the Continent. There is no doubt at all that he will come if I ask him, and taking his utter compliance with my wishes for granted makes me feel rather guilty. However, if I preface my request with a present, I think I shall feel less so."

"But why should you feel guilty?"

"Better you should ask why I want him."

"Well, then, why do you?"

"Because I foresee that you and I shall go off on all sorts of junkets in an effort to recover my statue. We shan't want Charles with us—you know how he can be—and yet there is no telling what mischief he will get into, left on his own."

"So . . . you want Mr. Kendrick to look after Charles."

"I shall pay for his passage, his room, and all of his wants," replied Arabella defensively. "Besides, Mr. Kendrick is fond of Charles. It will seem more like spending time with a cherished companion than caring for a dangerous lunatic."

"And yet, Mr. Kendrick will be joining us for the sole purpose of basking in your presence. It will vex him exceedingly to watch you going off without him."

"I know. I am a dreadful woman, am I not?"

"Yes," said Belinda. "Yes, I suppose you are."

Chapter 7

CALLING AT THE EFFING RECTORY

John Kendrick, Rector of Effing (who was sometimes called "vicar," although this wasn't strictly correct), lay coughing peevishly under a mound of blankets as his housekeeper entered with a bowlful of soup on a tray. She was the solid, square-ish, no-nonsense type, and there was not a shred of sympathetic understanding in her voice as she thumped his pillows and asked whether he felt up to receiving a visitor.

"Visitor?" the rector ejaculated. "How could you possibly think I might? My throat feels like the cat's scratching post and my nose is as blocked up as a miser's chimney!"

"All right, then; I shall tell Miss Beaumont that you are too ill to see her."

"Miss Beaumont?" he asked. "Miss Beaumont is *here?* Well, for heaven's sake, Mrs. Hasquith, why did you not *say* it was she? Show her in, by all means!"

Privately, Mr. Kendrick owned that he would not have engaged Mrs. Hasquith had he been permitted the freedom to chuse his own staff. But she was a relic of the previous rector's, and had come with the house.

"The rector is too ill to see anyone, ma'm!" shouted Mrs.

Hasquith over the banister, making certain her employer should hear her. "He says you can come back in a fortnight."

Arabella was quite nonplussed by this news. But before she could address the grizzled head that leered down at her from above, a roar of protest erupted from the sickroom.

"*Thought* that would get him," muttered the housekeeper with a grim smile. "Come upstairs and go in, miss, if you please."

Arabella found the poor reverend coughing weakly from the effort of his bellow.

"Hullo, Mr. K.," said she, plumping her offering down upon the bed. "I have brought you something to help wile away the hours until you are well again."

To his intense delight, the invalid found all manner of items inside to soothe and amuse him.

. . . There was a deck of cards:

"Oh! I am not supposed to have these, you know, but I suppose, if I only play with myself and don't gamble, it is bound to be all right."

Arabella could not help smiling as she momentarily pictured the rector "playing with himself."

. . . A flask of "cold medicine": "Cook put this up for you," Arabella explained. "It's an old family recipe."

Kendrick pulled out the stopper and sniffed the contents, which were sufficiently pungent to penetrate his blocked nasal passages.

"Brandy?" he enquired.

"I really don't know what Mrs. Moly puts in there. The ingredients are secret. It is wonderful stuff, though. She always makes some for Belinda and me whenever we are under the weather."

. . . A few good books (not Bibles).

. . . Newspapers.

. . . Dice and a cup: "Miss Beaumont, you are trying to lead me astray!"

. . . A little clasp knife, made in Switzerland, with all manner of clever attachments, which Arabella intended to borrow as soon as possible.

. . . A packet of tea, with a lemon and a small bottle of honey.

. . . And finally (this was Charles's contribution), a book of improper jokes, entitled *Very Bad Stories.*

"Ah!" cried Kendrick, delightedly stroking the cover. "Do you know, this reminds me of a joke I heard once, about an unpleasant old nun. She mistreated the girls who worked in the laundry . . ."

"Laundry?"

"A Magdalene laundry, it was . . ."

"Forgive me, Mr. K., but this does not sound at all the sort of joke I might appreciate. Doyle, my chambermaid, labored for years in one of those terrible places. And I doubt whether she would enjoy this story, either."

"Oh, yes, I know, but if you will just bear with me . . . the girls revenged themselves on the nun by adding extra starch to her habit, you see."

"It is so good to find you thriving and healthy again, Mr. Kendrick," said Arabella. "From your note I expected to find quite the opposite. I suppose you will be out of bed by tomorrow?"

The rector seemed to shrink before her eyes.

"Heavens, Miss Beaumont! I . . . I do not think so! I am feeling quite . . ."

" . . . well enough to tell jokes, and sufficiently hardheaded to force them upon your disobliging company," she finished, her eyes twinkling.

"Oh. But that was just a momentary flash of good health, you know, at the unexpected pleasure of seeing you. No, I really

am quite seriously ill; this happens every autumn. I am suscepti-
ble to river miasmas."

"That *is* a shame."

"Yes. Thank you for saying so."

"Because, you see, Charles, Belinda, and I are leaving for
Italy Tuesday week. I had hoped to find you well enough to
accompany us, as our guest. But I suppose you are really too
ill to be moved."

There was nothing Kendrick could say, and so he said
nothing, but his face was an eloquent record of the interior
agonies he was undergoing. Arabella toyed with him for a bit
whilst she gathered up her gloves and prepared to leave the
room. Then in the doorway she half-turned and said,

"If, by some miracle, you are better by the time we leave,
perhaps you would care to join us."

Chapter 8

CAT AMONGST THE FIGPECKERS

Unlike most persons of her station, Tilda Crouch, Lustings's scullery maid, could not conceive of anyone with a better job than herself. Of course, Tilda's wits were not all they might have been, but the fact that she was so happy in her work compensated for any discrepancy between this particular girl and her brighter but less satisfied counterparts in other households. Nevertheless, a scullery maid's lot is neither pleasant nor easy. So, when Arabella informed Tilda that henceforth she was to feed the birds in the aviatory, the child was ecstatic.

Readers of long standing will recall that the aviatory was Arabella's combination aviary and conservatory: a magical paradise of exotic plants and tropical birds, with a columned rotunda in the center. The task of feeding the birds had formerly devolved on the cook, but when Mrs. Molyneux actually suggested *roasting* Arabella's little bulbuls and precious bee-eaters, the mistress had decided to re-organize the duty roster.

There was, surely, no happier scullion in all England. The birds were happier, too, for Tilda didn't just feed and water them; she actually sat and spoke to her charges, and they, in turn, always had time for her, and never told her she was silly. The bolder ones perched unafraid upon her head and shoulders, and Tilda often appeared in the dining room now—for she was being trained to wait at table—with bird droppings in her hair. The scullery maid considered the aviatory to be a good place, a haven from the world, where no one reproved her, however kindly. And sometimes, despite the noisy avian chatter and oppressive humidity, the girl found it so restful here, that she actually . . . nodded off . . . just for a few . . . moments.

Naturally, Doyle was disappointed not to be going.

"But who is it will be lookin' after you and Miss Belinda, ma'm?" (Arabella's *femme de chambre* had been spoilt through having on several occasions accompanied her mistress to Bath. Now the little chit apparently expected to be taken to the Continent, as well.) "You'll be needin' somebody, surely, and if it isn't to be me, it'll be some sneakin' foreigner, most like, who'll sell you into white slavery and the Lord knows what-all!"

She was packing Arabella's toiletry case, fetching its specially designed comb, scissors, tweezers, nail file, shoe horn, back scratcher, sleeping tablets, *sal volatile,* and tooth powder from various places around the room, and because each item had its own compartment, and no two compartments were the same size, the task was less like packing than assembling a jigsaw puzzle in three dimensions.

"White slavery!" cried Arabella delightedly. "How exquisitely diverting! Should you like that, Bunny?"

"Should I like what?"

Belinda was trying to pack a lavender beaded evening shawl so that it should be neither crushed nor snagged in transit, and she had only ever been able to concentrate her attention upon one thing at a time.

"Being sold into white slavery?"

"Oh, probably. The harems of the Orient are said to be lavish to the point of decadence. And then, of course, I should get to be the pasha's favorite wife or concubine or whatever it is, and tell the other women what to do."

Arabella was sorting through her silk stockings, checking for holes and then discarding or rolling them up in pairs, accordingly. They had been custom-made for her, and were longer than was usual, since that courtesan supreme, that styler of trends and setter of fashions, had proclaimed knee-high stockings to be unflattering. The leg was shewn to greatest advantage, she insisted, when one's stockings—particularly dark-colored ones—extended to mid-thigh. Locating the garter up there was fetching, too.

"No; *I* shall be the favorite, Bunny," she said. "*You* could be second favorite."

"Oh, well. We shouldn't both be sold to the same pasha, in any event. A set of brothers, I should think. Then you could be preferred in your harem, I should be exalted in mine, and we would both of us have heaps of eunuchs to do our bidding."

"But as it is," said Doyle sourly, "you will both of you be on your own, as far as help goes, without so much as a eunuch between you! I cannot imagine how the pair of you will ever survive in them foreign parts!"

"A eunuch between us?" asked Arabella.

"Foreign parts!" cried Belinda. "I say! Do you think we shall experience any?"

"Without doubt. The Italians are said to be an extremely amorous race. Attractive, too." Arabella sighed, regarding the shoe she was wrapping up. "Do you suppose they'll have started wearing heels again on the Continent? I absolutely detest these dull, flat slippers!"

Doyle had finished with the toiletry case, and was now using a series of tiny silver funnels to fill a collection of leather-clad traveling bottles with eyewash, face creams, and scent. Frustration had been mounting within her, and at last she dropped the funnel, turned toward her mistress, and stamped her foot. Such a gesture, in any household but this one, would have immediately earned her the sack.

"My point exactly," said Arabella. "You see? Stamping one's foot looks ridiculous in soft, flat shoes! For such a gesture, one really requires a raised heel!"

The chambermaid was practically in tears now.

"Madam! Miss Belinda!" she cried. "My rightful place is with you ladies! What am I to *do* if I stay behind?"

Arabella saw at last that the poor thing was actually quite provoked. She also realized that a hand with a bottle in it, shaking under the influence of strong emotion, was almost certain to result in a waste of expensive scent.

"There! Do not be vexed, Doyle! You can keep things tidy here for our return, and catch up on your mending. If you like, I shall ask Mrs. Janks whether she would enjoy having a maid for herself whilst we're—"

"HELP! HELP!"

Tilda hurtled down the passage toward the kitchen staircase, as though all the scimitar-wielding eunuchs in the East were trying to slice off her behind.

"Mrs. Moly! Mrs. Janks! *Help!*"

She nearly tumbled down the steps in her haste, and the cook and housekeeper met her at the bottom of the stairs.

"Why, Tilda! Whatever is the matter?"

By the time she was able to speak, the rest of the household had run downstairs, too.

"Snake!" She gasped. "In the aviatory!"

"Snake?" asked Arabella. "But that is preposterous! Describe it!"

"I only saw its tail, miss. It was orange, with stripes round it."

"Stripes *round* it?" asked Belinda. "Do you mean rings?"

"Yes, miss. And . . . and it was hairy."

"Snakes are not hairy," said Arabella decisively.

"But it *was,* though. It was fair covered in fur!"

"Tilda, my girl," said Mrs. Janks firmly. "Has them stable boys been giving you funny things to drink, again?"

But Arabella had been meditating on the facts, as she was ever wont to do. "Fur?" she asked suddenly. "And you only saw the orange tail, you say? Quickly, everyone! To the aviatory! It's a cat!"

It was indeed a cat; a big ginger tomcat that made no attempt to hide from the wild-eyed women who burst in upon his solitude. In fact, he walked graciously out to greet them, waving his tail, as much as to say, "Welcome to my aviatory. What do you think of it?"

Mrs. Molyneux picked up the animal and bore it away.

"Well! This is most peculiar!" said Arabella. "How do you suppose that creature came to be in here?"

As if in reply, a loud whistle cut through the background bird chatter. Fisto the mynah, former resident of the morning room, had finally come to live in the aviatory despite, or actually because, he was such an uncanny mimic. He had grown quite tame with familiarity, and usually flew straight to Arabella's shoulder whenever she visited. Not today, though.

"Fisto," Arabella called. "Come here, sir, that I may stroke your head!"

But the mynah bird remained in the palm tree, flitting from branch to branch in agitation, and shrieking his vulgar whistle.

"Has the cat upset you, darling?" said Arabella, moving toward him. "It's all right. Cook has probably drowned the nasty thing by now. Come, Fisto. Let Mama smooth your feathers."

But as soon as she drew close, the mynah dropped from the tree onto the ground. And Arabella, leaning down to him there, discovered an empty space where one of the glass panes should have been.

"Ballocks! Bunny, come see this!"

The practical Belinda snatched up a pair of umbrellas before dashing across the room to her sister, and the two stood in silence beneath them, inspecting the damage. Then they blocked the opening with a large rock, to prevent any of the birds from escaping.

"That's got it," said Fisto in a deep voice.

A remarkable talent of this wholly remarkable bird was his aptitude for reproducing the voices of individuals. Those present now heard him discourse in the gruff tones of a common navvy.

"What you want to do is put the cat in easylike. See?"

And now the bird's voice rose to a tenor: "Can I leave 'im in the sack, Stan?"

"Naw, 'course you can't leave 'im in the sack! What've you got, shit for brains? If the sack stays tied up, 'ow's he gonna get out to eat the birdies?"

"But what if he bites me, Stan?"

"Untie the sack, then put the sack in the winda, and squeeze 'im out gently. Like paint from a tube."

"I know that voice!" cried Mrs. Janks indignantly. "It's Stan Biggs! Lady Ribbonhat's groom! He's always making that lowbrow remark about brains!"

"Lady Ribbonhat!" Belinda fumed. "What a low, contemptible woman! When she finds she cannot legally wrest this house from us, she vents her spleen by turning a cat loose on Bell's beloved birds!"

Arabella regarded her avian fauna with a mixture of affection and relief, as Mrs. Janks took a lump of sugar from her apron pocket.

"You've done a good job, Fisto," said the housekeeper approvingly. "Who's a clever bird, then?"

The mynah flew to her wrist and accepted his reward.

"But I don't understand how they managed to remove the window pane so neatly," said Arabella.

"Oh," said Mrs. Janks. "They used a glass cutter, I expect."

"What is that?"

"A diamond blade, miss. Mounted in a handle."

"Really? You mean a contrivance that cuts glass like scissors cut paper? Without leaving any jagged edges at all? What a wonderful idea! I shall have to get one before we leave!"

"You will have to think up some suitable form of revenge, too," said Belinda as they strolled, thoughtfully, toward the exit.

"Oh, I shall. But not now," said Arabella carelessly. "After all, the cat has done no harm, and you know what the Italians say about letting revenge cool to room temperature before ingesting."

"The Italians said that? I thought it was Talleyrand."

"He may have said it, too. It is impossible to track the exact source of a proverb."

"Bell, I do not understand you," said Belinda. "Why aren't you furious?"

"I am, really. But since we are speaking of proverbs, another springs to mind: 'Before embarking on a journey of revenge, dig two graves.' But I would rather not, you know; I should prefer to let Lady Ribbonhat dig her own. That way, there need only *be* one."

For the next week, Lustings was upside down with preparations for the journey. The sisters talked of Italy, dreamt of Italy, and Arabella had Mrs. Molyneux prepare Italian meals, instead of the usual French ones, that they might accustom themselves in advance to the unfamiliar cuisine.

The large library table was put into service as a map center, so that Arabella could chart their route. They would be sailing from Plymouth to Spain, where a British navy squadron was patrolling Spanish waters.

"We shan't put into port there, but will take on supplies mid-ocean," she explained. "With any luck, one of the admirals may ask us to dine."

"Lovely," murmured Belinda. "A battleship! Full of men! And ourselves the only women for leagues and leagues in any direction!"

Belinda was unabashed in her admiration of the male animal, and especially partial to *groups* of men, preferably young ones, mutually engaging in manly activities. She liked uniforms, too. But only the officers wore those.

"Then," Arabella continued, "our ship, the *Perseverance*—aptly named, don't you agree?—will pass through the Strait of Gibraltar, sail on to the Mediterranean, and so come at last into the Bay of Naples."

"Will it be safe, do you suppose?" Belinda asked. "Shall we be allowed to dock there, despite the fact that the queen is Napoleon's sister?"

Arabella looked up sharply. "I hope you are not having second thoughts at this stage," she said, tapping, with her finger, the Isle of Ischia. "I provided you with numerous chances to decline to accompany me when you were first informed of my intentions. I should not be going at all, if I did not suppose you were coming, as well."

"I have not changed my mind," said Belinda hastily. "I was just curious."

"We shall be perfectly safe. Mr. Soane says that the king of Naples is very cozy with Britain, just at present."

"And how long are we to stay there?"

"Well, I shall probably find my bronze at once, you know, and then . . ."

"How?" asked Charles, entering the room. "When you don't even speak the language?"

"Through an interpreter, if need be, although it will probably do to merely ask, 'where . . . ?' and then make two horns behind my head with my index fingers, and execute a couple of eloquent pelvic thrusts . . ."

Arabella demonstrated how she proposed to do this, eliciting peals of laughter from Charles and Belinda. She was being perfectly serious, however, and did not appreciate their reaction.

"I shouldn't advise you to use those gestures," said Belinda, wiping her eyes. "I'm fairly certain they'll be taken as insults."

"Well, anyway, once they understand what I am after, they will bring the statue to me, and I shall pay for it—again—and take it home."

"But who is this 'they' who are going to return your statue?" Charles persisted. "Whom are you going to ask?"

"I don't know," she grumbled, annoyed. "Anyone, I suppose."

It was beginning to dawn upon Arabella that her "caprice," as she called it, might turn out to be a dangerous waste of time and a stupid waste of her money. But she disliked looking ridiculous almost as much as she hated giving up. And so the poor creature was in a quandary, indeed. The only thing she could do now was to forge ahead, regardless.

"You will need to find an eyewitness, won't you?" Charles asked. "And there probably aren't any."

"Then," said Arabella, addressing Belinda as though Charles were not in the room, "it will only remain for us to wait there until Toby's scandal is forgotten. Fortunately, winters in Italy tend towards the mild and pleasant, so we may be prolonging our visit until the spring. But for heaven's sake, don't let on to Mrs. Janks, whatever you do! You know how she worries, and I have told the dear soul that we shall only be gone a few weeks."

If Charles and Belinda were not so accustomed to relying upon Arabella for everything from fashion advice to food on the table, they might have had some serious misgivings about this journey. But Arabella was in charge of it, so there was really nothing to worry about.

"For the number of trunks she's packed, you'd think she was planning on staying over there permanentlike," observed Mrs. Janks as the servants sat around the big kitchen fireplace with their evening cocoa. "I don't understand it: After what nearly happened to 'er last year, you'd think she'd want to keep away from crimes and criminals, rather'n go barging in after 'em!"

But not only did Arabella *not* wish to avoid the criminal ranks—she was practically determined on joining them, herself. The concept of the glass cutter had fetched her exceedingly, and also served as the springboard for another idea.

"Do you know what I have been thinking, Bunny?" she asked as the three siblings dawdled over dinner. "A professional detective really needs a kit full of tools: steel and flint, candles, string, a pocketknife with multiple attachments, a glass cutter, and so on, just like a thief does!"

"How will those actually help get your statue back, though?" asked Charles, pushing his food about with his fork and making little decorative piles at the edge of his plate. "And won't the tool bag be rather heavy to carry?"

"Probably," Arabella admitted. "But there is no telling what type of situations I am likely to encounter, and it is better to have a housebreaking kit without requiring one, than to desperately need such a thing and not possess it."

"You know," said Charles. "I, too, have been thinking. If the removal of a window pane is as easy as all that, Lady Ribbonhat's men may also have taken out a larger window, which has not yet been discovered. Perhaps they intend to return later, and come right inside the house."

Belinda laughed nervously. "Whatever makes you say that?"

"I don't know; I was recalling the tale of Lankyn, for some reason. You remember, Arabella; Molly used to tell it us, when we were children. Lankyn was a workman of some kind," he explained to Belinda, who was too young to remember their nursemaid, Molly. "He revenged himself on a welshing nob by creeping through a window whilst the fellow was away, and murdering the nob's wife, his baby, and all of the servants, besides. Do you suppose *he* had a glass cutter, too?"

Arabella looked at Belinda.

"He must have done," Charles continued, building a tumulus, strand by strand, out of spaghetti, "because Nurse told us that the man had impressed upon his wife the importance of locking up the place as tight as could be. And any woman left alone in a house on the edge of a moor, especially one with a baby, is going to follow that particular directive to the letter. I think he *must* have had a glass cutter."

"Stop it, Charles," said Arabella. "You're upsetting Belinda." She poured herself another glass of wine and called over her shoulder, "Fielding! Could we have the *pasta con funghi* again, please?"

There was no reply.

She rang the bell.

"Fielding . . . ? Mrs. Janks . . . ?"

"I don't believe there is anyone in the butler's pantry," said Belinda quietly.

"Or at least," said Charles, "none of the *servants*. But there could be . . . someone else . . . couldn't there? Someone who is standing in there, waiting until . . ."

"They've probably all gone down to the kitchen," said Arabella swiftly.

"But why should they do that," asked Belinda, "before we have finished our meal?"

Charles wore an odd sort of puckered expression, and Belinda goggled at him in mute terror.

"Of all the infernal . . . !" Arabella flung down her napkin, as though it were a gauntlet, and rose from the table. "Hellooo!" she called down the passage. "Is anyone there?" When no one answered, she went to the pantry herself, retrieved the pasta bowl, and plumped it onto the table.

"The butler's pantry," she announced, "is vacant."

"D'you know," said Charles, who had made a funereal pile of his mushrooms, "I am not really partial to Italian food. I think I shall get dinner at my club."

So saying, he got up from the table and quitted the house. It was true enough that he had scarcely touched his pasta, but the timing of his departure reminded his sisters, who were in no real danger of forgetting, that Charles was not a source of strength in a crisis.

Arabella had therefore to go downstairs alone. And her pace slowed as she neared the kitchen, for she half-expected to find her staff strewn about the room with their throats cut. Well, she told herself, if they are all busy in the kitchen, they won't have heard me ring. For there were no bells in that room, owing to her own insistence that the preparation of food was too important to interrupt with mundane requests from upstairs. Still, if the servants *were* in there, she would be able to hear their voices from where she now stood. And Arabella could hear nothing. All was as quiet as a graveyard after curfew.

Pausing at the threshold, she sucked in her breath and pushed the door open.

There was no blood on the floor, but what she found instead was almost as upsetting. Every member of her staff was gathered round the ginger tom. They were feeding it cream and stroking its fur, and they all looked up at the same instant to see their mistress regarding them from the doorway with extreme irritation. She had gone all white round the nostrils, which was always a bad sign.

"I want," said Arabella, massaging her temples, "I want that animal out of here by the time I return from Italy."

A DOUBLE-CROSSING

The sea was not so rough as to debilitate the voyagers, and Arabella was by all accounts only slightly bilious. She was just sick enough to be rendered peevish, in fact, and the Reverend Kendrick was attempting to divert her, during one of the sun's rare appearances, by reading aloud. Under happier circumstances, she would have enjoyed this, for the tome he'd selected was a history of the ancient world, comprised entirely of the writings of persons who had lived in it.

"'... and forthwith, he banished Zeno to Cinaria,'" read Mr. Kendrick, "'home of the artichoke.' Is that not wonderful, Miss Beaumont? I can fairly picture the hapless Zeno!"

"And I can picture the artichoke," Arabella replied. But Mr. Kendrick smiled, as though her sarcasm were contributing to the general joy of the moment.

"Suetonius was not the only one who wrote in that fashion," he said. "This is what Juvenal says of the many-storied city dwellings in Rome's residential section: 'When a fire burns one of these buildings down, the last to die are the poorest, who cannot get out, living as they do in the cheapest rooms beneath the eaves, where the gentle doves lay their eggs.'

"Do you see how cunningly the thing is done? The sentence begins by discussing something of great import, and then suddenly finishes with an engaging irrelevance. I should give *anything* to be able to write like that!"

"But you do write like that, Mr. Kendrick," said Arabella. She stretched herself beneath the heavy blanket and yawned. It pleased her, in this mood, to be insulting. "There is nothing in all the world so dull as a sea voyage," she said when she had finished her yawn, "unless one has the good luck to be violently ill, or swept overboard in a storm."

" . . . or carried away by pirates," added Belinda brightly. Her hands were buried in a muff the size of her own head plus two more, and the ends of her shawl flapped wildly in the stiff breeze.

"Yes. I am sure you could become quite carried away by pirates, Bunny," said Arabella, "but we are not likely to see any on this trip. The British Navy has the area too well secured."

"Pirates would never be dull," said Belinda dreamily. "Imagine! An entire *crew!* All those lusty Spaniards . . . and Africans . . . and Arabs . . . and oneself a helpless captive!" A seraphic smile stole across her features.

"The state of being dull is subjective, you see," Charles explained to Arabella. "You should have said, 'there is nothing in the world so dull as a sea voyage . . . *to my way of thinking.*'" He had secured his top hat to his head with a scarf tied under his chin, and looked a perfect prat. "Belinda finds fantasizing about her pirates anything *but* dull, and old Kendrick is invariably content, provided *you* are close by. As for me, there is always a lively game of knucklebones on offer between meals in the mess. Which brings me to the point rather nicely. Could you lend me some blunt? If you don't, I shall have nothing to do, and become as dull as you are."

Charles was never dull so long as there was gambling in the vicinity. He would bet on anything at all: the number of times Penderel Skeen would say "piffle" in a given conversation, what color shoes Miss Worthington was likely to wear with her badly cut puce-colored gown, and whether Cuthbert Savory-Pratt, observed from across the street, would turn to his right or his left after exiting from his hairdresser's.

None of this would have mattered, were Charles's luck not so infernally consistent, but the fellow nearly always lost. Consequently, he was a damned nuisance, eternally plaguing his sisters for money. Arabella had once observed that Charles seemed to have substituted one vice for another.

"You must have noticed it," she said to Belinda. "His behavior is fixed in stages: First, he spends twenty minutes or so begging—generally from *me*. The instant his suit finds favor, he goes straight for the game, in a wild lather of general excitement, but once engaged, his pleasure becomes focused and intense. After that, it builds swiftly to a climax, and then, all of a sudden, it's over. He crawls from the table to an easy chair, totally spent, and slumps there, either sleeping or eating, until his strength returns. I am not complaining. Merely noticing. At least, *this* vice has the merit of not producing offspring and requiring childcare from us."

Taken altogether, the voyage was fairly humdrum: entirely devoid of pirates for Belinda, a fond return of love for Kendrick, and big wins, or wins of any kind, for Charles. Nor did Arabella get swept overboard, despite her frequent forays out on deck in bad weather to relieve her mild seasickness symptoms. But midway through the crossing, the party were invited to dine aboard the *Minerve,* a British man-o'-war under the command of Rear Admiral Cockburn. Naturally, Charles pronounced the name phonetically.

"Come again?" asked Kendrick.

"Ignore him," Belinda suggested.

Charles, to whom the invitation had been conveyed via the captain, grinned like a basket of chips and said nothing.

"I apprehend the joke," said Arabella. "What, pray, is the officer's *real* name?"

"I knew you would suspect me of making it up!" cried Charles gleefully. "Both the name and rank together! Yet I swear it is true! Kendrick will bear me out!"

He handed the invitation to the rector, who peered at the print and confirmed the unfortunate appellation, though he colored up whilst he read it.

"You mustn't worry, old chap," said Charles, throwing his arm across the rector's shoulders. "I shall protect you from our wicked host! But you must also do your part, by remaining seated as much as possible!"

Whereupon, to the general merriment of the assembled company, Mr. Kendrick fled the saloon for the privacy of his own quarters.

Yet the dinner proved fairly stultifying, for all that. Rear Admiral Cockburn, despite his saucy name, was a man "exceeding dry." The sisters thought him stodgy. And Charles, afterward, reviled the battleship's plain fare at great length. There was but a single occurrence of note. One of their fellow guests, a passenger aboard the *Minerve,* changed ships that evening in order to continue on to Naples in the *Perseverance.*

Arabella believed herself to be on intimate terms with all the best and brightest men in London. Yet she had never heard of Cecil Elliot. Never heard of this paragon, who seemed to possess all the qualities that she herself had pronounced most agreeable in a partner, and she wondered at their not being previously acquainted. He was somewhat vague on the subject of his profession, and Arabella gathered that it had something to do with government or diplomacy or one of those subjects in which she took no interest.

"But why are you so averse to the subject of politics?" he had asked her at dinner.

"When one is not permitted a vote, Mr. Elliot, surely the process of determining who gets in and what measures will or will not be passed cannot be interesting."

Nevertheless, Arabella found whatever Mr. Elliot said to be of *profound* interest, and would willingly have listened to him holding forth upon the corn laws the whole night through, had he wished to go on speaking that long. Capable minds always impressed her, and Cecil Elliot was charming and attentive into the bargain. Handsome, too, in that unusual, individual way that she liked, and obviously powerful. But most compelling of all, he had known who Arabella was, and what she was, and yet, after a week's acquaintance, had still made no direct attempt at seduction. Instead of trying to bed her, he seemed intent upon getting to know her better. Nothing intrigues a courtesan more than this type of behavior, so striking in its novelty.

"If you would not think it obtrusive of me, Miss Beaumont," said he, "I should like to know the reason for your coming to Naples. It can scarcely be amusement or recreation this late in the season."

"You have hit the nail squarely upon the head, Mr. Elliot," she replied. "Recreation it is! I am engaged in the pursuit of art. Quite literally, in fact."

She thought it better to keep back the details, not because she feared his disapproval, but to encourage him to talk more about himself, and in so doing, fall in love with her. So far, he had managed to turn the tables, and she was falling in love with *him*. It was not supposed to work this way. But there was plenty of time. Arabella planned to see a great deal of Mr. Elliot—every inch of him, in fact—during their stay in Italy.

But they had no sooner reached the Bay of Naples, than the *Perseverance* met with the *Sea Lion,* a xebec bound for England. Both ships hove to, and a boat was rowed out from the one vessel to the other, to facilitate the transfer of Mr. Elliot and his valet back to London, whither the regent had commanded his immediate return.

"The regent? What does he want you for?" asked Arabella, who was so distressed at the thought of his leaving that she steeled herself to listen to a lengthy discourse on the details of political in-fighting and government protocol.

"God knows," said Elliot gloomily, watching his valet pack the rest of his things. (There wasn't much to be done, above cleaning and re-packing his fork and knife. The *Perseverance* had been about to dock, after all.) "I shall be candid with you, Miss Beaumont. The regent is a man quite given to fits of whimsy. Everyone knows that, of course, but only those of us in close contact with him apprehend the *extent* of it. If you were to offer me diamonds enough to fill this cabin, on the sole condition that I change places with the regent's valet for a week, I should not do it."

"*I* might," said Elliot's valet, sotto voce.

"I wonder whether you would, Malton, if you actually knew what you'd be letting yourself in for."

"Will you not give me an example?" Arabella asked.

"An example? Dear lady, I could give a thousand! Instead, I shall give you two. Often, in the night, the regent wakes, and wants a glass of water. That is natural enough. A carafe and tumbler stand filled and ready on his nightstand for this very purpose. But he ignores them, and instead rings for his valet. Because he wants the water *handed* to him, do you see. At three or four in the morning. And this can happen up to seven or eight times on any given night.

"He also keeps his watch there, next the carafe. But when he wants to know the time, which he frequently does—he only ever sleeps in fits and starts—the regent rings. Because he does not want to turn his head and *look* at his watch. He wants to be *told* the time. And consider: His requests for the time are separate from, and *in addition to,* his requests for water."

Elliot turned to Arabella. "I'll give you odds that when I arrive in London, his reason for bringing me home, whatever it was, will have passed, and he'll say, 'I don't want you *now,* dammit! I needed you five *days* ago when you were not here!'"

At the word "odds," Charles pricked up his ears. "You're on!" he cried. "Shall we say, half a crown? Half a crown, for a half-witted sovereign!"

"No, Charles," said Arabella. "I am opposed to regicide on general principle, but I think I might be persuaded of its efficacy, under certain circumstances."

"What would be the use? In that event we should just get one of his brothers on the throne, all of whom are, to varying degrees, vulgar, witless, mad, and corrupt."

"It is good to have a monarchy, though," she ventured. "If only for the holiday afforded by the king's birthday."

The captain knocked upon the open door. "Dinghy's ready when you are, sir."

Elliot turned to Arabella. "Miss Beaumont, would you think me presumptuous if I gave you my card? It might be amusing to meet in London and compare notes after our respective adventures are concluded. I must confess to a great curiosity about you, and I should very much like to hear how your journey turns out."

"That is a delightful suggestion, Mr. Elliot! I have not brought any of my own cards with me, but I shall be delighted to write to you."

He handed her a piece of pasteboard, which read:

CECIL ELLIOT, DDD
WHITE'S CLUB
ST. JAMES STREET
LONDON

"What does the triple *D* signify?" she asked.

"Duty, diplomacy, and discretion. It's a sort of joke, really, but an apt one. Those are the tenets by which I endeavor to live and conduct myself. *Adieu,* Miss Beaumont," he said, kissing her hand. *"Adieu et bonne chance."*

Whilst they had thus been making their farewells in Elliot's cabin, Belinda had remained on deck with Mr. Kendrick. Sympathetic girl that she was, she had divined his unquiet feelings, and endeavored to distract him with whatever the marine vista should have on offer. Just now, it was the *Sea Lion,* which would shortly be bearing away the source of the reverend's discomfort, and she pointed at the red, rakishly slanted sails.

"Look, Mr. Kendrick," she cried. "Did you ever see anything so dashing?"

"Splendid, isn't she?" said the captain, who happened to be passing by. "Our navy captured that one off the Barbary Coast, and re-christened her." He chuckled in an avuncular manner, which grated on Belinda's nerves. "Her original crew were as fierce a bunch of Corsair cutthroats as ever slaughtered gallant Christian seamen!"

"Do you mean she was a *pirate* ship?" Belinda asked.

"Aye, ma'm. Fastest thing afloat in her day. Would have got clean away from our lads, but she was badly outnumbered, and by the time her captain decided to make a run for it, we had her surrounded."

"What . . . happened to the crew?" asked the girl, fearing the answer.

"Hanged! In chains, too, bedad! No need to worry your pretty head about *them* sea robbers, miss! They're all in hell by now, turning round and round on the devil's own roasting spits!"

The captain, who had shewn a marked partiality toward the younger Beaumont sister since the first day out, could not have known that she would take this information in anything

other than a positive light. He had even entertained some
vague hopes of winning her admiration of his narrative tech-
nique to the point of convincing her to come back to his
cabin with him. But Belinda was, in fact, horror-stricken.
Moreover, as the man himself presented a most reassuring
and un-piratical appearance, she was not having any of *that,*
thank you. Even so, she lingered a while in his company after
Mr. Kendrick had gone below for his coat, because, despite
the wind and the gathering storm, the captain had begun to
tell her a story. It was a most curious tale, too, and Belinda
lost no time afterward in relating it to her sister.

"Rubbish," said Arabella flatly.

"But there was no reason for the captain to lie, Bell. He
did not even realize that he was relating anything of which I
was not already cognizant."

"That Elliot requested the transfer *himself?* But why
should he do that?"

"I don't know. Do you suppose he could have got wind of an
insurrection or an epidemic on shore, and wished to avoid it?"

"Before you told me this, I should have said that Mr. Elliot
would never think of saving himself from danger and leaving
the rest of us to face it, unprepared. But I should also have
said that he would not lie to me about his actions. The fact
that he has clearly done the one thing does not necessarily
mean he has also done the other, but sadly, I cannot rule it
out, either."

Accordingly, she removed his card from her glove, tore it
to fragments, and dropped them into the wastebasket next to
her bunk. "Come, Bunny," said she, "let us go out and catch
our first glimpse of Naples."

The *Perseverance* was just now on the point of docking,
and Mr. Kendrick strolled ebulliently over to join the ladies.

"I believe I shall write a poem about that xebec!" he exclaimed.

"What xebec?"

"The one which has borne Elliot off. Such sleek lines! Such a trim little ship! She was a bonny little brig, was she not?"

But of course, Kendrick had liked her for quite another reason. A reason that was rather odd, when you came to look at it, for he had never been jealous of the men who actually slept with Arabella.

"O heavenly, harmonious ship!" he intoned, waxing ecstatic. "O vision of loveliness, most sublime!"

Arabella lowered her eyes to the dock, where a venerable old gentleman stood, waiting patiently and holding a sign that said BOWMENT.

"Quite," she remarked. "And thus pass we, with scarcely a pause, from the sublime to the ridiculous."

Chapter 10

RELICS, HUMAN AND URBAN

John Soane's ancient friend had come to meet them himself, clad in scholar's robes, which made it all the more preposterous that he should be standing on the dock and holding up his little sign amidst a sea of touts and riotous shills. From where she was standing, Arabella could see that the hair had melted away from the crown of his head, leaving the top as naked as a baby bird's behind, but along the sides it fell almost to his shoulders in brittle, gray locks of differing lengths. Or would have done, had the wind not been whipping it across his face and straight up in the air. A hat would doubtless have been a great improvement. She could not quite picture him in a hat though, save, perhaps, the type worn by wizards.

Once the voyagers disembarked and had the chance to see him up close, the professor appeared to be in his seventies, with strong features and deep furrows extending from the sides of his nose to the corners of his mouth. But one could only notice these details later, owing to the immediate and horrific impression produced by his eyes. Professor Bergamini wore spectacles over them, tinted so dark a green that Arabella and Belinda could not see his actual eyes at all. On their approaching him, he had produced a hat from somewhere and clapped it on, when, of course, the usual thing when meeting ladies for the first, or any, time, was to take one's hat *off*. Arabella had been quite wrong about the style of it. This hat was the very opposite of a wizard's brimless cone, if anything as complex as a hat can be said to have an opposite. The crown was low, and a wide, loose brim cast the wearer's face in perpetual shadow. Staring out from beneath this generous awning, the tinted spectacles looked spectral, indeed, like the ocular holes in a skull.

Still, except for donning his hat, the professor was cordial enough. He had even arranged to have three carriages waiting at the dock to convey the Beaumonts and their luggage to the hotel . . . and Mr. Kendrick, too, of course.

"Bell," whispered Belinda. "He keeps . . . staring at me!"

"Does he? How can you tell?"

"I . . . I do not know! But I can! And I am all over goose-flesh! Look!" She drew back her glove, exposing the little, raised bumps on her forearm.

"Dear me!" said her sister. "Yet, I am not surprised."

"I cannot share a carriage with that . . . *monster!* You must do something!"

"All right, darling. I shall tend to it." Arabella detached herself from Belinda's clutches and approached the others. "Gentlemen, you will greatly oblige us by riding together in the first coach, where you will be free to discuss your manly plans without our tiresome interference."

Although they had no manly plans, so far as they were aware, Kendrick and Charles were happy enough to comply with her wishes—apparently tinted spectacles held no horrors for them—and so the party started off to everyone's satisfaction. Five minutes after they left the docks, the heavens split open, and the rain poured forth like steely beads.

"He means me no good, I am sure of it!" cried Belinda, shouting to make herself heard above the clattering racket.

"The old fellow must be evil, or mad!" The rain, on a sudden, lessened. "And his eyes," she continued, in a normal tone of voice, "could we but see them, should betray him at once. He resembles a gigantic house fly, attempting to disguise itself as a professor."

Her sister explained that tinted lenses were often used to correct vision problems, or sensitivity to the sun.

"But it is raining today," said Belinda.

"Yes. Well, perhaps he is sensitive to any light whatsoever."

"Or perhaps he suffers from syphilis . . ."

"Perhaps he does."

" . . . and perhaps," Belinda persisted, "the ravages of the disease have left him looking older than his actual age, and he is really only a young man of five and twenty!"

They were laughing now. It was not really so amusing, but they had not got much sleep the previous night, and that, coupled with Arabella's disappointment over Elliot's departure, and Belinda's terror of Bergamini, had rendered them both a trifle giddy. When their mirth subsided, they fell into a kind of reverie that resembled stupefaction.

"Bell," said Belinda, rousing herself at last, "shall we have to keep company with that dreadful old man *all* the time?"

"Well, the poor fellow has taken the trouble to secure our comfort. He is certain to know a great deal about antiquities, and perhaps he will be able to advise me on how best to deal with the customs officers once I find my statue. But I can see him alone, if you do not wish to accompany me whilst you are here."

Tired though she was, Belinda caught the import behind the words.

"No. I am the one who convinced you to undertake this journey," she said. "It would be very bad of me to desert you now, and I won't; I just wish that we might keep our contacts with . . . with dubious characters to a minimum."

Arabella smiled, and took a small edition of Boccaccio—travel-sized, for convenience—out of her necessities bag. "I expect you will get used to him, darling," she said. "He strikes me as the sort of man who grows on one."

And she began, quietly, to read, while Belinda looked out of the window, and thought about tumors.

After a time, the little caravan reached Resina, the contemporary town constructed unawares above the ancient one, and pulled up before a comfortable-looking hotel there. The landlords ran out to the new arrivals with umbrellas and hurried them indoors, where they passed through a medieval reception hall and up a grand staircase to a cozy suite of rooms. They were to have a large salon, with four bedchambers opening off it on two sides, and a private parlor at the farther end.

"I trust you will find it comfortable here," said the professor. "Signor and Signora Fiorello will see to your every need. There is even a doctor next door, should you require medical attention, though I sincerely hope that you will not."

Belinda had to admit that the old man had a wonderful voice, with the merest hint of a thrilling continental accent. And she decided that she might be able to bear his company in the days to come, so long as she did not have to actually look him in the face.

"This is the best hotel in Resina," he continued. "The owners are personal friends of mine. Here you can bathe, rest, and have dinner, and tomorrow I shall escort you to the scene of the murder."

"But what if it should still be raining?" asked Arabella.

"It will not rain tomorrow, *signorina*. This is just a small storm. It will pass over quickly."

He bowed, and Arabella barely had time to thank him before he was gone. Then she went down to supervise Mr. Kendrick's supervision of the fellow who was supervising the disposition of their luggage.

"In which room should you like them to put your valise,

Bunny?" she called over her shoulder. But there was no answer. Belinda had walked into the first bedroom she had
come to, and fallen facedown upon the bed.

On her way back upstairs, Arabella met her brother coming down.

"Shouldn't you like to have a nap, Charles?"

"Presently, presently," he replied, and she guessed what
was afoot, for prior to separating at the customs house, Arabella had given him money with which to pay for the carriages. And he had done; she had seen the lire pass hands. But
not understanding the rate of exchange, she had probably
given him too much, and Charles must now be looking for a
way to lose the amount left over.

Mr. Kendrick would have liked very much to take a nap.
But with impressive alacrity, he had grasped the true reason
for his inclusion in the party, and now he followed in
Charles's wake without a murmur of complaint. Because he
loved her.

When a sudden pang of remorse stabbed at Arabella like a
stiletto on the staircase, she ignored it. Mr. Kendrick, she
knew, would not want her to suffer on his account. He adored
performing these services for her. They were what he lived for,
and nothing was required of her in return save that she permit
him to anticipate her slightest wish. At least, that was how she
saw it.

On entering the room that would be hers, Arabella was
aware of an odd, suffused brightness. Her mind, by this time,
was somewhat dulled by fatigue, so it took her a moment to
identify the source: a sunbeam, stealing through a crack in
the shutters. Without so much as a glance at her inviting bed,
she threw open the French doors and stepped out onto a
small balcony. The sun was once again in possession of what
little was left of the day, and now, by its mellow light, Arabella beheld the ruins, which lay cupped beneath her in a kind
of crater, like a small-scale replica in a dish: columns, arches,

partial walls with shrubs sprouting from their cracks or ivy dripping down their summits, fragments of streets, the remains of sunken gardens, and oddly shaped mounds that she guessed to be unexcavated buildings. Here and there, a cypress pointed a slim, accusatory finger at the sky, from whose impassive blue expanse the ancient gods had once beheld the destruction of the faithful.

All was quiet, save for an occasional bird note echoing in the stillness, and the air sparkled with the prisms of quivering raindrops, refracting the golden sunlight of late afternoon. The resurrected city appeared to be sleeping. Arabella had not realized that the hotel was so close to it. She hurried inside and quickly dressed to go out, her fatigue vanished upon the instant. When she came downstairs, she glimpsed Charles playing vingt-et-un in the parlor with a puffy-looking fellow who had seemingly just arrived, for a vast collection of trunks and travel cases was once again piled in the lobby. Kendrick stood behind Charles's chair, looking exhausted. Arabella did not want to talk to them. She paused beside the parlor doorway, gathered herself together, and swiftly plunged past it, without being noticed.

The air outside proved chillier than she had expected or prepared for, but a path ran round the rim of the sunken city, gradually spiraling down to merge with one of the ancient streets, and by taking this at a brisk pace, she was quickly able to restore the warmth to her limbs. Like an explorer arriving on an undreamt-of continent, Arabella broached gardens, peered into windows, and paced through rooms that had once been studies and libraries and private kitchens. The spell of the past descended upon her consciousness like a gossamer scarf. A part of her mind was still grounded in the nineteenth century, but another part felt itself to be rooted in the distant past, as if she were somebody else, clinging to an existence that lay buried beneath the rubble, and seizing the chance to revisit its beloved city through the agency of a living body.

The sensation was a novel one, yet it did not distract Arabella from her purpose. Somewhere in this place, an exceptionally well-endowed Pan statue had lain unclaimed and undiscovered for seventeen centuries. Now it was here no longer, and a man lay dead because he had tried to procure it for her. Where had the murder occurred? From where had the bronze been taken? And more importantly, where was it now?

She walked through the silent streets as late-forming clouds returned to obscure the sun once again. There would be no sunset, now; just a gradual fading of light and color, reducing the world to a uniform gray before the darkness took over. Herculaneum was mostly gray, anyway. She shivered as shadows began to lengthen in the ancient doorways. A burst of cold air sprang up from nowhere, blowing her bonnet askew.

The certainty of knowing oneself to be the only living soul in an empty city is one that few will ever encounter, and thankfully so. But Arabella was enjoying the sensation. To be walking and thinking in a place uninhabited for a thousand years was a memory she would cherish for the rest of her life.

But then, she was *not* alone, after all.

Awareness of this fact broke upon her in subtle stages, building up so gradually that it was more like the subtle seepage of fluid through a porous membrane than a clear moment of certainty. But the instant she detected a slight movement out of the corner of her eye, an occurrence that coincided with the audible dislodgment of a pebble, her mind reacted immediately, and she turned to confront this intruder on her solitude, only to find the street empty.

She realized, with a jolt, that she might actually be in *danger*. But Arabella continued to saunter along the pavement, to all appearances unaware of the escort who stalked her just beyond that row of shops, because she was seeking the road by which she had come, and the way back to safety. There was not a soul down here excepting herself . . . and one other. Now and then, she thought she saw a partial face peeping at her from behind a date palm, or fingers emerging from a gap between the ancient bricks. In the waning light it was becoming harder to see. Where, oh, where was the exit road?

Arabella had completely lost her bearings. She could no longer recall which streets she had walked along, or where the hotel had stood in relation to them. Now she was aware of her own heart, thumping in her breast, and she began to walk a little faster. But only a *little* faster, lest her fright be perceived by the "other," and the time judged ripe for pouncing on her. Was that just the wind soughing through the umbrella pines? No. It was someone whispering.

Dear God. There was more than one of them. Either that, or the only one there was . . . was insane. Arabella keenly felt her vulnerability now. She was alone and unprotected in a strange place, where she neither spoke the language, understood the customs, nor knew how to find her way back. John Soane had spoken truly: She had got herself embroiled in a mad scheme. Upon regaining the hotel precincts, the first thing she would do would be to get a map of this place. But . . . what if she never got back to the hotel? She must not think like that! She *must* not! Because then she would panic, and panic was a type of surrender, and she was not made that way.

Now she could make out multiple human shapes in the gathering darkness. The people who had worshiped Pan were said to "panic" when they were filled with the divine presence, weren't they? She wouldn't, though, because she did not want the god; only his statue. She would find it soon and take it home, and relax with a cup of tea and her feet propped up on something, and she must keep on with this inner monologue, this inner, mindless chattering, so as to keep from thinking about those people following her on both sides of the road, and how more of them were appearing up ahead and coming toward her. She was being surrounded.

Suddenly, Arabella broke into a run, and fled down a side street. The movement was so unexpected that her pursuers failed to react for a moment, but soon they were giving chase, a pack of hounds hunting a stricken doe. She left the street and zigzagged across a series of alleys, praying to God, to nature, to her dead grandmother, but knowing it was only a matter of time before she would fly unwitting down some cul-de-sac and come up short against a wall of solid stone.

And then, on rounding the next corner, Arabella saw some sort of official up ahead—a night watchman, perhaps—shoveling a dead animal into a sack. She was struggling to draw sufficient air into her lungs to scream for help and still running as hard as she could, when someone stepped directly in her path.

"*Signorina!* Hello, *signorina!* You need a guide?"

A small ragamuffin in an oversized man's shirt was grinning up at her, and Arabella had a fleeting impression of white teeth in a dirty face. Mortified by the shriek that she had been unable to suppress, and still panting for breath, she brushed past him toward the watchman, with a hastily mumbled "No, thank you. Not just now."

"Not just now?" he persisted, jogging along at her side. "So, how do you think? Later is possible? I am good guide! I know all these houses and secret buried places. My name is Pietro! When later comes and you are ready to look, ask for me! I can show you anything, anytime you like!"

Her pursuers had stopped running behind her, and now she saw that they were children, also. But unsupervised children, Arabella knew, could be every bit as dangerous as adults. She halted and looked at the boy. "Anytime?" she asked. "Don't you ever go home, then?"

"This my home!" he cried, with a sweep of his arm that included his compatriots. "I . . . they . . . *all* of us, live here! In Ercolano!"

They were the filthiest children she had ever seen, and Arabella was a Londoner! Pitifully thin, and shoeless, with pointed little feral faces. The watchman shooed them away like chickens and admonished her. His English was not as good as the boy's, but his meaning was clear: The children were bad. She should not speak to them. She should go home. He brought his lantern and showed her the way out.

Returned to the hotel at last, Arabella dragged herself upstairs, where she found Belinda revived, refreshed, and dressing for dinner.

"There you are!" cried her sister gaily. "I wondered where you'd gone! Should I wear pearls in my hair tonight? Or do you think them too sophisticated for Resina?"

"Too . . . sophisticated . . ." Arabella gasped. "The silk baby's breath is much . . . more suitable. Bunny . . ."

"Hmmm?"

"Bunny, I think I need to lie down for a bit before dinner. Would you mind?"

"Well . . . we haven't much time, Bell. You should have had a nap, like I did, rather than go exploring right away."

And then, for the first time, she had a really good look at her sister.

"Bell! Are you all right? Here, lie on my bed! I'll ring for a glass of . . . whatever it is they drink here!"

A short time later, Arabella was propped up with a lot of pillows and a glass of . . . whatever it was they had brought her. She was feeling much better.

"Thank goodness!" said Belinda with heartfelt relief. "You gave me a terrible fright just now!"

"Yes, well, I'd had one myself, you see. But it turned out to be only fancy on my part. There was actually nothing to be afraid of, at all."

By the time the dinner bell sounded, the fair explorer had recovered her healthy complexion so completely that she was able to wear pale green brocade, without it making her look the least bit jaundiced.

Chapter 11

AN INDECENT PROPOSITION

A welcoming fire was crackling in the *sala da pranzo,* and the aromas wafting in from the kitchen (a circumstance that would have been regarded as a travesty in an English household) excited the appetites of the expectant diners, with the exception of Charles. But Arabella was irritated to find eight persons already seated when she entered the room. And where she had expected to see a number of tables, or in any event, two, there was only the one. Evidently, the guests would all be obliged to dine and converse together, whether they would or no.

Later that night, she described her fellow guests in the CIN. On her only other detection adventure, Arabella had used her crime investigation notebook solely to record her impressions pertaining to a murder. But she had not been traveling then. In the present instance, moreover, she had forgot to bring a separate travel diary with her. And so, having surmised that little detection work would be required of her this time, she was using the back of her CIN to chronicle her travels.

The head of the table was occupied by a broad, powerfully built priest of middle age, his square face set off by stiff salt-

and-pepper hair and a Vandyke beard. He wears pince-nez, and though he affects the standard cassock and collar of the Catholic lower clergy, he is evidently a **Primary Force** of considerable importance, for he also wears impressive jewelry, and is followed about wherever he goes by three silent monks. He somewhat singularly failed to rise from his seat when Bunny and I entered the room, and if I am not to take umbrage at his behavior, I must conclude that the practice is not observed amongst adherents of the Roman faith.

Our landlord and host effecting the introductions. I learned that the **Primary Force** hails from Palermo, and goes by the name of Father Terranova. I was mildly surprised that no ecclesiastical titles were appended to his name, but I suppose that the prelate—for I am certain that he is one—has his reasons for not wishing to use them.

His mother, Simonetta Terranova, resembles him. But she is shorter, possibly broader, and her beard is not so well-trimmed as his! Signora Terranova orders everyone about in superior tones, an affectation of which the great man himself has no need, and basks in the reflected brilliance of her shining son. Her sister, Ginevra Rinaldo, is wan and unassertive, where the Signora is robust and imposing.

Ginevra's grown children round out the family group. Renilde has premature jowls, and a long-bridged nose with a blobby tip. She scrapes her hair severely back from her heavy face, a look which does nothing for her, and plucks her eyebrows ridiculously thin. This gives her a hard look, and I think she **is** hard. Miss Rinaldo sat like a hobbledehoy during the introductions, rudely spooning her soup as though we were not there. She did look up, though, and I thought I saw her eyes glint with interest, when Charles and Mr. Kendrick were presented.

Osvaldo, her half brother, is the puffy fellow who was playing cards with Charles when I went out this afternoon. He's an utter beefwit, with affected English mannerisms. So, predictably, his two main occupations, in which he indulges with such frequency that they seem more like behavioral tics, are the taking of snuff (even at the table!) and repetitive recourse to his quizzing glass. The hair of his head is brushed forward from behind, à la execucion, and it peeps over the top of his exaggerated collar in a manner suggestive of vegetation. When viewed from the side, this extraordinary style choice produces an impression of a grass hummock, spied above the upraised wing of a duck. One simply cannot make out the profile at all. Nor can his face really be seen from the front, owing to the quizzing glass perpetually pressed against the socket of one eye.

There is also a trio of sycophantic monks, who were not introduced to us. I have concluded that they are not important in themselves, but merely constitute a kind of fashion accessory for the **Primary Force.**

Once introductions had been made and the Beaumont party was seated, soup was served to these latest arrivals, and the silence that now seized the company had more to do with the English group's fatigue, and both parties' desire for privacy, than with concentration upon the food. Belinda was fading again after a brief revival—her nap having been either too prolonged or not long enough. Charles did not like the soup and stirred it about without taking any, brooding over the two or three games of vingt-et-un lately lost to Osvaldo. Arabella was in a state approaching stupefaction from the combined effects of her tiring day and her scare in the ruins. And Reverend Kendrick, who had been kept constantly busy tending to the luggage, signing the register, seeing the passports safely secured, and watching over Charles, had been unable to procure a restorative of any kind, and nearly fell face-first from exhaustion into the *pasta puttanesca*.

After a while, though, when Arabella attempted to invest the occasion with a modicum of civility by recounting her recent adventures in the buried city, he mustered sufficient energy to rebuke her for having ventured out without a chaperone.

"Anything might have happened to you, Miss Beaumont! Please remember that a murder occurred in that place only recently! The watchman had a shovel, you said? Isn't that what the victim was killed with? Perhaps it was the very murder weapon itself you saw! I implore you to exercise more common sense, in future!"

"The murder weapon!" Arabella exclaimed. "You are right, Mr. Kendrick! It could have been the very one!" And she might have been killed whilst the spirit of the ancient Roman had been occupying a part of her consciousness. How sad for the poor soul, waiting over seventeen hundred years to reanimate in a receptive mind, only to be killed again, almost immediately, with a shovel this time.

"The reverend is indeed right, *signorina*," said the priest, nodding sagaciously. "You must not allow your eagerness to run away with you. Otherwise, some vagrant, seeing how easy it is, will try to run away with you, also!"

The other members of his party laughed gently at their leader's little sally, except for Renilde. She had the sort of face that looks a stranger to laughter.

"It is, if I may say so," added the prelate, "an unusual season for sightseeing."

"That is why I have chosen it," Arabella replied. "I cannot bear crowds. Has your journey been a long one, Mr. Terranova?" She would not address him as "Father." He was not *her* father, and she was not of his faith. Arabella was determined to shew this fellow that he was no better than she was:

After all, in their respective universes they were both stars, each with its host of orbiting bodies.

"It has, indeed," he replied. "We should have arrived before you, but for a slight accident which delayed us some hours. 'Don't worry, Felice,' I say to myself. 'You will be there soon enough. There will be few people traveling at this time of year, and Osvaldo can go on ahead to procure the rooms. Just trust in God.' So I do. And what happens? I find your group already here, and in possession of the very suite we were to have had!" He shrugged. "Such things, they happen. Who can say why? Those of us with faith, trust that God knows what He is doing."

"And *you* have faith, of course!"

He smiled. "I do not always have it, but I always *try* to have it. *Signorina,*" he said, addressing Arabella, but looking at Charles. "Do you think that your brother would consider changing rooms with us?"

"No, I do not think that he would. This is *my* expedition, *signor,* and I make the decisions. Charles has no say in what we do here."

"Oh! But this is most unusual, yes? Even for the English?"

"Quite. Yet I can assure you that it is the case."

"Then, would *you* consider changing rooms?"

"No. I like the balcony, and am partial to the view it affords. Why do you ask?"

"Because," he said grimly. "I, too, am partial to that particular view."

Perceiving the conversation to have reached an impasse, Arabella now addressed herself to the garlic bread, whilst on her right, Mr. Kendrick and Father Terranova commenced the sort of religious discussion in which she took no interest. With Osvaldo on her left, there was no one to talk to, for the fellow was inspecting her through his quizzing glass as though she were a museum exhibit.

Across the table, his sister was asking impertinent questions of Belinda concerning her relationships to Charles and Mr. Kendrick, since Renilde had been too absorbed in the soup course to mark the landlord's introductions.

"Of course," said she, with a toss of her head, "we might have taken a more exclusive hotel than this one, but my cousin had very specific reasons for wanting to be here. And the beds are tolerable, I suppose."

"Yes, they are very comfortable," said Belinda, and she could not for the life of her think of anything else to say. Because in the whole of her life she had never before sat for such an extended period in such close proximity to such a thoroughly disagreeable person.

"I know who you are," said Osvaldo abruptly, addressing Arabella and pocketing his quizzing glass.

"You can hardly expect me to be impressed by that news," Arabella replied. "*I* have known it for years. I also seem to recall being introduced to you a short time ago at this very table."

"Yes. And I think at once that your name, she's familiar. But only this moment I remember where I see you before. You are Arabella Beaumont, the London courtesan, are you not?"

Osvaldo had chosen to make this remark during another lull in the conversation, so that it was heard by everybody in the room.

"Yes," said Arabella simply. "I am."

The priest's mother and aunt hastily excused themselves from the dinner table. They tried to induce Miss Rinaldo to come with them, but unfortunately for Belinda, they were unsuccessful.

"Quite so," lisped Osvaldo in a horribly accurate imitation of a typical London dandy's voice, without the typical London dandy's command of English. "My Mayfair friends, they point you out to me at the theater, once. I spend fully much of the time amusing to myself in London, you see. I am-a, how you call, a natural son of the Duke of Clarence."

And how many times had she heard *that* before? Foreigners were ever wont to claim relatives amongst the nobility of one's own country, although, as a matter of fact, Osvaldo *did* somewhat resemble the duke, with that pear-shaped head.

"Where I come from, sir," said Arabella frostily, "illegitimacy is considered a severe social disadvantage!"

"Ah!" he replied. "And where you come-a from, the courtesan, she is also the social outcast, no? But this is not so much true in Italy. Not if one can boast of noble blood in one's veins!"

The guests now found it convenient to withdraw to the coffee room, where Mr. Kendrick attempted to join Arabella on a small divan. But the *Powerful Force* got there ahead of him, settling his bulk emphatically down upon the cushions and practically tipping the side with Arabella on it up into the air.

"So!" said the priest, with evident relish. "This is a most unusual circumstance! I do not believe I have ever shared after-dinner coffee with a whore."

Arabella told herself that perhaps the man did not mean to be rude.

"As a matter of fact, *signor,*" said she, "I am a *courtesan,* not a whore."

"There is a difference?"

"Indeed there is."

"And what is that, may I ask?"

"Self-respect."

He chuckled. "Most interesting! And just how do you justify this profession, whatever it may please you to call it, to God?"

"There is no need for justification," she said. "All creatures fornicate, with God's complete approval. The Divine Injunction bids us go forth and multiply, is it not so, Mr. Terranova? And humans must earn their bread. Thus, I earn my bread like a human being, by fornicating like one of God's creatures. How can He possibly object to that? How can *you* object to it?"

"But I do not object to it," he said, smiling. "Your profession gives my profession the means of earning its bread, also. Until a short time ago, the church even conceded the necessity of brothels. After all, in Italy there are many whores, and every one of them contributes to the church collection basket!"

"While your ignorance is perhaps understandable," said she, "it is also insulting. There is as vast a difference between a whore and a courtesan as there is between a novice monk and an archbishop. Although the difference between the examples *themselves* is perhaps not so great."

Confound the man! He actually had the temerity to laugh!

"That was well said!" he cried. "And I do beg your pardon for insulting you, my dear . . . lady. Is that an insult, too?"

Arabella shook her head.

"You see," he explained, "as a courtesan from a Protestant country, you probably think the Church is your enemy. But consider: The same system that made you an outcast has also made you wealthy, and as your excellent friend, Mr. Kendrick, informed me at dinner, you generously provided the funding for the roof repairs to the Effing church. Do you see? All things are connected, and every part works together."

This man was either very wonderful, or very terrible.

"You must be a Jesuit," said Arabella. "I have heard about your order. It is said to combine the best and worst features of all the others."

"That is true," he said pleasantly. "And here you see before you the best and worst, combined in one *man*. You should have heard me swear when our carriage lost a wheel at Messina! But we could debate the Church's position on whoredom for the next sixty years, quoting contradictory passages of the Bible at one another. The Bible is designed that way intentionally, you know. The exercise might even prove interesting: You are probably cleverer than I am, but I undoubtedly know the Bible better than you do. Nevertheless, after dinner I would rather eat dessert than quote Scripture. Will you allow me to fetch you one of those little cakes?"

"Thank you, *signor*. I would rather chuse for myself. But I should like to know why *you* have come all this distance in the off-season. Are you attending a Church conference here?"

What some might have called a beatific smile spread itself across his features. Others would have pronounced it smug, perhaps. In any case, the entire room was listening when he said, "I am here on a sacred mission, to baptize the ancient dead of Ercolano. And when I have completed the task, I intend to perform the same service for the poor, pagan souls of Pompeii."

The three monks sat back in their chairs with little smirks of satisfaction, as they awaited the expected exclamations of wonder and delight from the English tourists. But they were destined to be disappointed.

Kendrick, teetering on a small gilt chair with one dangerously slanting leg, had been on the point of sleep only a moment before, but the priest's pronouncement startled him awake.

"Indeed!" said the rector. "I had not realized such a thing was possible!"

"Normally, it would not be," Terranova replied. "But as the dead of Pompeii and Herculaneum, or 'the Pompulaneans,' as I call them . . ." (Here, his followers smiled again, in a superior sort of way) " . . . were all Romans, we feel that they should be considered Catholic by association. All that remains is for someone—myself, for example—to sprinkle holy water on the site and say the litany, and it is done."

"Wonderful!" exclaimed Belinda, who had to pass behind them on her way to the coffee pot. "Now all those poor little unchristened dead babies can finally be sent to heaven! I hope that you will see to them first, Father!"

The priest appeared discomfited.

"I wish I could, *signorina*," he said, "but modern infants come under a different jurisdiction. The mass baptism which I have in contemplation will not affect them."

"Rot!" muttered Arabella. Aloud, she asked how he proposed to sprinkle holy water over an entire city.

"That is simply done," he replied. "I need only stand on a high place, as His Holiness, the Blessed Pope, does, to perform the rite over the entire area at once."

She had a sudden intuition. "Which high place do you mean?"

But Terranova became extremely absorbed in stirring his coffee just then, and the voice of one of the monks was now heard for the first time.

"I am certain the *signorina* cannot object. The balcony of your suite, she afford-a the pear-fect . . ."

"I am sorry to have to correct you," said Arabella, "but the *signorina* certainly *can* object. And she *does*."

In order to signal the matter closed, our heroine rose at once and crossed to the dessert table, where Osvaldo found the opportunity to join her. He had taken out his quizzing glass again, and seemed to be committing every detail of her physiognomy to memory. Arabella never minded admiring scrutiny from prospective clients, but she had a notion that this particular noodle was seeking imperfections with which to regale his mother and aunt later on. Accordingly, she turned away from him, as if to better assess the sweets on offer.

Mr. Kendrick, meanwhile, had taken a more comfortable seat, and was now chatting somewhat uncomfortably with Miss Rinaldo, who had wedged herself next to him in a chair wide enough for exactly one and a half persons. Initially, she had attempted to have a conversation with Charles, but he had looked right through her, as though she were a ghost interposed between himself and the gaming room.

"Upon my word!" Kendrick was heard to exclaim. "What a magnificent pianoforte! Do you not think so, Signorina Rinaldo?"

"Yes," she replied simply. "I wonder whether you would accompany me on it, Mr. Kendrick, in the event that I should feel like singing?"

"Renilde often feels like singing," said Osvaldo helpfully. "Unfortunately, we do not-a often feel like listening."

Undaunted by the fair prospect of Arabella's back, he had simply gone round to the front and come right up to her, where he continued his invasive examination at the closest possible range. She might have reached out and touched him without fully extending her arm. In fact, she decided that she *would* touch him, for this puppy badly wanted its ears pulled. Accordingly, Arabella dunked her thumb into the sauce boat and smeared a glob of warm, sticky syrup of peaches across the lens of his inspection device.

"Oh," she said tonelessly. "I am so sorry. Am I in your way?"

And she swept through the room with all the affronted majesty of a powerful pagan empress.

"Miss Beaumont!" cried the rector. "Surely you do not mean to leave us so soon!" He struggled desperately to rise from his seat.

"I am afraid I must, Mr. Kendrick. I have some letters to write."

But after she had left, Arabella also, paradoxically, lingered behind, for Mr. Kendrick's mind was full of her, and Signorina Rinaldo was thinking about her, too.

"Have you known Miss Beaumont long, Mr. Kendrick?" she asked.

"Yes," he replied, smiling. "Ever since we were children. I spent nearly every school holiday with her family."

"I see. You are old friends, then. And now you have come to this place with your old friends on holiday. But why so late in the season?"

"We are searching for a statue which Miss Beaumont recently bought from this part of the world. It's gone missing, and . . . well, it was stolen, actually."

"But Italy is full of statues! Surely your friend might have chosen another, or had one made, without coming all this way?"

"Quite. But this is an old statue. Very, very old, in fact—it was discovered in Ercolano, and there is not another like it in the entire world."

"Is that so?" Renilde affected surprise, and then, placing a hand on the rector's leg, as if to steady her nerves, she said, "Would this be connected to the art theft and murder that happened here last month?"

Kendrick jumped at her touch, and attempted to ease his leg from under her hand without giving offense.

"Yes," he said.

"I know quite a bit about that. You see, the matter involves my family."

"Your family? Oh, I say!"

"Yoo-hoo! Mr. Kendrick!" Belinda called from across the room, cupping her hands around her mouth. "Father Terranova has asked me to sing. Would you be good enough to provide accompaniment on the pianoforte?"

He rose to oblige her, inclining his head toward Renilde. "I should be most interested in hearing your story, Miss Rinaldo!"

"Yes? Well, I shall tell you about it another time," she replied in a low voice. "But we must talk privately, for I am not supposed to discuss this with anyone. Now you had better go, for my cousin wants a song, it seems, and where his pleasures are concerned, he is a very impatient man."

Chapter 12

POSSIBLE SUSPECTS

Dear Mrs. Janks,

The weather in Resina is all one might wish at this time of year, and we are very comfortably accommodated in a good sort of hotel, where the food, though not a patch on Mrs. Moly's cooking, is fresh, plain and substantial enough to keep us from hunger and stomach complaints.

There is no news of the statue yet, as we have only just arrived, but I did go down to view the scene of the dastardly crime. Herculaneum, or "Ercolano," as the natives call it, is "hauntingly beautiful" by daylight, and plain "haunting" after the sun goes down. Only think of all the ghosts that must be bound to this city, where their human forms perished centuries ago, all within moments of one another!

Now I wonder, Mrs. Janks, whether you can have heard any news pertaining to the "family scandal"? Do people still talk of it? Are we still

ostracized and reviled? Or have things begun to
settle down, at last? My mind misgives me upon
the subject. I have already written several letters
to friends and relatives, but have heard nothing as
yet. We cannot come home until the whole sordid
mess is forgotten. Please write as soon as you can,
either to relieve my anxieties . . . or to confirm
them.

With warmest regards to you and all the
Lustings staff,

A.B.

Arabella blotted and folded her letter, carefully placing it
between the pages of *The Decameron* for safekeeping until
she should have occasion to go upstairs, for she was presently
sitting in the hotel parlor, away from the annoyances of the
coffee room. She would infinitely have preferred to be both
downstairs *and* alone, but she had been obliged to compromise, for the dour landlady was in here, polishing her Venetian goblet collection. Fortunately, Signora Fiorello was not
the garrulous sort, as persons with a limited command of
one's own language so often are, and Arabella respected the
fact that her landlady was a fellow collector. There were no
presumptuous priests here, or invasive, pear-headed morons
to shatter the tranquility, and reopening *The Decameron* to
the page where she had lately left off reading, Arabella began
to relax.

But there is no rest for the wicked: She had just nestled into
the cushions, having come to the part where the nuns are en-

joying the services of the well-endowed deaf-mute handy-
man, when she was distracted by the hotel cat, drinking
lustily from its water bowl in the corner.

"Signora Fiorello," said she, "you would greatly oblige me
by removing that animal from my presence."

The landlady stooped to pick up the bowl with one hand,
puss with the other.

"Don't-a you like-a cats?" she asked fiercely, cradling the
animal against her well-upholstered shoulder. In Signora
Fiorello's world there were only two types of people: those
who loved felines and those destined for a special hell all
their own.

"I concede their usefulness as vermin catchers," said Arabella, "but I dislike listening to their love songs whilst I am
trying to sleep. Nor, as now, do I enjoy the sound of a lapping
tongue in my near vicinity that may lately have lapped the
blood of some disease-ridden rodent."

"So. You *don't*-a like the cats," said Mrs. Fiorello, in a tone
that placed Arabella squarely in the camp of the damned. And
she strode from the room, her head high, and her cat's somewhat lower.

Arabella could probably have had the room to herself for
as long as she wanted it now, but rather than remain there
and risk another unwelcome interaction with her fellow creatures, she decided that the fates were impelling her upstairs,
and upstairs she accordingly went.

"Mrs. Janks," said Fielding, "don't it seem odd that we've
had no word from the missus, tellin' us as to when she's coming home?"

"No, Marianne, it don't seem odd a bit! I'll tell you, *I*
shouldn't want to come back at this time o' year if *I* was in
Italy!"

A storm was at that moment battering Lustings's outer
walls and hammering against the drawing room windows,

where the staff reclined in sated bliss after an enormous evening meal.

You are shocked, are you not, to find servants in the drawing room? Admittedly, it *is* a trifle unusual. But before she left, Arabella told the housekeeper that the staff might treat her home as their own whilst she was away. Except for Tilda, of course, who had a tendency to break things, and had to be watched for that reason.

"Is Italy nice, then?" asked Doyle. She had the happy ginger tomcat on her lap, and was rubbing his chin.

"Oh, yes; it's ever so warm and pleasant there. *Tsk!* I wish my lady's clients would learn to follow the *seams,* 'stead o' just ripping away in the middle like they does!" (Mrs. Janks was mending one of Arabella's delicate nightdresses, which a prominent parliamentarian had torn practically in half with his teeth.) "Italy's where they grow the grapes, you know," she added.

"Grapes!" cried Fielding.

"And oranges. Grapes and oranges grow wild all along the boulevards, which aren't proper streets, but rivers. That's all they have there—rivers. All the buildings are on islands that bob about ever so, till a body feels right sick. But it's sunny and warm, with monkeys and parrots in all the grape trees, and the Pope himself going up and down in a giant shell boat, pulled by dolphins."

Mrs. Molyneux was French by birth, and had once been to Italy. But she quietly attended to her mending, and allowed Mrs. Janks's pronouncements to stand unchallenged, because, reader, Mrs. Moly had worked in other establishments, including Lady Ribbonhat's, and had learned to prize a peaceful household above high wages and titled employers. She also understood the importance of cherished beliefs, and would never destroy the inner visions of anyone she liked, no matter how silly or inaccurate.

"Sometimes," Mrs. Janks continued, "the buildings come

loose from all the bobbing and lean way over, so that to get into one you have to pass underneath it and be pulled up through a window. What's wrong, my dear? Are you all right?"

"I zhust . . . have somesing in my eye," said Mrs. Molyneux, bending over her lap and hiding her face in her apron. "Zere!" she said, sitting up straight. "I am quite all right again!"

The cat was now smiling to itself on Fielding's lap, and purring loudly.

"We shall have to get rid of this fellow before the missus gets home, " said the housekeeper.

"Oh, but Rooney's such a *nice* cat, Mrs. Janks," Tilda protested. "Maybe Madam will fall in love with him and keep him for always."

"Rooney? Is that what you call him? Whatever for?"

"I named him Rooney," said Doyle. "Because he is so noble. He is called after a boy I knew in Tipperary once, who had just the same red hair and princely manners."

"You don't say so! Well, I must admit he *does* have the nicest manners as ever I saw in a cat," said the housekeeper, patting his tail. "But we shall have to wait and see what the missus says when she gets back . . . if she ever *does* get back, that is. "

Long after Arabella had left the others, Belinda staggered through the door to the Beaumont party's private parlor, and dropped onto a chair next the desk.

"I must remonstrate with you, Bell!" she cried faintly. "After you left, I was made to sing all the English ballads the world has ever known!"

"How could that be my fault?" Arabella asked, busily writing the aforementioned description of her fellow guests.

"Because, if you had only been there, you might have had half of them. It was very ill-mannered to leave us so abruptly."

"Ill-mannered? *I* was ill-mannered? What about the others?"

"I fully understand your exasperation with that horrid Osvaldo fellow," said Belinda, "but I fail to see why you cannot be more amenable towards Father Terranova. After all, he only wants to throw some water off your balcony and mutter a few meaningless words. What is that to you?"

"All words are meaningless, in and of themselves, Bunny. We make them mean something by the intention that impels their utterance." Arabella shut the notebook. "And I do not care for that man's meaning. I disliked him the moment I saw him. He wants to intrude himself into our rooms and leave his noxious stamp upon them, like some . . . randy tomcat. I do not want him in here, I do not want him on my balcony, and I particularly do not want him baptizing the helpless dead, who are in no position to object."

"Well, I don't see that it matters," said Belinda. "They *are* dead, after all."

"No, your sister is quite right, Miss Belinda," said Mr. Kendrick, stepping through the open doorway. "To those of us who believe in any sort of an afterlife, what is done to the soul, either before or a thousand years after it leaves the body, matters very much indeed."

"I believe in an afterlife," said Belinda. "However, I do *not* believe that the actions of a living person can have an effect on anyone's soul but his own."

"That is true for most people. But clergy are different, you see. We *do* have authority over the souls of others, and our authority comes straight from the Almighty. If Father Terranova baptizes everyone who lies buried in Herculaneum, those souls will all go to heaven. The question is, do they have the right to be there?"

"More importantly," said Arabella, "do they want to be snatched from whatever pagan twilight they now inhabit with their friends from all over the ancient Roman empire, to spend eternity with a lot of Christians? What could those two groups possibly have in common, apart from the accident of having been born on the same peninsula? The ancient Romans hated the Christians. I do not think they would like it at all."

"What a silly conversation," said Belinda, yawning. "What were you writing, Bell, when I came in, just now?"

"I was making an entry in my new CIN."

"Oh?" asked the rector interestedly, believing he had heard the word "sin." "Is it anything for which I may be of assistance?"

"No, thank you, Mr. Kendrick. A 'CIN' is a criminal inquiry notebook."

"I thought you said it stood for 'crime investigation notebook,'" said Belinda.

"I daresay I did. But 'criminal inquiry' sounds well, too. In fact, I think it sounds better. Last year, Mr. Kendrick, I kept a blue one, if you remember. I find it helps to store all my findings in one place." She stroked the cover. "This time, I've chosen a parchment-colored book," she said, "to remind me of my own dear parchment-colored ponies. How I should love to be able to ride one of them now! All that time spent on the ship was most debilitating."

"What have you written, then?" asked Belinda eagerly. "May I see?"

"It isn't much yet," Arabella admitted, handing her the book, "but I hope to have more to add very soon. The part pertaining to the crime is in the front."

1. *Were there any witnesses? —perhaps.*
2. *Was that shovel I saw the murder weapon? —possibly.*
3. *To whom does it belong? —I cannot say.*
4. *Where is my statue now? —I have no idea.*

"Do you know," said Belinda slowly. "I think I am only just beginning to appreciate how difficult this is going to be. The trail must be quite cold by now."

"Yes, but I am not going to give up before I have even started! Besides, we must needs stay here, statue or no, until London has had time to forget about us. I only wish that I had some leads to investigate."

"Oh! But you *do* have a lead!" cried Kendrick, who was so fatigued that he had quite forgotten about it until that moment. "Signorina Rinaldo says that her family was involved in the theft! We have not yet spoken about it at any length. But she claims to possess considerable knowledge on the subject."

"Well, that is splendid, if it is true," said Arabella doubtfully. "Will you examine her tomorrow, Mr. Kendrick?"

"I live but to serve you, Miss Beaumont!"

"Truly?" she asked with a smile. "And what about God?"

"Oh. Well, yes; God, too, of course. But you, dear Miss Beaumont, are second only to Him in my eyes."

He took her hand, in an excess of feeling. And as he bowed over it, Arabella noticed something swing out from his neckcloth.

"What is that?"

He removed the chain from around his neck and handed it to her. "It is a St. Christopher medal. He is the patron saint of travelers, you know. Father Terranova gave it me, in appreciation of tonight's musical performance."

Arabella arched an eyebrow. "A graven image? Received from the hands of a papist? Does not that contradict your beliefs, Reverend?"

He smiled. "Not a bit. I believe God to be everything: the universe itself, and all it contains. After all, one can scarcely see or hear or smell or touch anything that is not part of the universe."

"Then, when you said just now that I come second to God

in your eyes, were you telling me that you serve everything else in the universe first, and me last? I must say that I find that more than a little insulting!"

"Pray, ignore her, Mr. Kendrick," said Belinda. "Your actions speak for themselves. As for the medal, I have always believed that protection is a good thing, whatever its form."

She turned to the next page of the CIN. "What is this?" she asked Arabella.

"My current theories on the case. You may read them aloud, if you like."

Possible Suspects:

1. *a rich art collector, who, wanting the Herculaneum treasures for himself, arranged to have the dealer killed. But a single collector would never risk, or even know how to risk, having so many workers conspiring in a murder. It would be too easy for them to turn him in for the reward, or blackmail him. No, it would have to be:*
2. *someone capable of ensuring the loyalty of every one of the looters. Like Robin Hood. Or, perhaps:*
3. *an organization. The Church? Some church, anyway, or:*
4. *possibly a secret society.*

"I am making an effort to mentally reconstruct the crime, you see," Arabella explained. "Suppose this Alfred Jones, the man who sent me the sketch and to whom John Soane and I gave our money, was paying his workers a pittance to dig the site, hunting for swag. Then one day they tunneled into a villa, and found the most magnificent items ever discovered here. Imagine those fellows, dirt all over their faces, holding up their small oil lamps and gazing on things not seen for seventeen hundred years! It fair gives me chills! All right. Now imagine that *you* are one of those workers. The artifacts have been found and covered up again, and Alfred Jones instructs you to return with him on a certain night, with a cart, to retrieve the goods in secret. You know that these things are worth a lot of money, but *he's* going to get it all. So what do you do?"

"Kill him, and take them for myself," said Belinda promptly, shocking the rector.

"Yes?" Arabella pursued. "But *then* what do you do? You cannot sell them, because the murder is too well publicized. Everyone is on the lookout for you and the artworks, and you will surely hang if you are caught."

"Could she not store them someplace and wait a few years for things to calm down?" asked Kendrick.

"She could do that. But what if she had already found a buyer, *before* murdering Jones, between the time she found the treasure and the night she went to collect it? That would make it easier, would it not? And then, you see, Belinda would have a place to take the statue right away, so that she should never be caught with the contraband."

"What we need to do now, then," said Belinda, "is to find that buyer."

"Quite," said Arabella.

"So! Here you all are!" exclaimed Charles in a voice slurred by alcohol. He stood unsteadily in the doorway, stoutly supported by Osvaldo.

"Well," said Arabella, slamming her notebook shut. "We all have a long day ahead of us tomorrow. I shall therefore go to bed without more ado."

"Who is 'Moradu'?" Osvaldo leered. "And might I persuade you to let-a me take his place?"

She regarded the Pear-Head with acute dislike. Had he just attempted a witticism? Or was he merely abysmally dim? It scarcely mattered; Osvaldo was at once the most obnoxious and the silliest-looking person she had encountered since coming abroad. Arabella shifted her gaze from his portly form and began vaguely to gaze about her, as though in search of some misplaced object.

"May I help-a you find something, *signorina?*" he asked eagerly.

"Yes," she replied, looking him full in the face, and through him at the same time. "I am searching for the *peach sauce.*"

This was possibly the moment at which Osvaldo realized the hopelessness of his position. But being possessed of an empty, and therefore buoyant, sort of head, it did not disturb him overmuch. In fact, he fixed on a remedy almost immediately, and resolved thereafter to transfer his amorous attentions to Belinda.

Chapter 13

DREAMS AND THE BURIED CITY

Arabella's bedroom was cold, and she dreamt of penguins. In fact, waking in the small hours and wanting a drink, she discovered a thin crust of ice upon the water in her bedside carafe.

"Well, you *will* sleep with the window open," said Belinda at breakfast next morning. "What did you expect?"

"I am not complaining," replied Arabella, calmly buttering a roll. "It was quite exhilarating, in fact. I was merely noting that the weather is changing, and I promised Mrs. Janks we should be home by Christmas. Was there any post this morning, Charles?"

"Nothing for you," said he, "though I've had notices from three creditors, already. How the devil they knew where to find me beats all understanding!"

Belinda, who had taken the seat next Osvaldo's, gave a sudden, visible start, and regarded him with a shocked expression, whilst he, in turn, leaned in toward her with a meaningful smile, and penetrated her with his stare.

"Do you always leave your window open, Miss Beaumont?" asked the rector, pushing his chair back from the table in order to let Belinda out.

"Yes, Mr. Kendrick. But if you were thinking of climbing up to my balcony some night, I should not advise it. The railings are certain to be slippery when frost-covered, and I would hate to have to tell your family how you came to break your neck."

A year ago, such a statement, made before virtual strangers, would have caused him to blush deeply. But the rector had by now grown used to Arabella's sallies, and the slight flush raised by her words was barely even discernable, though Renilde marked it.

"No," he said, "I merely ask because I, too, keep my window open at night. The fact is, I cannot sleep if my feet become overheated."

Arabella nodded. "For my part," she said, "I cannot endure a hot pillow."

"Oh!" said he, "I am suddenly reminded of the dream I had! Charles and I were wearing togas and selling food from a stall in Herculaneum—some sort of dumplings, fried in hot fat. I fished them out with a wire scoop, and they looked just like little pillows."

"I don't suppose I bought any from you, then, my feelings about hot pillows being what they are."

"No, Miss Beaumont; regrettably, you were not in the dream."

"I, too, have had strange dreams since coming here," said Renilde, biting suggestively into a grape. "They are . . . deeply sensual. They are also long, and require some time in the telling. And since you and I are the only ones who are interested in dreams, Mr. Kendrick, I should hate to bore the rest of the company with them. Perhaps we should remove ourselves to one of the smaller coffee rooms."

This remark, besides being in bad taste, was not even true, since everyone at the table had a dream, either dreamt on the previous night or several nights ago or when they were small, that they were most eager to share with the others.

"I . . . I pray you will excuse me, *signorina,*" stammered Kendrick, "but I really must . . . that is, I cannot be . . . I . . ."

Fortunately . . . or not, depending on one's viewpoint, Professor Bergamini popped his head in at that moment, and Belinda, on moving from Osvaldo's immediate vicinity, had taken a chair directly opposite the door. This, her second shock of the morning, nearly caused the poor girl to jump out of her clothing, though she did preserve sufficient presence of mind to stifle her shriek with a table napkin.

"Ah!" said Bergamini. "You are still at breakfast, I see!"

From this, you might expect that he was referring to the entire party. But the professor only had eyes—or so one might assume from the direction in which his nose was pointing—for the rattled Belinda. He smiled broadly and executed a courteous bow. "I am ready to escort you to Ercolano, whenever you wish."

"Thank you, Signor Bergamini," muttered the rector, setting his knife and fork closely together on his plate. "I rather think that we are ready *now.*"

"Why didn't you interview Miss Rinaldo?" Arabella hissed at him as they left the room. "When she offered you the perfect opportunity to do so?"

"There will doubtless be other opportunities," he whispered back. "Besides, I should not have had the time to interview her properly, unless I had missed the excursion."

To this, Arabella said nothing. But having thoughtlessly brought her napkin with her from the breakfast table, as they passed through the hall, she flicked it with frustration at the suit of armor, and left it hanging from the articulated arm.

After they had gone, Signora Terranova appealed to her son.

"Felice, can't you do something?"

"I flatter myself that I can do plenty of things, *madre mia.*"

"You know what I mean! People of our caliber should not have to mingle with common *puttane!* You must speak to the landlord and have them put out at once!"

"By no means," he replied. "I have not enjoyed such stimulating conversation since my seminary days. Besides, what harm are they doing you?"

"Better you should ask what harm they are doing Renilde!"

He affected surprise. "Oh, but surely they are *not* doing Renilde? I think she would have told us! Although, I *did* see her talking the ear off the unfortunate Mr. Kendrick last night. Are you worried lest she should strain her voice from overuse?"

"Felice! You know very well what I mean! Those *puttane* are setting your cousin a bad example, and the men have evil designs upon her!"

"Hmm. And what is your opinion, Aunt Ginevra?" he asked, passing the preserves.

"To be fair," said she, "the English are well dressed, and speak like educated persons. However, the women have brought no maid with them, and who travels like that but mountebanks?"

"Why does no one ask me what *I* think?" Renilde demanded.

The rest of the family fell silent.

"Renilde," said her aunt at last, "you will oblige me by having no further intercourse with either of those men. They will only upset you, dear!"

"A singular choice of words," murmured the prelate, with a smile.

"I do not like Signor Beaumont," Renilde said. "But there is no harm in talking to Reverend Kendrick. *He* shan't make me angry!"

"No, probably not. Very well, then, you may speak to the rector. But not alone, mind! Osvaldo or someone must always be in the room with you. And do not go getting any funny ideas about him," she added. "Remember, he's C of E!"

"If Renilde really has the chance of marrying, Mama," said Terranova, quietly, "I should not care if the fellow worshiped grasshoppers and were king of the monkey people. Should you?"

She snorted. "He has no money! And why is a man of the church, even a Protestant church, traveling with *puttane?*"

"I expect that it is rather a complicated story."

Herculaneum was sparkling in the morning sunshine, looking . . . well, almost new, as the Beaumonts and Mr. Kendrick and the professor strolled along the wide pavement beside the ancient roadway. The wonderful thing about these ruins was that they hardly looked like ruins at all—many of the buildings still retained their roofs and wooden balcony railings. One could walk down streets that were almost perfectly intact, and conjure a sense of the city before the eruption.

"I wonder what everyone thought when they came back afterwards—the people who got out, I mean," mused Belinda. "Could they tell that their city had been buried, or did they think it had been burnt to nothing, or swept out to sea?"

"The survivors left no record of their reactions," said the professor, "and when they died, the disaster was all but forgotten. Pompeii and Herculaneum came to be regarded as mere legends. Eventually, someone discovered Pliny the Younger's eyewitness account, but unfortunately, that is the only record we have."

"Why 'unfortunately'?" asked Kendrick. "I should have thought it fortunate indeed to have such a record!"

"Because," said Arabella, who could never resist showing off what she knew, "Pliny the Younger only observed the eruption from the safety of his drawing room window in Naples, and never bothered to write about it at all until years later, when Tacitus asked him to. One has to wonder how accurate his recollection was."

Charles cleared his throat as a caution, but there was no stopping her now.

"His uncle, Pliny the Elder, a naval officer and a man of science, attempted to rescue the Pompeians who were stranded on the beach. He was fascinated by the eruption, and left the safety of Naples with a small fleet, to get as close as possible."

"This little Pliny went to mark it," sang Belinda, "and *this* little Pliny stayed home!"

"Whilst this little Pliny ate dormouse," added Charles, "which he had at a restaurant in Rome!"

Arabella was not amused. In fact, she was on the verge of vexation.

"What about the uncle, then?" asked Kendrick. "Even *I* have heard of Pliny the Elder! Why don't we have his account?"

"Because he never wrote one. The poor man died on the beach, probably from a combination of poisonous fumes and heart failure."

Throughout Arabella's little showing-off lecture, the professor had said nothing, leading his group through the ancient streets and keeping his own counsel. Arabella glanced over now and then, to see whether she was impressing him, but the tinted spectacles and broad-brimmed hat effectively concealed his thoughts from her. Presently, he brought them to a halt.

"This is where the murder occurred," he said quietly, indicating a mound with a tunnel opening at its base. "The bronze in which you are so much interested, *signorina*, was taken from the villa which lies buried in there, and brought outside, to this spot." He pointed out the places with his walking stick, where the ground had been scarred and scuffed about.

"Good," said Arabella. "I should like to inspect the tunnel, as well."

"That will not be possible, I am afraid. A section of the roof has collapsed since the statue's removal, and it is no longer safe."

Viewing the tunnel and the villa to which it led could not possibly have helped her investigation, but she should have liked to see them all the same. Perhaps there were other interesting pieces down there that the looters missed. And then she noticed a dark stain, splashed across the wall of the neighboring house. Arabella did not need to ask what it was, and she stared at it, horrified.

Misinterpreting her interest, Bergamini began to describe the building:

" . . . A fairly typical construction of its type. We shall explore it after lunch, to give you a general sense of how the ancients actually lived."

Charles caught the word "lunch," and his flagging spirits revived somewhat. He had felt no desire to come out here in the first place, but Kendrick had wanted to, and Arabella, as ever, was adamant that Charles not be left by himself.

"We could eat now, you know!" He had to shout this, for he had lagged behind the others, in order to poke at things with his stick. Food and a sit-down would make a change from walking around, trying to avoid listening to Arabella.

"Is it just my imagination," he asked, catching up with the rest, "or are those little brutes following us? Drive them off, Professor, there's a good chap. Tell them that we're foreign devils who want to roast and eat them."

The urchins Arabella had encountered on the previous evening—or different ones, perhaps—were watching from a distance and keeping the group in sight. Yet they made no attempt to approach them directly.

"Oh, let them alone, Charles," she said. "They're not bothering us."

She took the pencil from behind her ear and began sketching the murder scene into her CIN.

"I don't see what good that will do," said Charles, peering over her shoulder.

"Neither do I, but one never can tell. Professor, before I forget, will you show us a vomitorium?"

"I beg your pardon?"

"You know: the room where the Romans went to be sick during orgies, so that their stomachs could hold more."

A child's laugh reverberated off the stones, and Pietro skipped over to their side of the street.

"Is not true, *signorina!* It means 'go out.' You see?" He pointed to a partially standing public building, where the word was painted over a doorway.

"'Vomitorium' means 'exit'?" she asked. He nodded vigorously. "It is not true, then? There were no special rooms for . . . I mean, the Romans never did that?"

"They never! One crazy man, perhaps, or two." He shrugged. "But they were not normal. Who could like to eat again after being sick?"

"Myself!" cried another boy, emphatically stabbing his own little chest with his index finger. "I would eat and eat and eat, and if there was more food, I would throw up the old food and eat that, too!"

The other children were creeping forward now, under the guise of interested listeners.

"Bell," said Belinda quietly. "These poor children are hungry! We must do something for them!"

"Yes, indeed," said Arabella. "Let us invite them to share our lunch."

Bergamini was against this, but Arabella prevailed.

"Come along, darlings," called Belinda, taking up the hamper and waving her hand. "We've plenty of food here!"

The children were soon surging round her like happy porpoises, and Belinda, from sheer goodness of heart, ended by giving away the basket's entire contents. In just a few moments, the children had run off with all the cheese and salumi, like midget barbarians, shouting in triumph and waving their long bread loaves. Pietro observed the scene with evident satisfaction, as though he himself had been its architect. And so, in a way, he had been.

"How do you come to speak such good English?" Arabella asked him.

"English, German, Spanish, French, Russian," he said, counting them off on his fingers. "We learn from visitors who come this place. Now is not the season time, but if you come back when the weather is gooder, I can change for you any kind money. One time, I even had Chinese!"

"Remarkable," said Arabella. "Would you tell me something, if I gave you a sweet?"

"*Si, signorina*. If you give me sweet I tell you something. But if you give me money I tell you *three* somethings!"

"Then I shall come right to the point. Can you find out whether any of your friends saw the murder which took place on this spot?"

"I saw it my own self!"

"You *did?*"

"*Si*. We all did. The man was killed with a shovel, right there!" He pointed to the spot she had been sketching. "Do you see this?" he asked, drawing her attention to a wheel rut in the dried mud. "I will tell you about it. I will tell you all of it. Information, she is my . . . how do you say? *Specializzazione*."

"Talent?"

He nodded. "But I do not give it away for free, *signorina*. I cannot afford to."

"No, of course not," said Arabella. "I operate in much the same manner myself."

When Pietro held out his hand for payment, she reached for his other one to place beside it, and proceeded to fill them both with coins.

"*Dio mio!*" cried the boy. "I wish my hands was bigger!"

"Where can we talk?" Arabella asked him.

"At your hotel." He began tearing shreds from the bottom of his already tattered shirt, and tying up the coins inside them. "I see you on the balcony. I know your room. I will climb up tonight when the moon she is out."

"I am much obliged to you. And the more you help me, the more I shall pay."

"No sweets?" he asked, with a grin.

"No sweets," she said. "This will be strictly a cash transaction."

"Good," he said. "I no like-a sweets."

Chapter 14

FORTUNE'S FOOL

"Pay no heed to the *bambini, signorina*," said the professor. "They lie. They will say whatever they think you want them to say, as long as they believe they'll have something to gain by it. Avoid them; they are nothing but street rats."

"I forbid you to call them that!" cried Belinda indignantly. "They are human children, even as you yourself once were!" (Privately, she did not really believe this.) "I wish we could help them!" she added.

Kendrick agreed with her. "They most definitely want looking after, with regular religious instruction, bedtimes, and schooling."

"I don't know whether they actually *do* want any of those things," said Arabella. "They strike me as being quite resourceful children. Probably they would prefer food and money to church and school."

"It's more a question of what they need, than what they want," said Belinda.

"Well, I'll tell you what *I* jolly well want, and that is lunch!" said Charles. "If you had not seen fit to give away all our food, my stomach would be a lot happier than it presently is."

"I am sorry you have missed your luncheon, *signor,*" said Bergamini. "We shall return to the hotel at once, and the kitchen will prepare something to your liking."

"I doubt that," Charles grumbled.

They gathered up their things, and were on the point of leaving, when one of the children popped out of an alley with an object under her arm.

"Wait, *signorina!*" she cried, thrusting a clay figurine into Arabella's hands. "This she fall from that cart, on the bad night, yes? She bring-a you luck!"

Arabella eyed the figure with suspicion: a crudely sculpted female, the head too large, the hands and feet too small, holding a cornucopia full of "coins." There was a dwarf crouched at her feet. Or maybe it was an infant. But it looked like a dwarf.

"Who made this?" Arabella asked the girl.

"It come from here! From the dead city!"

"I think it was made by a friend of yours."

"No! It is Fortuna! She bring you luck!"

"Oh, yes?" said Charles, taking the figure from his sister. "She doesn't seem to have been particularly lucky for *you,* my little wench."

"She *will* be," said the child. "Because one of you will pay me for her."

"Hmm. Well, that's a point. Fortuna, did you say?" He studied the piece with evident interest. "Who's this little chap at her feet?"

The girl shrugged.

"That's Dispater," said Bergamini. "Also known as 'Plutus,' the god of wealth."

"Really? Oh, I say! I think I had better have this! Bell, would you . . . ?"

"No."

"Why ever not? You can certainly afford it!"

"That is not the point, Charles. You are always insisting that I buy you this or that. If I enjoyed being pestered to buy people things, I would have had children."

The girl stared up at her, with a wistful face, and Arabella, blushing to the roots of her hair, bought the statuette without further ado.

But, despite his insistence that she get it for him, Charles was disinclined to carry the figurine back to the hotel, and he determined to place it in the luncheon hamper in order that somebody else should do the hefting. For, as the proverb tells us, and as Charles most certainly would have remarked had he known about it: "Fortune wearies with carrying."

"I thought you gave all our food away to the urchins, Belinda," he said, opening the lid and peering in.

"Their need was greater than ours," she replied piously.

"Apparently not," he said, removing a loaf of bread and a wedge of cheese from the interior. "Look at this! My luck is turning already!"

Now that Charles had found something to eat, there was no immediate need to leave, and Bergamini was a fascinating lecturer . . . if one liked that sort of thing. Arabella truly did. Charles truly did not. Mr. Kendrick and Belinda fell somewhere in the middle, but neither was seriously hurt.

"The floors are badly buckled here, I am afraid," said Bergamini apologetically. "You had better hold on to my arm, *signorina*."

They had been touring the house with the stained outer wall when Belinda caught the toe of her slipper on an upraised tile. Her cheeks remained pink for some time after Bergamini had helped her to rise, but the color of her nether cheeks is not known, for these were covered up again, moments after her fall. At any rate, she looked adorable, which may have been why the old pedant stroked her arm and squeezed it a little. Probably he was only trying to comfort her.

Mr. Kendrick's injury was more serious, for he twisted his ankle on a crumbling step, and was obliged to sit upon the edge of the impluvium, the rainfall catchment area in the center of the atrium, whilst the rest of the party completed their tour of the house. He had no trouble hearing them, wherever they might wander, because so many of the walls were missing. And Arabella obligingly lent him her CIN and the pencil from behind her ear, to amuse himself as best he might.

" . . . This, I take it, was the dining room?" she asked Bergamini.

"One of them. The Latin term is 'triclinium.' Most big houses had two or more. The summer dining room is through here," he said, leading the way. "As you see, it is open to the ocean breezes on three sides."

Belinda smiled. "How enchanting!" she breathed. "If I were a Pompeian, I should love having my meals in such a room as this!"

"I should love to eat a meal *at all*," muttered Kendrick, for Charles had not shared his bread and cheese. At length, Arabella joined him on the edge of the impluvium, whilst Bergamini bore off the reluctant Belinda, and Charles had a quick snooze in the corner.

"Have you made a sketch?" she asked.

"I have made a list," Mr. Kendrick replied. "Ercolano is exceedingly evocative, is it not? I have been imagining myself an ancient inhabitant of this place during the week prior to the eruption, a man who has had a presentiment that he shan't live much longer. This is an enumeration of all the things such a man would have loved best."

"I had no idea you were given to fancies, Mr. Kendrick!"

cried Arabella. "What a delightful dimension this adds to my knowledge of your character! May I see your list?"

"I'll read it to you," he said.

"'*New sandals. The drone of bees in the thyme. Cypress trees, silhouetted against the moon. Fried dormice. A pouch-ful of brothel tokens.*'"

"This being the pre-Christian era," he explained, "you understand there would have been no harm in that.

"'*Opening night at the theater. A drizzly afternoon, spent entirely at the public baths, with a massage to follow. Winning at knucklebones. The birth of a healthy son. Finding myself in a position to help someone who needed it. Planning the garden at the new villa. Besting a clever friend in a philosophical argument. Coming home from a wonderful party and seeing the sun rise. Listening to flute music near a fountain in late afternoon. Having someone wonderful fall in love with me. A beautifully set table. The smell of roasting pine nuts. A comfortable bed with sweet-smelling linens. A song in the evening.*'"

Arabella was moved, and felt, once again, that she was having a kind of communion with the ancient dead.

"If you were to use this as the basis of a sermon," she said, "what lesson might your congregation draw from it?"

"Well," said the rector, "I do not know that I *could* compose a sermon, a positive one, I mean, from such unlikely subjects as gambling, pride, and decadent foodstuffs."

"And brothel tokens. You must not forget those!"

"If I were actually to write a sermon based on this list, I think I should say: 'Though a man travel the world to acquire the rare and the beautiful, at the end of his day, he shall find that the greatest gifts await him on his own doorstep.'"

The sentiment was a respectable one; even poetic in its way. But Arabella took it as a personal criticism.

"Is that what a man shall find?" she asked hotly. "Because, speaking for women, I can assure you that acquisition of the rare and the beautiful remains the chiefest joy for our entire lives."

"In your own case, perhaps," said the reverend quietly. "But I do not think you can really presume to speak for *all* women."

"Exactly. Nor can *you* presume to speak for all men."

"And yet," he replied with a smile, "that is what rectors are paid to do."

"We should be starting back now," said Bergamini, entering the atrium with an unhappy-looking Belinda on his arm. "Mr. Kendrick? Can you make it up the hill? Or should you like to wait here, and have me send a carriage for you?"

Charles sulked all the way home because Arabella made him lend his walking stick to Mr. Kendrick, who obviously could *not* hobble along and carry the lunch hamper, too. Charles even tried to make Belinda carry it, arguing that since she had so rashly given away the contents, she should be made to do penance. Belinda nearly complied, if only for the excuse to disengage herself from the professor's proprietary grasp. But Arabella told Charles to stop whining, and said that even though they all knew him for a selfish ass, he was not to behave like one or she would be revoking his financial supplements for the duration of their visit.

And so the little band made the return journey with Bergamini and Arabella in the lead, followed by Belinda, who had at last detached herself from Professor Fly-eyes in order to help support Mr. Kendrick up the path. Charles straggled behind the rest, muttering imprecations now and then, but taking care that no one should hear him, lest his sister make good her threat.

By this time, Arabella had decided that she liked the professor despite his dark spectacles, for he certainly knew his subject, and she was a great admirer of experts.

"Signorina Beaumont," he said. "May I ask how you propose to recover this bronze? Do you think, supposing you find any witnesses, that they will disclose to you what they would not disclose to the police?"

"Possibly. After all, I shall be offering a substantial monetary incentive."

"But, dear lady," he exclaimed, "the murder took place in the dark and the rain, in the city of the dead. No one could possibly have seen what happened to the statue, and even supposing they had, what could they tell you? Only that it was put into a cart, probably, and taken away. But no one actually *did* see anything, because everyone was sensibly at home at the time."

"You seem very certain of that."

"I merely state what is generally known," said Bergamini. "Forgive me, but I do not think you have the snowflake's chance in hell of recovering this piece."

"Fair enough. But why should you wish to discourage me from conducting my own investigation? It cannot possibly make any difference to you what I do here."

"It does, though," he said. "You have seen what Ercolano is, and I perceive that the spell of this place has touched you deeply. How, then, can you want to take away a piece of it that does not belong to you?"

"But it *does* belong to me," she insisted. "I paid . . . well, a lot of money for it. Besides, it's not in Ercolano any longer— somebody else has it. Somebody with less right to it than I have. If the local authorities should find the statue before I do, they will surely not be replacing it in the ground."

"True," said Bergamini. "I did not mean that it should be re-buried; only that it should remain in Italy, and be treated like the national treasure that it is. If I have anything to say about it, the statue will go to the museum, in Naples."

"Really? Are you at all familiar with this bronze, Professor? It's Pan, you know, in a state of . . . extreme arousal, with a double phallus. Are you telling me that you would actually put that on public display?"

"Not on display, perhaps. We keep such things in a special room, with access restricted to . . . with access restricted. But it would at least be made available for viewing to scholars and serious art lovers."

"And so will it be, at my house, in London."

"But London is not where it belongs."

They walked on in silence for a time. Then Arabella said, "Are women allowed to see the art in this 'special room'?"

"No. Women and children are excluded, of course."

"Why 'of course'? And why do you include women in the same category as children? We are adults, even as you are. Do you think that women are likely to go mad from shock when they see sexual things? Or are you merely trying to prevent us from discovering exactly what it is that our husbands and lovers are doing to us beneath the bedclothes?"

Bergamini made no answer. He walked by her side with his hands folded behind him, and his face seemed to wear a puzzled expression, though it was difficult to ascertain this for certain without being able to actually see his eyes.

"That, alone, is reason enough for me to claim the bronze," said Arabella. "Anyone who calls upon me at Lustings will be welcome to view my Pan and all of his parts. Anyone at all. As for finding it, I shall continue to seek for clews here, and allow events to unfold in their own time. I think you will be surprised, Professor Bergamini, when I am victorious in the end."

"Yes," he said quietly. "Very surprised."

*   *   *

Before going to bed that night, Arabella wrote:

The mind looks for patterns in everyday life as reflections of the spirit, which seeks to know the unknowable. The spirit asks: Where is God? Is there life after death? By what signs may I know this? The mind, on the other hand, asks: Who has my statue? Where is it now? How do I get it back?

Why has the professor warned me off? Is this something other than a straightforward art theft? If so, I do hope it is nothing to do with politics.

Chapter 15

TÊTE-À-TÊTE

"I sees a man," said the old tinker woman, staring at Lady Bendover's palm. "A tall one, an' hansum. He's . . ." She gave a little, practiced gasp, and leaned forward to whisper in the lady's ear. "He's your footman, mum!"

The subject gave a delighted squeal and glanced coyly round at the assembled company: a parlor full of women like herself, rich, aging, idle, self-centered.

"Why, it's true, Hermione!" she burbled to the hostess. "I have never in my life experienced anything like it!"

Now it was Lady Ribbonhat's turn. The tinker woman already knew a bit about her, as she did about all the guests, having gotten their names from the hostess beforehand and sussed out the gossip on each one.

"I sees a house," she said promptly. "A house as is yours, but you ain't got it, has you?"

"Yes!" said Lady Ribbonhat breathlessly. "I mean, no! That's Lustings!"

She had been hooked from the moment she received the invitation to come and have her fortune told by "the best pregnosticater in the British Aisles!"

The Countess of Wattle was a very great lady. Perhaps her

spelling was a little lax, but in all other respects she was terribly strict, and she always insisted upon the best. So, if *the countess* said this "pregnosticater" was a marvel, then a marvel she must be.

"Yer husband's not happy about this."

"My husband is dead," said Lady Ribbonhat.

"That he be," said the fortune teller promptly. "I ware talkin' of his speret!"

A close one! But neatly managed, withal.

"His spirit?" asked Lady Ribbonhat, uncertainly.

"Aye. He wants to shew ye how yer to get the house back agin."

The tinker woman looked up from the seeker's withered palm and stared at the wall, as though gazing into realms beyond the physical one. Actually, she was gazing at the escritoire across the room, its stack of letters neatly arranged in a filigree letter rack.

"There be a cache of letters," she said. "Letters what you don't know about. They'll prove yer rights." She nodded to herself. "Aye, they'll prove 'em, all right."

"Where are these letters?" asked Lady Ribbonhat excitedly. "How can I find them?"

"Yer husband knows where they are," replied the tinker, as the countess's Persian cat entered the room. "His speret's in a cat, an' the cat will lead you to 'em."

"A cat?" Lady R. felt her heart sink. "It wouldn't be an *orange* cat, would it?"

"Aye."

"But I . . . gave that cat away! Haven't the slightest idea what's become of it!"

"Success will be yourn arter trials overcome," droned the fortune teller, dropping Lady Ribbonhat's hand and holding out her own. "Cross my palm wi' sil'er, if I've told ye summat of benefit."

*   *   *

That evening, the Beaumonts and Mr. Kendrick were obliged, once again, to be sociable with the Terranovas. This was something of a strain, given Arabella's former rudeness, but even so, Father Terranova reclaimed what was becoming his customary seat beside her upon the small divan.

"It seems strange that you have chosen to see Herculaneum, *signorina,*" he said. "Most tourists to this part of the world prefer to visit Pompeii."

Since Arabella had not been asked a direct question, she did not find it necessary to respond.

"Ercolano is smaller," he continued, "and there is not so much of interest here. No brothels, for instance. But there are several at Pompeii. I should think you would like to see those."

"And why should you think that?"

"Well, one would naturally suppose that you would want to pay homage to the birthplace of your profession."

Arabella fought down her fury, but those who knew her intimately could still hear it in her voice. "Prostitution did not begin with the Romans, *signor.* It is much older than that, probably dating back to prehistoric—"

Mr. Kendrick cleared his throat. "That reminds me of a joke."

And this time, whether owing to the fact that he was somewhat incapacitated, with his bound ankle propped up on a footstool, or simply because nobody could think of anything else to say, Arabella let him tell it.

"Well, it seems this nun, who was outrageously vicious to the laundresses, got her habit back from the laundry just before a high holy Mass. It was so full of starch that she could not sit down in it. The only thing she could do was to stand bolt upright, although she could also manage an awkward sort of kneel. There was no time to send it back before the Mass, so she had to wear it and make do, standing up for most of the day, and even afterwards at the party, when everyone else was seated and taking their ease.

"Finally, after ten hours or so, we are told, 'her feet could stand no more'—I love that part!—and she sank down into the wretched kneeling position which she could only just manage, while the priest was passing by with a cup of wrack punch and a plate full of chicken.

"I thought of that myself," he added modestly. "Nice little . . . little detail, to help you picture the scene, you know."

"Do get on with it, old man," said Charles with a yawn.

"Right. Well, so the priest said, 'There's no need to kneel *now*, Sister,' and she said, 'I know, Father; force of habit!' "

In the quiet air of the *salotto*, Kendrick's final words seemed to echo faintly through the stony corridors of an abandoned city, before being finally absorbed into the walls and dying away forever.

"It was funnier in print," he mumbled.

The loud, artificial laugh that burst from Renilde the moment after he said this was worse, even, than the silence had been.

"A fine story, Mr. Kendrick," said Terranova, crumbling a bit of cake with his fingers, "though a little too close to home, perhaps: Some of my best friends are vicious nuns."

There was genuine laughter at this, but Signora Terranova, who had taken a sip of coffee, spluttered it out again and had to be thumped on the back by her sister.

"Felice!" she gasped, when she had once more been set to rights. "That was unforgivable from a man of your station!"

"Then I apologize, Mama," he said with a smile.

Brushing an invisible crumb from his lap, Mr. Kendrick arose and limped over to Arabella with the biscuit plate.

"Why, thank you, Mr. Kendrick!"

"There is really no need to thank me, Miss Beaumont."

"I know," she replied, smiling up at him. "Force of habit."
She leant forward and lowered her voice. "Will you not take
Renilde aside, and tactfully try to discover what she knows?
She seems most anxious to please you."

This proved unpleasantly accurate, for when Kendrick offered to hear her story, Renilde insisted that he take her to
another room, where they could be alone.

" . . . Because my cousin, he will be *furioso* if he hears
what I am to tell you."

"But why?" Kendrick asked, once solitude had been
achieved, and Renilde had shut the door. "Is the statue in his
possession?"

"It might be. Yes, it is possible."

She removed her shoes, and moved closer to him on the
sopha, tucking her feet under her in a suggestive manner.
Then she pretended to pluck a leaf fragment from his collar,
which Kendrick suspected she had had with her all along.

"Look," she breathed, holding the scrap close to his eyes,
"what sort of plant do you suppose this came from?"

"I have no idea, *signorina*. The light is dim to non-existent
in here. Would you mind telling me how your family is connected to the Pan statue, and to the murder of Signor Jones?"

"Do you know what I think?" she asked.

"What?"

"I think this was a fig leaf. Just like the one that covered
the private parts of Eve, when she realized . . ." Renilde's
voice dropped to a whisper, ". . . her *sin!*"

At the word "sin," Kendrick thought of the buff-colored
notebook, and of how much Miss Beaumont was depending
upon him.

"Signorina Rinaldo . . ."

"I wish that you would call me Renilde."

"Please tell me everything you know about the missing
statue. From the beginning."

"Why should I?"

"Because you said you would."

"Is it so very important to you?"

"Yes, it is!"

"And what will you give me, if I tell you?"

Renilde had moved even closer, so that she was practically sitting in his lap. Now she was twining her fingers in his hair and blowing softly upon his face, in what was evidently meant to be a seductive manner. And so it might have been, if she had been prettier, nicer, and less devious, and if her breath had not smelt quite so much of unbrushed teeth, with overtones of garlic sausage in red wine, and coffee to finish.

"I . . . well," said Kendrick, thinking furiously, "that depends entirely upon the nature of the information. If you tell me some small thing, you will receive something trifling in return, and if what you have to say is important . . ."

"Yes . . . ?"

"Oh, this is futile! You do not actually know anything about it, do you? You have been deliberately wasting my time. To what end, I know not."

Kendrick pushed her off him and endeavored to stand up, but in this he was betrayed by his twisted ankle, and Renilde easily pulled him back onto the sopha. She tugged at her gown's neckline on both sides, baring her shoulders, and exposing more of her cleavage, such as it was.

"What are you doing?" cried the unhappy cleric. "Unhand me, madam . . . !"

"Listen," she hissed close to his ear. "My cousin Felice was the one who gave the orders that the statue . . . and the other things . . . be taken from the buried villa. He was the first to know they were down there."

"And how did he discover that?" Kendrick was certain that the young lady was inventing tales at random now, in an attempt to keep him there.

"Felice has many people working for him. They tell him what is going on."

"Ah! How convenient! What has he to do with artifacts?"

"I don't know. But someone else learned that they were going to be dug out. And . . . and he . . . this other person . . . went and dug them out first."

"Who was this person?"

"I don't know who he was. Just somebody. But he was very stupid, because Cousin Felice is a powerful man. He has . . . spies. Everywhere. And they . . . his spies . . . killed this other, stupid man. Then they took away all the statues and things . . . I think, maybe, they took them back to my cousin."

It seemed to Kendrick that Renilde was simply making it up as she went along, and searching her mind for what to say next.

"There!" she cried. "I gave you everything! Now you must give *me* everything!"

And she attempted to throw herself into his arms, but Kendrick was too quick for her. He leapt to his feet just in time, ignoring the pain in his protesting ankle.

"You have not told me very much, after all, Signorina Rinaldo," he said. "But I shall give you this." He took the St. Christopher medal from around his neck and placed it in her hand.

Renilde stood up, too, sensing that she had lost the moment.

"Won't you at least help me put it on?"

She was trembling, and there were tears in her eyes, which glistened in the faint gleam of the candle. They were only tears of rage, but Kendrick was not to know that. To him, they were just tears—of distress, perhaps, or grief or humiliation—and he felt a surge of pity for this unattractive young woman, who had the misfortune to desire a man who would never return her feelings. Probably this had happened to her before. And probably, it would happen again.

"May the saint protect you on your quest for a mate," said

Kendrick gently, fastening the chain round her neck, "and may he keep you safe from unscrupulous persons until you are safely married."

Renilde collapsed, sobbing, onto the sopha. The reverend limped to the door to fling it wide with fury; fury at the unfeeling universe and its indifference to the sufferings of the discarded and unloved creatures whom nobody wants. The tearing open of the door was a gesture of defiant contempt for the cosmos, for the general unfairness inherent in the Way Things Were. It was a stand against apathy, a resounding NO! to the eternal Who Cares? It was one man's crusade against the absurdity and senselessness echoing down all the days of creation since the beginning.

At least, that was what he had been *going* to do.

But Renilde had locked it.

"*Help!*" shouted Kendrick, banging on the door with both fists. "Please! Somebody! We are trapped in here! Help!"

"Stop!" cried the young woman, leaping up. "If we should be found together, it will look very bad!"

"Help!" he shouted again. She clapped a hand over his mouth, but he shook her off. "Help!"

"If they find us, we shall both be ruined!" wailed Renilde.

"Give me the key, then," Kendrick demanded.

"*No!*" she shrieked. "No-no-no-no!" And with that, she commenced a feral howl that froze the rector's blood. It sounded as though she were turning into a werewolf.

Someone in the corridor commenced pounding on the door.

"Signorina Rinaldo! Are you all right? Open this door at once!"

Renilde's howls, which continued unabated, had evidently roused the household, for now a gabble of voices could be heard without. Mr. Kendrick stood as if rooted to the floor, afraid to turn round, lest the sight of Renilde's metamorphosis should cost him his sanity. The howling continued to escalate in both pitch and frequency. Kendrick covered his ears, praying silently to God.

Outside in the passage, the landlord and his wife and servants, Terranova, Renilde's mother, brother and aunt, the three monks, and Charles and Belinda were all shouting at him to open the door. Well. Probably Charles wasn't. Finally, somebody forced it, with a loud bang, and Renilde abruptly stopped shrieking.

For the space of four heartbeats, the two parties faced each other across the silence. There stood the Rector of Effing, his face pale, his hair mussed and his cravat undone; Renilde, shoeless, with the sleeves of her gown pulled from her shoulders and her heaving bosom displayed (only the upper part, but still), and the pair of them—the people, not the bosoms—standing now in the light cast from the wall sconces in the passage, with the room behind them in almost total darkness. Added to which, the realization of how all this must appear to the others gave to the rector the guiltiest expression that ever was seen.

"Reverend Kendrick," said Terranova, squinting past him at his cousin. "Isn't that the St. Christopher medal that I recently gave to *you?*"

Upstairs, Arabella was awaiting Pietro's arrival, supposing that the hullabaloo downstairs was occasioned by some asinine parlor game. But the noise had effectively obscured the subtler sounds of someone climbing up to her balcony, so that when the boy knocked upon the French window, she was startled nearly out of her wits.

"Come in," she whispered, holding the window wide so that he could slip past her. When she lit the candle, Arabella saw that Pietro was shivering, for the night was cold, and the barefoot child was dressed in the thinnest of rags. She wrapped him in the spare blanket. "You keep that," said Arabella. "I shall square it with the landlord. Now, quickly! Tell me what you have found out!"

"I have talked with the others," he said, "but no one knows the man who killed the Englishman. We did not see him ever before, and he has not come back."

"Oh," said Arabella sadly.

"This Englishman who died; you loved him very much?"

"Why, no! Not at all! That is, I hope that you will not think me a bad person, Pietro, but I do not care so much about the murder. It was a terrible thing, to be certain, and I am sorry the man was killed, but I never met him. Do you see? I bought a statue. I have already paid for it, and I very much want it found. That is the only reason I have come here. Did you see where the cart went?"

"No, *signorina*. But I showed you the wheel prints in the mud, remember?"

Arabella felt her heart sink. The boy was not going to be helpful after all.

"Pietro," she said gently. "How can you know for certain that those wheel ruts even belonged to the cart that took the statues? They might have been made by any cart that has gone through there recently."

"No, *signorina!* Those wheel tracks lead to the old goat path. My friends and me, we saw the cart leave that way! No one ever uses that road anymore!"

Her pulse quickened. "And will these tracks lead me to the statue?"

"No, *signorina*. The wheel marks lead to the main road. Then she disappear."

Dashed again! "Pietro," she said, "this does not really help me."

But the boy was nodding, rapidly. "One of the wheels," he said. "She is chipped on the inside edge, so that when she go round, there is a mark like the moon look when she is . . . not round. I do not know where your statue is, but I know where the man lives who owns the cart that took it away."

"You do? But why should you notice a little thing like a chipped wheel rim?"

"Because *I* chipped it! The man pretends he is a farmer, but really he is a smuggler. I mark his wheel, then I report what he does, where he goes, to people who pay me for *informazione*. Do you see?"

"You clever boy! Can you take me to the house of this man?"

"No, *signorina*. I check before I come here. He has gone to Naples to wait for a shipment of . . . a shipment. And he has taken his cock with him, which means he will be staying with his cousin."

"His *cock?*"

"*Si.* His fighting cock. It always win. And his cousin own the cockpit. But you would not be safe there. The place is full of bad mens. Is better to wait here until he returns."

"Oh, very well! But will you promise to take me to this smuggler, or farmer, or whatever he is, the moment he should come home?"

"I will take you to the road outside his house. Then I must leave you. This man has never seen me. That is why I am safe from him. He is dangerous, *signorina*. You must bring other men with you when you go there, in case of trouble."

Chapter 16

FELLATIO . . . ORATIO . . . OSVALDO!

The next morning, Arabella was up with the proverbial larks—all 7,328 of them. "There's a to-do!" she grumbled, getting up to slam the casement closed. But then she stopped, and stared at a sunrise that looked more like the last sunset of a dying world. The horizon appeared to be composed of rippling, radiating cloud tentacles, in hot pink and rose gold with violet linings.

"*Quel spectaculari!*" she breathed. (Arabella was inclined to invent new words and phrases when she did not know the correct ones.)

A servant came in with a tray and set a cup of coffee down upon the nightstand.

"Look, Geppetta!" cried Arabella, pointing to the window. "*Malto bella, no?*" (Also, her Italian was not very good.)

But the woman only scowled, muttering and crossing herself as she turned from the window. Then she screamed aloud, and clapping a hand over her mouth, pointed to the wall where a miniature scroll, some three inches long, had been nailed over the bed.

"*Maledizione!*" croaked Geppetta, as if through a severed

windpipe. Then she fled the room without asking whether the *signorina* required anything else.

Reaching up, Arabella tugged out the nail and removed the scroll. The message inside was short, crudely lettered, and written in Italian, but she guessed, both from the look of the thing and the servant's violent reaction to it, that it was not exactly a love poem.

When she went down to breakfast, Arabella encountered Bergamini and Father Terranova having a whispered, yet heated, argument at the bottom of the staircase. They ceased immediately at her approach, and stepped hastily away from each other.

"Good morning, Signorina Beaumont!" cried Father Terranova heartily. "How fortunate for me that I am arrived in time to escort you to breakfast!"

The professor bowed to her. "I shall wait upon your leisure, *signorina*," he said, "but please try not to prolong your meal. Pompeii is some miles distant, and the roads are not what they were in the old days. Above all, we need to get started before the streets become congested. You will find me in the library when you are ready to start out." He bowed again, and withdrew.

"I had no idea you two were acquainted," said Arabella as she and the priest walked down the passage together.

"We are not," said Terranova. "That is to say, we have only just met. Did you happen to see that beautiful sunrise this morning?"

"Oh, yes, indeed! But when I tried to point it out to the maidservant, she crossed herself and would not look at it."

"I am not surprised. People here are very superstitious. They believe that a morning sky like that is an omen."

"Of what?"

"Who knows? Some foolishness about the displeasure of the Roman gods. I would not trouble myself over it, if I were you."

"*Roman* gods? But she crossed herself!"

"Yes; the old beliefs live on here, despite all we do, and mingle incestuously with present-day Church practices. I think, if you and I could see inside Geppetta's head, we would both be very surprised by what we should find there."

"And what about this?" Arabella asked, showing him the scroll. "It was nailed to the wall in my room."

He took it from her, frowning, and crumpled it in his hand after reading it.

"This is nothing," he said. "Peasants are very stupid!"

"How do you know it was a peasant? It does not appear to be signed."

"Because only peasants think like this! An educated person would not be capable of conceiving such a thing!"

"I did not think peasants even *could* write."

"Some can."

"But what does it say?"

"Nothing," he insisted, tearing the paper to pieces. "What you do not know can not hurt you, yes? Please! Oblige me by forgetting you ever saw it!"

The uncomfortable feeling with which Arabella had begun her day carried on through breakfast and beyond: She had assumed that the whole party would be making the trip to Pompeii with her, as the professor had hinted at having got up something rather special for their benefit. But Mr. Kendrick could not go, on account of his ankle, and Charles begged off—"If you've seen one buried city, you've seen them both"—because he had begun a phenomenal winning streak, and had set his heart upon attending some gambling venue or other. He proposed to take Kendrick along with him in a Bath chair. So the ladies and Bergamini were to be on their own.

"Bell, I don't think I shall come after all," whispered Belinda. "In the absence of Charles and Mr. Kendrick, I am afraid the professor will increase his odious attentions to me to the point where I shan't be able to bear it! In any event, I shall not enjoy myself."

"Professor Bergamini arranged this for us on purpose, Bunny. It would be most ungracious to refuse him. Besides, I shall feel ashamed to go home having seen Herculaneum and not Pompeii. Everyone will be asking us about them . . . if we still have any friends, that is. I am sorry if ruins do not interest you like they do me, but your only alternative is to spend the day at the cock fights with Charles, wheeling Mr. Kendrick around in his Bath chair."

When she put it like that, Belinda saw reason, and climbed into the carriage without further argument.

"Now there's an odd thing," said Arabella, looking out the window where Bergamini stood making arrangements with the driver. "The professor is wearing a tiny faggot through his buttonhole."

"A what?"

"A faggot. You know; a stick of kindling wood. At least, that is what I think it is. It looks to have been cast from pewter, or some other dullish metal."

"That *is* strange," said Belinda. "Father Terranova wears a hatchet pin on his cassock."

"I'm afraid I do not follow you."

"Well: a stick of kindling, and a hatchet to cut it with. Father Terranova's pin also looks to be pewter. Do you suppose the two men are connected in some way?"

"I do, *now*. I had thought they were unacquainted until I saw them arguing on the stairs this morning."

"Well, that does not signify," said Belinda. "Charles is always having arguments with strangers."

"But they were *whispering*."

"Whispering?"

"As though they were afraid of being overheard. Of course, they were speaking Italian, and I should not have understood them in any case, but they left off the moment I appeared, and Terranova whisked me off to the dining room."

"Bell," said Belinda suddenly, "I do not like this place. We should go home."

"Nonsense! It is an excellent spot! We have wonderful weather—warmer than England, anyway. And romantic views, and delicious food . . ."

"Charles does not like the food."

"Hang Charles! He would find something to complain about in Paradise, not that he is likely ever to see that place. Why do you not like it here?"

"I sense things going on beneath the surface; sneaking, horrible things. You feel it, too, don't you? The Italians are very kind, very courteous, and yet, everything is *sub rosa* and *sotto voce*. The professor, with his dark spectacles, and Father Terranova with his pointed beard. . . . D'you know," said Belinda, straying from the subject, "I think I may abhor the beard even more than the spectacles?"

"Don't be silly. Beards are the fashion over here. I expect they soon will be in England, too."

Belinda shuddered. "Then I shall die a spinster."

"Well, I am sorry if it makes you uncomfortable, but I am not going home without my statue. You volunteered to come along—I should never have come here at all but for you. Then you insisted I bring Charles, and now you both want to go home before I am ready to oblige you. Why cannot the two of you follow Mr. Kendrick's example? *He* never complains."

"No. And yet the rector has more reasons for dissatisfaction than even Charles and I do," said Belinda.

"What do you mean?"

"You are using him, and you are being unkind, as well. Mr. Kendrick only came out here because he loves you, Bell. You are taking unscrupulous advantage of a decent, honest gentleman. And he is not an imbecile. One day he will shake you off like a summer cold and get on with his life, ennobled by suffering, while you . . . you will be the poorer for the loss of such a man."

"Nevertheless," said Arabella, "*he* does not complain, whilst you and Charles do little else."

"I suppose, then, on balance, it equals out," said Belinda not unreasonably. "We shall probably be asked to leave the hotel, in any case, owing to the indiscretion lately committed by 'the man who does not complain.'"

"Do you think so?"

"Certainly. After last night's wretched Renilde affair, the landlord will have no choice. You and I know that Mr. Kendrick was only trying to get something out of her, but I fear that everyone else thinks he was trying to put something *into* her. And the proprietors, being good Catholics . . ."

" . . . will do exactly as Terranova bids them," Arabella finished. "*He* won't have us put out. After all, Mr. Kendrick is a fellow professional."

Belinda had told her sister of the previous night's doings insofar as she herself was acquainted with them, but she had not actually seen very much, and there were gaps in her knowledge; Mr. Kendrick had been either unwilling or unable to acquit himself; and Charles, who had probably seen more than Belinda, had done nothing but roar with laughter when asked about it, till he'd passed out from too much wine and too little food.

"There seems to be a great deal about this statue affair that we do not know, and never *can* know," Belinda said. "But then, you like mysteries, don't you? This one should satisfy even *your* peculiar tastes!"

They had been waiting more than a quarter of an hour for the professor, but so engrossed were they in their conversation that Arabella had only just realized it. And for the first time, she noticed how thronged the street was. But Bergamini appeared at the instant she decided to go in search of him, fighting his way through the masses—where had so many people come from?—to reach the carriage.

"What is happening?" asked Arabella as the professor took a seat next to Belinda. "What is the meaning of this crowd?"

"Hmm? Oh. They are only peasants. No one in particular. I expect they have come for the festival."

"What festival?"

"Some local festival. In honor of a saint."

The professor did not seem to know which saint it was, though. And then they were off, somewhat slowly, due to all the people clogging the road. The so-called celebrants had a grim, determined look about them, and they seemed entirely too quiet for a holiday crowd.

Arabella made several unsuccessful attempts to engage the professor in conversation, but as he appeared to be lost in thought, she picked up the thread of her discussion with Belinda, and behaved as though *he* were not present, *either*.

"I do not really care for a mystery," she said. "I only wish to find my statue and take it home!"

"Ah," replied Belinda, arching her brows. "But it is your duty to seek the Mystery. For if you are less than diligent, the Mystery will find *you*."

"How do you mean?" asked Arabella, paling.

"I don't know," her sister replied with a dismissive shrug. "I read that in one of your volumes on Sufi mysticism."

Arabella was not comforted, despite her affinity for the wisdom of the Dervishes. She thought again about the curse scroll, and decided not to mention it to Bunny. There was no point, after all, since she was never to know what it said.

If Pompeii is less well preserved than Herculaneum, it is also larger, so there is more to see, and one's feet become tired before one has half been over the place. After only three quarters of an hour in the famous city, Belinda was quite worn-out, and begged leave to sit down upon a bench astutely placed for that purpose by the site administrators. Bergamini and Arabella continued to explore nearby, for nothing imparts energy to the body like feeding the mind, and these two persons were in their element here.

" . . . The disaster was capricious," the professor was saying. "Most of the bronze statues from Herculaneum, including, probably, the one you are seeking, *signorina,* have been recovered in beautiful condition. But here in Pompeii, the rain of pumice stones which hit this place has pockmarked and oxidized all the bronzes we have found here so far. Like this one." He indicated a bronze tableau, depicting a gladiator beset by lions and pitted by lapilli.

It had not occurred to Arabella that her statue might be marred. She mightn't want it, after all, in that case! No . . . no, she *did* want it, but she fervently hoped that it had not been damaged. At any rate, as it had not come from here, she could be reasonably certain that it had not been damaged by lapilli.

"Professor," Belinda called, when he and Arabella had wandered back in range of her voice. "Are we the only visitors? I had understood that Pompeii was quite a popular destination."

"It is, *signorina.* But because I have arranged this tour for you today, the site is closed to everyone but ourselves."

Belinda was astonished. "How ever did you manage that?"

"Through my connection with the university."

"Yes, I see," she said, half to herself, "but even so . . ."

Arabella was sniffing the air. "Do you know? It is the queerest thing, but I believe I can smell meat roasting!"

"That is nothing," said the professor. "Now, if the *signorina* Belinda has quite recovered, I shall take you into a buried villa through a tunnel that is quite safe. We have just time to explore it before lunch. Please follow me closely."

Of course it was dark in the tunnel. All tunnels are dark.

But the mists that slipped, serpentlike, through the passage-
ways were somewhat unexpected, and the cold water and
slime that dripped from the ceilings and walls gave the place
an uncanny atmosphere. One might imagine death to feel like
this, if one could manage, somehow, to be both dead and
frightened at the same time.

Then the tunnel curved, and Arabella caught her breath.
"There's a light!" she whispered, and knew not why she was
whispering. "Up ahead!"

"Is there?" asked Bergamini. "That is odd!"

They had reached the door of the villa, and light was, indeed, issuing from beneath it. Arabella later wrote John
Soane a long letter all about it:

> ... *The door was opened from within by a
> handsome servant dressed as a Roman slave, who
> escorted us straight through to the triclinium.
> Here, tall bronze oil lamps had been placed about
> the chamber, illuminating the wall paintings.
> Three were of delightful if prosaic subjects: fruit
> bowls, fish, and dishes of eggs. But the fourth wall
> featured a disturbing depiction of a sphinx,
> devouring a hapless traveler.*
>
> *In the center of the room stood a table of bronze
> and marble, surrounded by three wooden couches.
> These were inlaid with silver, ivory and mother of
> pearl, and heaped with cushions of all shapes and
> sizes, sensuously soft and saturated in rich colors.
> Professor Bergamini had had them brought in, of
> course. I presumed the originals had long since
> disintegrated.*
>
> *The table was set for three persons, with plates
> of ancient silver. We were much amazed to see,*

*laid out in the center, and also upon a kind of
sideboard, a great variety of foodstuffs, which,
fortunately, were of more recent vintage than the
paintings, furnishings and tableware!*

The diners were allotted a couch apiece, and the "slave" who had greeted them at the door was now joined by three attractive companions, bearing ewers of water to wash the travelers' hands.

The table, as Arabella had said, was laid with an abundance of food, such as salads, cheeses, olives, and *lucanica* sausages, flavored with orange peel and fennel, accompanied by loaves of bread that had not changed in appearance for more than seventeen centuries. And the "slaves" kept bringing out more dishes. There were peahens' eggs, cooked in ashes; honey-roasted dormice, stuffed with minced pork, sage, and pine nuts (Belinda wouldn't eat these, but Arabella, more adventurous, pronounced them delicious); smoked duck; wildflower bulbs in vinegar; a dish of moray eel with razor clams; honey in the comb; and cheesecakes.

Finally, Arabella was presented with a platter of tiny birds, which the professor said were roasted nightingales, served with peppered mayonnaise.

"That is what the Romans called this dish," he explained. "But of course, they're not really nightingales."

"Aren't they?" she asked.

"Heavens, no! Nightingales were kept as pets, and were very expensive. These are just local songbirds."

"I see," she said, picking up one of the fowls in her fingers. The tiny bird had been done to a turn, and was all steaming and fragrant with herbs, the crisp skin lacquered to a rich mahogany. "What are they, really? Some type of warbler?" And she thought, with fierce satisfaction, of the infernal larks that had disturbed her slumbers that morning.

"In English," said Bergamini, "it is called a Figpecker, I believe."

Arabella stopped in the very act of taking a bite, and set the morsel down on the plate before the flesh had touched her lips.

She kept Figpeckers at home, in her aviatory. When Mrs. Moly had once suggested roasting them, even as these birds had been, Arabella had nearly thrown a fit. Why, though? She had been ready enough to eat the Romans' beloved nightingales. But that was a species with which she was unfamiliar. Upon learning that these were, in fact, Figpeckers, she would no more entertain the notion of eating it than if someone had suggested she devour a puppy. It was strange that familiar association could make such a difference.

> *... Into goblets of ancient Roman glass, the servants poured out a mixture of boiled wine and honey. An array of little sauce pots and pitchers stood in the center of our table, whilst the other dishes were whisked on and off it. The ancient Romans were devoted to sauces. Most were made from various vinegars, honey, herbs, and spices, but the undisputed favorite, according to your learned friend, was garum.*

"It's in that fat pitcher, there, if you would like to try some," said the professor. "This is a modified version, for I doubt whether even I could have withstood the original."

"And what was that made of?" asked Belinda.

"Fermented fish intestines," he replied. "It was very salty."

> *... We are much indebted to you, sir, for our introduction to Professor Bergamini, and for the*

> *most remarkable meal we have ever eaten! Bunny*
> *and I were quite overwhelmed by the magnificence*
> *and the scope of it, but when we tried to say so, he*
> *graciously deflected our thanks, and reminded us*
> *that Belinda had once expressed a wish to eat in*
> *an ancient dining room. Was it not a handsome*
> *gesture? He is ever the considerate host. When we*
> *had finished, he gave us each a silver toothpick, as*
> *a useful souvenir.*

But Arabella did not add what had transpired after that, for when the plates were cleared away, and she was about to suggest they start for home, the "slaves" suddenly blew out the lamps, plunging the room into darkness.

"What is it?" she cried. "A cave-in? Professor? Bunny? Are you all right?"

"Oh!" shrieked Belinda. "Oh-oh-oh . . . ah-ah . . . oh! . . . *oh!*"

Bergamini said nothing at all, for he was extremely busy just then, eliciting the aforementioned response from Belinda direct. Arabella soon found herself similarly accosted by the handsome fellows who had served them at the table. And, although she had professed herself unable to eat another thing only moments before, she now found her mouth full again. Not that she minded.

"Do you never tire of winning, Beaumont?"

"Tire of winning? Is that even possible?"

"Well, some people might find it a trifle predictable," said Kendrick, smiling as he tucked his own winnings into his wallet. "Though I must admit it is rather heady following you around, backing your choices and collecting money."

"I tell you, Kendrick, that little statuette has changed my life! I feel as though I could not lose if I wanted to! This last match has been so lucrative, I think I might be persuaded to stand you to lunch."

Cock fighting is a cruel sport. Its defenders will try to tell you that the birds do it naturally, so where is the harm in betting on the one most likely to win? But when two cocks fight under natural circumstances, the loser generally runs away. In a cockpit there is no escape, and in the absence of an owner's interference, the birds have no choice but to fight to the death.

"Like gladiators in a coliseum!" crowed Charles.

He was in excellent spirits, and wherefore should he not be? He was winning every card game, dog race, roll of the dice, or casual wager into which he entered, and his winnings were piling up to the extent that he was obliged to leave a portion of them under the protection of his sisters and Kendrick. For the first time in his life, everything was going his way.

"*Canestro!*" somebody shouted, and the rest of the company took up the cry. "*Canestro! Canestro!*"

Evidently, the owner of the losing cock, which now lay dead on the sidelines, had been unable to pay the forfeit. Charles and Mr. Kendrick watched in amusement as the man was put into a great basket and suspended from the roof.

"He is not accustomed to losing, you see," an onlooker explained. "His-a cock, she always win, so Tacito has brought no money with him."

They stared up at the captive; he glared down upon them in turn, and made the *corno*—a rude hand gesture—directly at Charles.

"Did you see that?" Charles asked indignantly. "What an abysmal sore loser!"

"The sign of the horns!" cried Kendrick. "Confound the fellow! I believe he has cursed you, Beaumont!"

"Not cursed, exactly," said the helpful onlooker. "He was

just taking away your power. That is the sign that we use against witchcraft."

"Against witchcraft!" Charles exclaimed. "It doesn't actually work, does it?"

The man shrugged. "Often enough to keep belief alive," he said. "The same as for any superstition." And he filed out with the others.

"I say, Kendrick, do you suppose that farmer actually has the power to nullify Fortuna's luck? . . . Oh, that's right; you're a man of the cloth. You don't believe in magic, do you?"

"Surely you are joking! We men of the cloth believe in nothing else," said Kendrick with a smile. "But I shouldn't worry too much about it, if I were you. You *know* your luck cannot last forever. Just enjoy it whilst you've got it."

(He had declined the Bath chair in the end, and was getting around rather well with a cane.)

"*Scusatemi, signori,*" said a respectable-looking fellow, leading a tiny white greyhound on a leash. "Which of you is Signor Beaumont?"

"Um . . ." said Charles uneasily.

"Who is asking?" said the rector.

"I have a letter for Signor Beaumont from Professor Bergamini," said the man, and he placed it into Charles's outstretched hand.

Forgive me for interrupting your day in this fashion, but I wonder whether you would do me the favor of presenting this dog to Miss Belinda, and pretending that the gift comes from yourself? You can tell her that the bitch was part of your takings, perhaps. Or that she won a great race and you were so impressed that you bought her, but regretted your decision by the time you reached the hotel.

"Confound the fellow!" Charles exclaimed. "Why involve me? Why not give her the blasted animal himself?"

You see, I fear it might seem a trifle presumptuous, coming from me.

"Very proper of him," said Kendrick approvingly.

The dog's name is Carrara, like the marble, both for her color and for the fact that in repose she resembles a statue. She is called "Cara," for short. And . . . this is very important . . . her collar must remain upon her neck at all times, for she is nervous, and it helps to keep her calm.
I realize that, as a brother, you cannot give a present to one sister without slighting the other. You will greatly oblige me, therefore, by stopping at Cristofalo's, in the Via Montedoro, and retrieving a cloak and a mask, previously paid for, to give to Signorina Arabella.

"Of all the damnable insolence!" fumed Charles. "As though I'd nothing better to do than play personal delivery boy for some decrepit old pedagogue!"

By now, reader, Charles's impatience should be readily apprehended. As this matter was neither about himself nor his pleasures, it could not possibly be of interest to him. Moreover, he would be required to perform an office for someone else's benefit. It was only natural that he should grow hostile.

"Well, I for one, think it's a charming idea," said the rector. "If you will not do it, I shall say it was my idea. I am an old family friend, after all. Gifts won't seem inappropriate, coming from me."

But then Charles pictured Kendrick as the center of his sisters' adored attention, receiving heartfelt thanks for the handsome presents.

"Oh, very well," he grumbled, taking the dog's lead from her handler. "So long as all I need to do is lie."

When they called at Cristofalo's, the shop man shewed them a gold, papier-mâché mask with a nose like a bird's beak, and a sumptuous cloak, or domino, of violet-blue velvet embroidered in gold. The costume was obviously costly, and whilst it was being wrapped, Mr. Kendrick wondered how the professor could afford such luxury on a modest university salary. He reflected with sadness that Bergamini's afterthought was far beyond his own means, even as a beforethought.

"Come along," said Charles. "I have just recollected that a rooster called Magnanimous is scheduled to fight this afternoon. It's a sign, is it not? If we hurry, we shall be in time to place a bet."

Thus, all the Beaumont siblings were carrying on that afternoon, in cockpits of one sort or another. Back at the hotel, however, illicit activity of quite another type was in progress.

"All is in readiness for you, Father," said the landlady. And as she knelt to kiss Father Terranova's ring, she simultaneously presented him with the key to Arabella's suite.

The instant he stepped onto the balcony, a wild cheer burst out from the crowd, and the prelate swept his arms wide in a gesture of universal benediction. Below him, standing shoulder to shoulder, to the limit of visibility, stood most of the good people of Resina, plus a great many others who had traveled from distant towns to be there. They had been gathering all that morning. Hundreds of them. Who knows? Thousands, perhaps.

Terranova's three monks stood behind him, watching with attentive reverence. Behind *them,* Signora Terranova had settled herself into a large armchair, so as not to miss a single word of her son's speech. And in the next room, Osvaldo was going through Belinda's undergarments, handling and sniffing the dainty shifts with enormous satisfaction.

But why are we wasting our time in here? Osvaldo is not very interesting. Let us instead join the enraptured crowd outside. Perhaps they will make room for us in the front row. Oh, look! Here are Charles and Mr. Kendrick, returned from town! They will let us in, surely. That's better! Now we can see and hear Father Terranova perfectly well. You don't speak Italian? Never mind—it is not so much *what* the man is saying as *how*. He is very animated, is he not? And mark the occasional phrases to which he gives particular emphasis. You don't? Oh, that's right. Well, my Italian is not very good, either, but I can understand a bit. Shall I translate for you? Let's see . . . "Courage in the face of tyranny . . ." something-something, ". . . resist to the last ounce of our strength." And . . . "fight the oppressors." Peculiar expressions for a baptism! And those expansive gestures he's making! They seem very emphatic, very explicit, don't they? Well, after all, this is not just a foreign language, but a foreign culture. We should not expect it to make complete sense to us.

His speech would appear to be drawing to its close now. And look there! Our satisfied little party of professor and ladies has just crested the hill!

"But she must eat *something!*" cried Kendrick. He was much distressed by Arabella's reaction at finding the priest on her balcony. She had refused to come down to dinner, refused to speak to anyone, and at this moment, was upstairs packing her trunks in a blind rage.

"Have you tried to talk to her, Miss Belinda?"

"Hmm? Oh, yes, I tried. But Arabella cannot be reasoned with when she is in this mood. I am afraid we shall just have to wait for time to take its course."

To tell the truth, Belinda had not tried so *very* hard, because just now her thoughts were chiefly occupied with her amorous encounter of that afternoon, and with Bergamini. Bergamini! He was hideous! Old! Doddering! And yet, in the dark, he had been *very* far from feeble. Still, how was it possible that she was feeling this way about him now? How *was* she feeling about him now? He had those horrid, death's head spectacles. And that dry, gray hair, liberally sprinkled with flecks of dried epidermis. And wrinkles! He was covered in wrinkles, and he wore that huge, silly hat, and those pretentious scholarly robes! She wanted to see him again, as soon as possible. She did not know how she would make it through the night without him.

"Whatever can it be ailing this sweet Signorina Belinda?" asked Osvaldo, having watched her spoon pesto onto her cannoli.

They were just four to dinner: Renilde, her mother, and her aunt had had trays sent to their suite. Father Terranova and his monkish retinue had been swept off to dine at the home of a local official. And Arabella, packing her trunks, was using language that was not fit for the dinner table in any case.

Speaking of the dinner table, the astute reader may wonder what the cannoli were doing there, during the meal. The answer is an interesting one. Signora Fiorello, having apprehended her guests' antipathy for one another, had wisely discontinued the tradition of after-dinner coffee in the *salotto*, and was henceforth determined to serve everything— antipasto, pasta, salad, entree, dessert, and cheese—all at once, higgledy-piggledy, so as to get the meals over with as quickly as possible. With the strange presentation, and so many empty places, dinner was proving a rather unsettling occasion. Kendrick had to ask Belinda to pass the Parmesan grater not twice but thrice before she responded.

"If I didn't know better, I should say the wench had fallen in love," muttered Charles.

Osvaldo was most gratified to hear this, for it doubtless

meant that she had already discovered the note that he had left beneath her pillow after fondling her underclothes.

"If you didn't know better?" he asked of Charles. "How do you mean?"

"Only that Belinda happens to have spent the day in the company of our sister and Professor 'Buggermini.' She has been nowhere else, to my knowledge. Not even up to her room."

It was true. Belinda had sat about the parlor in a daze ever since her return, not bothering to change for dinner. But now, at Charles's epithet, she was suddenly bristling like a boar.

" 'Buggermini!' How dare you, sir? I'll thank you to keep a civil tongue in your head when you're talking about . . . *no!* I *forbid* you to talk about that great man *at all!* You are not fit to lick his shoe!"

"Well, well!" said Charles quietly. "Kendrick, I fear we must bid adieu to 'Professor Fly-eyes' and 'Buggermini,' and usher in 'That Great Man.' "

Belinda dropped her fork upon her plate. "I am no longer hungry," she said, rising from her chair with blazing cheeks.

"No?" asked Charles, raising an eyebrow. "Won't you even finish your pudding? It's all covered in lovely pesto!"

"Your slimy insinuations have put me off pudding!" she cried. And without further ado she ran from the room, her eyes smarting with tears.

"Insinuations?" Charles inquired of the others. "I never made any insinuations. I merely said 'Bugg—' Oh!"

Osvaldo, who could not have been termed a bright man, smiled inside his gigantic collar, thinking that all this had something to do with himself. He had failed to comprehend that Charles's earlier remark about Belinda having not been up to her room meant that she could not have found his note. Nor had he grasped the import of the sudden silence that followed the utterance of half of Bergamini's name. That silence was prolonged for a time, whilst the three gentlemen pursued three different trains of thought, and yet all of them concerned the fair sex.

"I say, Kendrick," said Charles, having regained his composure and poured himself another glass of canary. "This is an unexpected turn of events, is it not? What do you make of it?"

"I think I'll just take a tray up to Miss Beaumont," mumbled Kendrick, who had been as deaf to the conversation as had Osvaldo. "She really must be persuaded to eat *something!*"

Chapter 17

A BLESSING IN DISGUISE

"I understand how angry you must feel," said Belinda, who was having another go at smoothing her sister's feathers, "and you are perfectly justified, of course, but you must remember, Bell: We are in a foreign country."

"To think," cried Arabella, slamming a pile of books into her trunk. "To *think* that that . . . *hideous* man should have invaded this room! *My* room! Against my expressed wishes, and with the complicity of the landlords! It is . . . it is beyond anything! This isn't my room at all, it seems! It belongs to the whole world!"

"I repeat," said Belinda. "We are in a foreign country. The ways of these people are not our ways, and religion is very important here. In fact, it is more important than anything else. You are a woman, with no husband or father standing behind you, and you are a foreigner. The Italians have actually shown great forbearance toward you—toward us, coming to their country, or whatever this is, and demanding our 'rights.' We *have* no rights, here. John Locke's idea is merely a relic we have brought with us. Can you not see how absurd we must look to them?"

Arabella plumped down on the bed. "I suppose I had not thought of it in that light," she admitted.

"Besides," said Belinda, pursuing her advantage. "If we leave now, where shall we go? Home? Without what we came for? You will make us all unhappy if you do that. You will not have your statue, Charles has not finished fleecing the local populace, and Mr. Kendrick . . . oh. He will be happy enough, I suppose."

"But you hate it here, Bunny! Only this morning you were trying to convince me to take you home!"

"I know I was," said Belinda. "But that was this morning. I want to stay . . . now."

Is it possible, dear reader, that a single amorous encounter in a lightless, underground vault can awaken a young woman to love? Love with an elderly man, whom she has held in abhorrence up to the hour preceding her sublime moment?

The subject of improbable attachment is truly one that requires meditation—not on the grounds of possibility, for such things frequently happen, and Belinda was genuinely in love with Professor Bergamini—but for the sheer strangeness of it. Such a pointless expenditure of emotion, veering wide of any clear biological objective! Yet, people do not always fall in love with viable procreational partners. They may fall in love with pug dogs, or ships, or even statues. As for Belinda, she had learnt an important lesson: Love is not necessarily blind, but it does, sometimes, wear dark spectacles.

"You are perfectly right, Bunny," said Arabella, coming over to kiss the top of her head. "I have been foolish. But at least I appreciate good sense when I hear it. And you are the most sensible little person that ever was!"

"Miss Beaumont," called Kendrick from without. "I have brought you a tray. Will you not try to take a little something?"

"By all means!" she cried, throwing open the door. "I am quite ravenous! How very good of you, Mr. Kendrick!"

"Oh!" said he. "I thought that you were . . . were . . ."

"I was. But I am over it now."

"You mean, we are not going to leave?" he asked.

"Why, no. I have not got my statue, have I?"

"This is splendid, Mr. Kendrick!" cried Belinda, inspecting the tray. "An extra-large helping of pudding! Bell, do you really want it? Because I was obliged to leave my own downstairs, and I'm sure they'll have given it to the goat by now."

At this point, Kendrick would have left the tray and retired to some place of seclusion, to ponder the changeability of the feminine temperament. But the sisters insisted that he stay. They fed him titbits from the plate and draped him with laces and ribbons, laughing uproariously the meanwhile, as they unpacked Arabella's things again.

"Miss Beaumont," said Kendrick, looking perfectly darling in a mohair shawl, which Belinda had thrown over his head and shoulders. And a bonnet, which Arabella had jammed over the top of it. And a golden tiara, set with amber stones and lapis lazuli, which Belinda had added as a whimsical afterthought. "I have formed a theory about what occurred here today."

"Please! Let us speak no more about it!"

"But this might have some bearing on the mystery! Well, it is highly mysterious, at any rate."

She made an exasperated noise, signifying at once her frustration with his obstinacy and her consent that he should proceed.

"Before your arrival, I was watching Father Terranova give the blessing."

"You were! Yet you made no attempt to evict him from our rooms?!"

"The crowd about the hotel was too dense to break through. It would not have been possible. But even supposing it were, what would you have had me do, then? Force the priest from your balcony, in full sight of a thousand people who wished to hear him? I am devoted to your service, madam, but I hope I am not stupid. Besides, he did not appear to be giving a blessing."

"What do you mean?"

"There was no holy water; no aspergillum. It appeared that he was merely delivering a speech to the crowd."

"Really?" Arabella was intrigued. "What did he say?"

"I've no idea. It was in Italian, of course."

Further discourse upon this subject was effectively curtailed by the arrival of Charles, bearing Arabella's costume and Belinda's greyhound, which he had previously secreted in his room. And to his delighted astonishment, he was fairly smothered in unaccustomed gratitude from his amazed and delighted sisters.

> *Dear Mrs. Janks,*
>
> *I really am beginning to feel as though the whole world has shunned me! That my gentleman friends should cut me is not so much a surprise, but that you, who have always defended me, would now ignore my pleas for information, is hard indeed! Charles invented the story about the dancing lesson in a misguided attempt to save Belinda from an imprudent marriage. Why will you not believe that? Please, Mrs. Janks, dear Mrs. Janks, I implore you to tell me what is going on there with respect to my current standing in society! If it would be unwise for me to come home now, why will you not write and say so?*

"No post . . . no Pietro . . . I am becoming a regular nervous Nelly!" Arabella observed to Belinda, as the sisters posted handbills in the little town. These had been translated into Italian, and advertised a reward for any news leading to the statue's recovery.

"In that order?" Belinda asked.

"What?"

"Which worries you more, Pietro's absence, or your lack of letters?"

"What is the difference? Sometimes, Bunny, I cannot fathom you at all."

They finished their task, and were making their way back to the hotel, when a large bush growing beside the road suddenly and unaccountably sneezed. The sisters halted in their tracks, and regarded the shrub with grave uncertainty.

"*Signorina!*" whispered the bush. "Come closer! It is Pietro! I cannot be seen talking to you!"

"What . . . ?"

"Ssshh! You are being watched, *signorina!* Pretend you are tired, and sit down in the shade."

She and Belinda sat upon the grass.

"The smuggler is back," he said quietly. "Meet me in town tomorrow, and I will fix a time to take you to his house. You will need to bring men with you."

"Will coachmen be all right?" she asked softly.

"Yes. Get big ones."

"Very well. Where shall I meet you in Resina? And at what time?"

"*Non è importante.* I will find you. Good-bye, *signorina.*"

"Do you really think you're being watched?" asked Belinda as they walked toward the hotel.

"Of course not! Why should anyone want to watch me? Other than for business reasons, of course. I think Pietro is just attempting to inject a little mystery into an otherwise dull assignment."

In any case, the fellow who *was* following them was just an ordinary man, going about his ordinary business, which coincidentally happened to lie in the same direction.

The following morning, Arabella and Mr. Kendrick went to Resina. Belinda had an assignation with her professor, and Charles, now that his luck had changed, was no longer in need of a minder.

"Where should you like me to take you?" asked the rector.

"I don't care where I go or what I do, so long as I may bask in the sunshine!"

"Then I think I know the very place! Your brother and I discovered a little taverna with outdoor tables, on that day you went to Pompeii with Miss Belinda. It was around . . . here, someplace . . . I cannot quite recall where, though . . . ah!" (He had spied a shop window with an ENGLISH SPOKEN HEAR sign.) "If you will wait just one moment, Miss Beaumont, I shall pop inside and enquire about it."

Arabella stood in the tender sunlight, idly humming, and swaying a little to her own music. It was a mild day, only slightly chilly, with the gush from the public fountain glistening in the sunshine, and the birds singing for all they were worth. She was feeling happy on the inside, and exquisite on the outside, dressed as she was in a soft gown of cream-colored wool, with Mameluke sleeves and gray ribbons, surmounted by a gray velvet spencer and a tippet of silver fox fur. In point of fact, the inner happiness was most probably occasioned by the outward display, and so engrossed was she in contemplation of this fact as to be not at all prepared when someone seized her roughly from behind and whipped a blindfold over her eyes.

"Help!" Arabella screamed, or started to, but a hand was quickly and firmly clamped over her mouth. Then she struggled womanfully to free herself, but that was no good, either;

her head and shoulders were the only parts of her anatomy she was able to move, and these are not very effective in amateur self-defense maneuvers.

Oddly enough, her assailant was making no effort either to force her into a carriage or to cut her throat. He simply held her immobilized in the public square for a few moments, as she strove ineffectually within a pair of arms that embraced her like iron barrel staves.

"Stubborn little idiot!" growled a voice in her ear. "You were warned, time and again, but you have failed to listen to reason!"

It was an English voice, and Arabella wondered, in her panic, whether that was a good thing. Where was Kendrick? Would he find her in time?

And then, as suddenly as she had been seized, she was released again, and the blindfold removed. (The reader may be interested to learn that it was a pocket handkerchief, tied into a loop so as to be easily dropped over her head.)

Arabella spun round and furiously confronted her assailant. "Gordon!" she exclaimed with an admixture of relief and delight. "My God, you nearly gave me heart failure!"

He laughed and kissed her.

"Hello, my darling! What are you doing so far from home?"

"It's rather a long story. What are *you* doing out here?"

"Searching for a decent cup of coffee, like everybody else."

"Look who I have got, Mr. Kendrick!" Arabella called as the rector emerged from the shop. "It's Lord Byron!"

The two men were not actually friends. One couldn't be, with Byron. By his own admission, the poet's only friend had been his dog, Boatswain. And Boatswain was dead. But Byron liked John Kendrick well enough for all that. They sat outside because Arabella wanted to admire the sky. She had to crane her neck a bit to actually see it above the sheer walls of the tenement buildings that hemmed them in, but it was better than nothing. Besides, craning shewed off her throat to its best advantage, and a couple of youngbloods on the other side of the street were making friendly kissing noises at her. Arabella smiled at them provocatively.

"Any number of people love their work," she preened, "but how many can claim that their work loves them back?"

"I can," said Kendrick. "My parishioners daily shew their gratitude for my presence in a thousand different ways."

"But that's hardly the same *sort* of love," Byron observed.

"Good heavens, I should hope not!"

Coffee was brought out to them in tiny cups, because it was so very strong.

"Do tell us about your adventures, Gordon!" said Arabella. (Byron's intimates all called him Gordon, as he had the misfortune to share his Christian name with the widely detested prince regent.) "When did you leave England?"

"I don't remember *when*," he said. "Only *why*: I left in order to get away from Caroline for a bit. She's a lovely woman, you know, but ever so slightly off-balance. I beg your pardon, that is most unfair . . . to all the slightly off-balanced persons in the world! Caroline is a raving lunatic. Usually I like that in a mistress, but not when it involves possessiveness.

"Anyway, I went first to Greece, where Lord Elgin's agent gave me a tour of the Parthenon. And when I saw the places where that bastard Elgin had ripped away the friezes and wrenched off the caryatids, I was blind with fury! That wasn't the agent's fault, of course, but it *was* his fault when he said, 'Thank God for Lord Elgin! What a friend to antiquity!' I nearly choked the life out of him."

Arabella shifted uncomfortably in her chair. Actually, the precise word for what she did is "squirmed." For she had remembered her handbills. She could even see one of them from where she was sitting. Thankfully, they did not bear her name, but they did give the hotel's address. And Byron was fluent in Italian.

"Nothing provokes my rage like the arrogance of British despoilers," he said. "The way they simply help themselves to the history of other cultures! What presumption! It is theft, pure and simple! If it were up to me, all such perpetrators would be hanged for the criminals they are! And one day," he added, setting the tiny spoon onto his saucer, "it might *very well* be up to me."

"What do you mean?" asked Kendrick.

"Oh, nothing, probably. But you see . . . well, there *is* talk. That is, some people are sort of suggesting that I shall end up as king of Greece."

"Crikey!" Kendrick exclaimed. "Wouldn't *that* be remarkable!"

"It would. Though I feel I can tell you that I do not believe myself worthy."

"Gordon," said Arabella. "Do not insult us by feigning humility. It suits you exceedingly ill."

"I know it does!" he laughed. "I should *love* to be king of Greece! To what more could a man aspire? And then I'd give those English despoilers what-for!"

Arabella avoided Kendrick's eye.

"But I want to know about *you*, Arabella! What has tempted you to leave fair Lustings and venture abroad?"

She cleared her throat. "Well . . . I . . ." Her voice faltered.

"You can tell Gordon, Arabella!" said Kendrick encouragingly.

Confound the man! What was he doing?! She couldn't tell Gordon about her quest for the statue! He'd—how had he put it?—"choke the life out of her!"

"Come, come," Kendrick urged. "Lord Byron is no stranger to scandal! Besides, it's none of your doing; you are a victim of your brother's poor judgment!"

"Oh!" she said weakly. "Oh, yes. Well, you see, Gordon, my brother Charles told a silly story at his club, which started a rumor . . ."

Byron slapped the table hard with his open hand. His listeners jumped, and the espresso cups rattled in their saucers.

"I *did* hear about that! Incest, wasn't it? Incest, amongst the three of you!"

"*You* heard about it? In *Greece?*"

"News travels fast, these days. So, you're lying low out here till the scandal blows over, I take it. You could not have picked a nicer spot to do it in: Mediterranean vistas . . . Roman ruins . . . and all the beautiful artworks of antiquity, spread at your feet."

"Gordon," she ventured, "have you heard anything? What are people saying?"

"I shouldn't worry about it," he said kindly. "Incest is such a little thing. I practice it myself, you know. Though of course, Augusta is only my half sister . . ."

"Tell us about Missolonghi," said Kendrick quickly.

"A beautiful spot! Savage! Raw! I ate with the Pallikar chieftains, and slept beneath the stars, wrapped in my cloak. It's just skirmishes now. But there will be full-scale war, eventually, and then I shall return, to fight side-by-side with my Pallikar brethren! The Italians, on the other hand, are ready to commence their own rebellion against tyranny, *now.* That is why I am here, in fact. I have joined the Carbonari, to help advance their glorious cause!"

"That sounds like a political organization," said Arabella suspiciously.

"It is . . . *but,*" he added, hastily, "it's a *secret society.* You dote upon those."

"I do," she admitted. "What are their aims? Please be brief, Gordon."

"Briefly, then, we are seeking Italy's unification, under one government."

"That doesn't sound like it need be kept secret!"

"Oh, but it does! You see, the Austrians are dead against it, and the papal states are insisting . . ." but he saw her eyes glaze over. "You must just take my word that it is a noble cause. We are in deadly earnest."

"I believe you," said Arabella, standing up and filling her lungs. "By heaven, what a morning! One could almost believe it was spring! Mr. K., might I prevail upon you to purchase a box of those exquisite little butter horns, and take them back to the hotel for me? Come along, Gordon! Let us go dabble our feet in some fountain!"

If Byron was shocked at her blatant contempt of Kendrick, he masked it.

"Another time, I should love to," said he, consulting his watch. "But just now I have a pressing appointment."

"What?!" cried Arabella, only half in jest. "Forsaking *me* for another woman?"

"No. I meant that literally. I am being honored this evening at a military dinner. Medals, you know, will only go so far in covering up the wrinkles on a man's jacket, and I'm told they do absolutely nothing at all for crumpled trousers."

A child in a tattered shirt hastened up to them, and Arabella saw with dismay that it was Pietro. He was panting, like one who has been running for a long time, or someone who is badly frightened. Or both.

"*Signorina,* I must speak quickly . . . !"

What was she to do, now? If she discussed plans with the boy, Gordon was almost certain to ask questions. And if he should discover that she was proposing to deprive Italy of one of its national treasures . . . !

"I am sorry, little fellow, but I have just spent the last of my lira on coffee," said Arabella untruthfully, for Byron had paid for it. She turned away from Pietro, as though he no longer existed, and saw Byron across the street, tearing down her handbill.

"Vandals!" he snarled. "Looters! This is precisely the kind of thing I was talking about!" He ripped the notice to shreds as a dog rips a handkerchief dropped by an enemy, letting the pieces fall where they might. Then he stalked off.

"Good-bye, Gordon, my love!" called Arabella, waving for all she was worth. "Be sure to do everything I wouldn't do! That was a near thing!" she said to Kendrick. "Where is Pietro? Pietro!" she called down the street. "Pietro!"

"I should not expect to see him again, if I were you," said Kendrick quietly.

"Whatever do you mean?"

"I think you know what I mean. That boy has been of invaluable help in your pigheaded quest for a statue that isn't actually yours. Has it occurred to you that he may have risked his life in coming to you just now? And you repaid the lad by treating him like a common beggar before your friends!"

If the rector had been a spitting man, Arabella's shoes would have stood in some danger. He was thinking, perhaps, of how she had tried to dismiss *him*, too, sending him for butter horns when she wished to run off with Gordon.

"I pay Pietro handsomely for what he does," she retorted. "In *cash*. We have no understanding about how he is to be treated in front of my friends."

Kendrick remained silent. And as Arabella called and called without result, his silence grew in eloquence. At last, she gave up, and turned back toward the hotel.

"Signorina!"

She whirled round expectantly, but the boy who ran toward her from across the street was a stranger. "I have message for you!"

"Where is Pietro?" asked Arabella.

"He cannot come. But I will take you to the house you want. Can you go on Wednesday? At nine o'clock?"

"Of course."

"And bring a nin . . . nintr . . . someone who speaks Italian, yes?"

"An interpreter?"

"Yes. One of those."

SOMETHING FUNNY ABOUT
THE COCOA

The redoubtable Mrs. Molyneux, a cook par excellence, understood the importance of details. They *mattered,* whether one was cooking for the aristocracy, or only for one's fellow servants while the mistress was from home. Unfortunately, after having saved a set of actual pigeon's feet to make tracks across the unbaked crust of her pigeon pie, she forgot that Tilda had to be closely watched in everything.

"*Wait!*" shrieked the cook. Dropping her saucier with a clang, she lunged across the pastry table and grabbed Tilda by the wrists only just in time. "You must first *wash* zee feets!"

Wonderingly, Tilda turned the bird claws over and saw that the bottoms were thickly coated with muck and feces from the pigeon coop.

"Oh," she said.

Fielding, the parlor maid–cum-butler-cum–kitchen assistant, was standing at the kitchen sink extension, cutting sippets with a bread knife. Not for that night, of course—who would want sippets with pie? But Mrs. Molyneux would be requiring them for the following day, and insisted that stale ones were best.

"Mrs. Moly!" said Fielding, glancing out the window. "There's an old peddler woman coming round to the door, with a sack!"

"Well, geeve 'air some food, eef she's ongry, but send hair away eef she tries to sell you anysing."

"New cats for old!" croaked a voice outside.

"What was zat she said?" asked the cook.

"Sounded like 'New hats for old,'" said Fielding. "That doesn't make any sense, though, does it?"

"*Non*, indeed! Go see what she wants, Marianne."

Fielding opened the door to as outrageously an attired pilgrim as the young woman had ever beheld, with a sack of squirming creatures slung over its back.

"Oh," said the parlor maid. "You'll be wanting to speak to Cook, I expect. Mrs. Moly! Could you come here a moment? It's somebody with rabbits or something!"

Mrs. Molyneux duly appeared, wiping her hands on her apron.

" 'Allo! Yes? What 'ave you thair? Leetle robeets?"

"Kittens," said the peddler, stooping down with her bag and pouring the contents across the threshold.

"Ah! Well, I'm afraid zat we do not eat keettens at zees 'ouse. You might try down ze road, at Justice Harbuckle's residonce. I am told zat zee jodge prefairs children, but keettens might make a nice shange. Good day."

Mrs. Molyneux tried to shut the door so as to scoop the cat cubs back out onto the step, but Lady Ribbonhat (for the astute reader will have guessed it was she) quickly stuck out her foot, just as Tilda arrived at the back door.

"Oh!" cried the girl, plumping down on the floor and gathering them into her skirt. "Kittens! Please, may we keep them, Mrs. Moly?"

"We may not," said the cook. "We 'ave already got zee wan cat, and I don't know 'ow zee mistress weel take on when she sees *zat* one! Besides, we 'ave no money to waste on kittens!"

"Oh, but you see, I don't want any money!" cried Lady Peddler-Ribbon.

"No?" asked the cook, startled. "What *do* you want, zen?"

"An exchange! If you will let me have your raggedy old ginger tomcat, I shall give you these three adorable black-and-white kittens, instead!" She held one of them up and cuddled it against her cheek. "You see? Their eyes are still blue!"

Mrs. Janks now joined Tilda and Mrs. Moly at the door.

"'Ow did you know we even 'ad a ginger tomcat?" asked the housekeeper, narrowing her eyes. "And what do you want 'im for?"

"Uh . . . well," said the peddler, "I only require one cat, for my particular line of work."

"And what might that be?"

"Well . . . I . . . travel about. From one place to another, you understand. And I am chiefly engaged in selling . . . um, various gewgaws and bric-a-brac. I cannot keep three felines with me. I mean, they will get lost, will they not? No, three cats is two cats too many. I merely require one good, reliable mouser!"

"And why should a peddler need a mouser at all?" asked the cook. "Eef she travel all zee time?"

"No," said Mrs. Janks. "No, thank you. We already have a cat, and we find him quite satisfactory! Come now, Tilda, give the woman back her kittens."

"Oh, no, Mrs. Janks!" cried the scullion tragically. "They're such cunning little things! And they'll get lost, she says, if . . ."

"She wants to trade them for Rooney," explained the housekeeper. "You don't want them *that* badly, do you?"

"Rooney?! I could never give *him* up!"

"So then," said Mrs. Janks reasonably. "Give the kittens back to Lady Peddler-Hat, here. I dunno why you want a cat that you cared so little for that you had your ostler put it through our window," she added, leaning in toward the "peddler," "but I can tell you this, my lady; if *you* want 'im, that's reason enough for us to keep 'im."

And Mrs. Janks shut the door in her face.

"Tilda, when you've finished trackin' that pie, wipe your 'ands an' go fetch me a pen and some paper. The mistress is not going to believe this!"

Fair mornings generally found Arabella seated on the sunny little balcony, in a cashmere peignoir, fretting over her non-existent post and sorely missing her beloved blue chocolate pot. No one drank chocolate in this part of the world, evidently, so one had to make do with coffee. And in the absence of any correspondence, Arabella read a book, or searched through odd, outdated English papers for news of the family scandal. But she never discovered any mention of it.

"How bad can it possibly be," she asked Belinda, "if the papers aren't on to it? So why does no one write and *tell* me? Have you received any letters, Bunny?"

"No, but then, I have not written any, either. I simply haven't the mental energy, at present. And if I had, all I should write would be 'Bergamini, Bergamini, Bergamini.' I should never tire of that, but I am afraid other people might."

"They might, indeed! But I cannot understand this universal silence," Arabella said, half to herself. "I have written to practically everyone I know."

"Perhaps the post is not as efficient here as it is at home. Perhaps nothing is getting through."

"But it *is,* though. Signor Terranova receives daily postal dispatches from all over the world, and Charles had another demand from his tailor only yesterday! I am exceedingly worried! Mrs. Janks has not even responded to my request for the household expense report, and you know that is just not like her!"

They were sitting in the sun, with coffee again, and Arabella was thinking how comforted she would have felt with a cup of chocolate between her hands.

"Hmm? I am sorry, I wasn't listening," said Belinda. "I cannot seem to concentrate on anything anyone says. But speaking of the post, here are two things that came in for you this morning."

She held up an envelope, together with a packet, and Arabella fairly snatched them from her. Then she groaned.

"These aren't from home! They were delivered *by hand.*"

"Well? Maybe they're clews, then, or a death threat, with a packet of poison powder. Post is post, Bell, wherever it comes from . . . where *does* it come from?"

"The University of Naples," she said, reading the envelope.

"Oh!" cried Belinda, scrambling up from her chair and coming round to Arabella's side of the table. "That is Bergamini's university! What does it say?!"

Arabella tore open the envelope and unfolded the note.

"It *is* from Bergamini," she said. "It is a response to the note I wrote to him yesterday. Here, I'll read it to you:

> *Dearest Madam,*
> *I am ready to act as your interpreter and escort you to the home of this smuggler person whenever you should like to go. In the meantime, and mindful of the incompatibility of my country's cuisine with your brother's stomach, I am taking the liberty of sending him, through you, a supply of English cocoa. I hope this may help to mitigate Signor Beaumont's indisposition*

*insofar as some of it may be caused by
homesickness.*

*I remain your obedient servant, and please
communicate my regards to your charming sister,
Belinda.*

"Ah!" cried Belinda, half-swooning with delight. "Read that last part to me, again!"

*"Please communicate my regards to your
charming sister, Belinda."*

"Again!"

"No," said Arabella. "Here, take the note." And she handed it over. "Now you can read it to yourself as much as you will. Just . . ."

"Please communicate . . ."

" . . . read it to yourself, please."

"Oh, but I want to *hear* it, Bell!"

"Fine," said Arabella, rising from her chair. "Then I shall visit the kitchen, and learn how to cook like an Italian."

On the following morning, Professor Bergamini called at the hotel at ten minutes to 9:00. Belinda flew across the room when he entered, and clung onto him like a mussel on a piling. For his part, though he still displayed his usual manner of gentle solicitude toward her, Bergamini's movements seemed charged with a new vitality. It would have been sweet to see them thus enthralled, the one with the other, were it not so strange. When they sat cozily together in the carriage they looked for all the world like a dear, doting old gentleman and his granddaughter, but for their little fingers linked upon the carriage seat. Yet who was there to disapprove?

Arabella had seen all manner of queer things in her time. Charles would have made fun, probably, but he had not been included in the party. And Kendrick, too, had elected to remain behind. He seemed to be avoiding Arabella's company since her rudeness toward Pietro.

It was nearly winter now, but one would scarcely guess this. The countryside at harvest time gladdened the eye in its magnificent abundance. But if the carriage seemed to bear them through the center of a lovely picture, the farm at which they eventually turned in was a veritable portrait of neglect. Weeds proliferated. The plow lay upturned in a puddle of rank water, corroded with rust. A few scrawny chickens picked despondently through the stones and trash in front of the house, as though they didn't actually expect to find anything, but felt the need to keep up appearances. Yet the house itself was practically new, and a fine riding horse stood saddled and ready in the drive.

"Clearly," Arabella murmured, as they climbed from the carriage, "the owner makes a comfortable living by some means *other* than farming!"

The man himself came out to meet them, and Arabella was alarmed by his appearance. He was a surly, swarthy fellow, with a curling mustache and one hard, brown eye that squinted. The other eye, which was blue and wide open, seemed to be fixed on something that stood next to and slightly behind him. He neither invited the visitors inside, nor brought them out chairs, so that they were obliged to remain standing during the whole of the interview. But in any case, their stay would not be a long one.

"Ask him, please, Professor," said Arabella, "whether he has any information about the art theft."

"It can scarcely be called a theft, I think," said Bergamini. "Those pieces did not belong to the person who was murdered. In fact, I think we had better leave the term 'theft' out of this, since technically, you yourself are a potential—"

"Oh, very well," she interrupted. "Ask him what he remembers of the murder, and whether he knows the statue's current whereabouts."

As the professor spoke to him in Italian, the smuggler stiffened, and his nostrils dilated with fear or with rage or possibly something else. Bergamini spoke quietly, but menacingly—to Arabella's mind, at least—like a Spanish inquisitor. Eventually, the man found his voice and replied at length, in a high-pitched, defensive chatter.

"He says," said the professor, "that he is a farmer. He knows nothing about any murder."

"What else?"

"I do not understand, *signorina*."

"He has been talking for the last minute or more. What else did he say?"

"Oh, you know these peasants . . . so superstitious! Just some nonsense about . . . a curse. He says he will be killed if he helps you."

It was now quite plain to see that the man *was* frightened. He would tell them nothing, not even when Arabella produced a wad of lire from her reticule, and riffled the edges enticingly with her thumb. At last she was obliged to give it up as a bad job. But after they had re-entered the carriage, the fellow's wife, who had hidden herself on the other side of it so as to escape detection from the house, reached her arm through the window, and caught Bergamini by the sleeve. She began to talk, low and rapidly.

"The artworks were wrapped in burlap and canvas," the professor translated. "They were brought here in her husband's little donkey cart, and the next evening they were taken away again, in a larger oxcart, which contained more canvas and burlap-covered items."

"Where was the oxcart going?"

"Napoli," the woman replied.

Arabella thanked her, and handed over the money.

"Naples," she repeated gloomily as the carriage proceeded down the road. "From Naples, it might have been loaded onto a ship and gone anywhere."

"No," said Bergamini with sudden animation. "I think I know *exactly* where it went! A few days ago I was speaking with the curator of the Naples Museum, when he excused himself to talk to a workman waiting in the hall outside. I heard the man complaining about a lot of junk that had suddenly turned up in the storeroom where he kept his tools. He didn't know what they were, he said. But there were a lot of them. And they were all wrapped up in canvas and burlap!"

"Professor," said Arabella. "How long would it take to arrange accommodation for us in Naples?"

That evening, the hotel kitchen staff prepared cocoa for all the guests, which, considering that they had never made it before, was a noble effort. Arabella had overseen its preparation, but forgot to mention that cocoa is usually served in cups, and the landlady had given orders for wineglasses to be set out upon a clever contrivance that rotated like a spinning platter.

The advent of cocoa cheered the Beaumonts no end. Charles actually smiled—something he rarely did away from his gambling hells—and Belinda kept explaining to everyone that the cocoa had been a gift from Professor Bergamini. Instead of being put off by the unusual wineglass presentation, Arabella had entered at once into the spirit of the occasion, which was reminiscent for her of long-ago nursery celebrations, and in a correspondingly childlike frame of mind, she believed that the excitement generated by the cocoa somehow related to her own extraordinary qualities as a person of note. For that reason, she disdained to use an ordinary glass, and instead appropriated—without asking—an expensive Venetian goblet from the cabinet.

Mr. Kendrick was subdued in the presence of Renilde,

whom he had not seen since the night she had tried to seduce him. (She had been taking all her meals in her room, and these days only came downstairs to collect the post.) Besides, the two parties had barely been on speaking terms after the unlawful breaking-and-entering episode. But the cocoa actually went a little way toward effecting a thaw.

"Well, now," said Terranova. "We have cocoa, and a roomful of people who must have encountered interesting stories, either true or untrue, in the course of their lives. Who'll give us a tale?"

"I know a story," Mr. Kendrick volunteered.

"That is good of you, Reverend, and of course we all remember your last one! But perhaps we had better have the ladies start us off."

In the end, and to no one's very great surprise, the honor devolved on Arabella.

"Once upon a time," she began, "there lived a garden slug, who was typical of his kind in every way but one: He wished to be a person of consequence.

" 'No one will ever notice me down here in the cabbages,' he sniveled. 'And I have such gifts! Such talents! Such brilliance to share with the world!' "

"And had he?" asked Belinda.

"What do you think? He was just a slug, after all."

"He sounds like Nero," said Terranova thoughtfully, stroking his beard.

"Well, for my part, I pity the poor creature," said Kendrick. "Imagine what it must feel like to know for a certainty that there will never be any way out of one's wretched existence but death."

"And yet, you have just described the condition known as 'life,' Mr. Kendrick," said Arabella. Signora Fiorello appeared with a pitcher and began pouring cocoa into the wineglasses. "But I do not mind in the least. Personally, I am finding life quite enjoyable, at the moment."

"Naturally," he said. "But you are a human being. Life cannot be nearly as rich or as satisfying for the slugs of this world!"

At that moment, someone began pounding the heavy iron ring that served as a front door knocker. Signora Fiorello set down the pitcher and hurried out to answer it. Her husband, too, came running at the summons.

The coffee room's occupants fell silent as an officious voice without was heard commanding or demanding something. This was followed by argumentative jabbering from the landlord, and the words "no-no-no!" repeated frequently. Terranova exchanged uneasy glances with his monks.

"Let us go and see whether we may be of any assistance," he said, rising. The rest of the company followed him into the entrance hall, where two gargantuan soldiers and their enormous officer loomed over the diminutive landlord. The signora was arguing, too, and trying to break into the circle to stand next to her spouse.

"What goes on here?" asked Arabella in her best imperious tones. "Do you gentlemen speak English?"

At the sight of her, all three soldiers removed their hats, and the officer, apparently mistaking her for the proprietress, said, "Sorry, *signorina,* for the disturbance. But we have had a report that a dangerous speech was recently made here, and we must investigate. Can you tell us anything about this matter?"

Arabella turned to look for Father Terranova, and was just in time to see him slipping out of the coffee room to rejoin the company. He had evidently gone back inside for some purpose. Now he stood waiting in the shadows, surrounded by his monks. He was beyond the reach of the central lantern, and completely at her mercy.

"Yes," she said calmly. "I can tell you all about it, in fact. That man over there was the focus of a large gathering some days ago, when he addressed a crowd from the balcony that overlooks Ercolano."

The soldiers all turned toward Terranova. "Yes?" said the officer. "And can you tell us what this speech was about, *signorina?*"

"Quite. He was baptizing the victims who died in the eruption of 79 A.D. Hardly a danger, *signor*. On the contrary, it was an act of mercy."

Then Father Terranova stepped into the light, and a gasp of recognition went up from the soldiers, who knelt and asked his pardon. The officer apologized for the intrusion, and the warriors returned from whence they had come. Terranova was evidently a man of some renown.

"Those men did not look like Italians," said Arabella.

"No," said Terranova. "They were Austro-Hungarians."

"Then, why . . . no, never mind. The explanation is doubtless political."

After the rest of the guests had returned to the coffee room, the priest detained her at the entrance for a moment.

"*Signorina,*" he said. "Thank you for that."

"For what, *signor?* You said that you were going to bless the dead, and I must assume that you have kept your word. For I, as you know, speak no Italian."

A glass shattered in the coffee room, and they entered to find a serving girl on her knees, mopping up a puddle of cocoa.

"The cat, she's-a jump on the table," explained the landlady. "Thanks to goodness, it was not my prize goblet that broke!" And after an accusing glance at Arabella, Signora Fiorello poured the contents of her Venetian masterpiece into an ordinary wineglass and set it on the revolving stand with the others. "Here," she said, handing the beautiful goblet to one of the maids. "Wash-a this, and then return it, *very carefully,* to the cabinet! If it-a should break, you will pay for it . . . with your next five years' wages!"

"It's probably all cold now," said Charles bitterly.

"Not a bit," replied Terranova, hefting one of the glasses

and feeling the temperature through it. "But you have changed seats, I think. Here, Signor Beaumont, this one was yours." And he turned the stand. "Signorina Beaumont, I believe your cocoa is in *this* glass, now."

He spun the platter in the opposite direction, and Renilde leaned suddenly forward. "But that one is mine, cousin!" she cried.

"No, Renilde. I do not think so. That is Signorina Beaumont's."

"It isn't," she insisted. "I have already drunk from that one, Cousin Felice. Pass it to me! Please!"

"No," he repeated, his voice heavy with menace. "That is *Signorina Beaumont's.*"

Renilde glanced at Arabella, her face eloquent with anguish.

Good God, thought the courtesan, is Terranova trying to poison me? She immediately took up the glass he had spun round to her, not in order to drink it, but to remove it from that murderously rotating platter. It smelt perfectly fine, although that did not signify. She toyed with it, and swirled the liquid around the glass for a while, before finally setting it down.

"Here is yours, Reverend Kendrick," said Terranova, continuing to distribute the cocoa via the "lazy Susan," " . . . and Aunt Ginevra's . . . and Signorina Belinda's . . ."

Finally, all the glasses had been served save one, and the priest took that for himself.

"Renilde . . . ? We are now one glass short, it seems," he said, smiling.

"I am not taking any, Cousin Felice."

"I insist. Cocoa is very healthful. It will calm your nerves."

"No, thank you," she replied. "I really do not care for cocoa!"

"Now, I *know* that's not true," he said. "I remember in London last year, you could not get enough of it. And look—

Signorina Beaumont is not drinking *hers*. Don't you like cocoa, *signorina?*"

"I like it exceedingly," said Arabella. "But I have some writing to do tonight, and I am afraid its well-known soporific effect will put me to sleep before I have completed my task."

He reached out, and placed her glass back upon the platter once more. "In that case," he said, "we shall not waste Professor Bergamini's generous gift. Renilde, you may have this glass, after all."

The girl fell back against her chair, and to everyone's surprise, began to cry!

"Please," she sobbed. "Please! I am very sorry, cousin!"

"You have been over-excited, Renilde," he said soothingly. "Drink your cocoa, and everything will be all right."

"I do not want it anymore."

"But I *insist*. It will calm your nerves, and put you to sleep. Drink it, Renilde. Drink it *now*."

The young woman suddenly seemed to master her weakness. She straightened herself, took up Arabella's rejected glass, looked at Kendrick, looked defiantly at Terranova, and tossed off the contents in a single draught.

"Now, if you will all excuse me," said Renilde firmly, "I am going to bed."

"Yes," Terranova agreed. "Your nerves have had a shock. Good night, my child. May God bless and protect thee, and may you feel better in the morning."

Was it Arabella's imagination, or did the girl stagger as she went through the doorway? Nobody else seemed overly concerned. As soon as Renilde had gone, the *Primary Force* turned his devil's beard in Arabella's direction, his pince-nez glittering diabolically in the light from the oil lamp.

"Your charming story was interrupted, Miss Beaumont," he said. "Can you recall where you left off?"

*   *   *

That night, Arabella wrote in her CIN:

1. **Has Renilde actually, knowingly, drunk poisoned cocoa?** *If so, Terranova must have done it when he slipped back into the coffee room, whilst the rest of us were talking to the soldiers.*
2. **Was the poison intended for me?**
But why would he do that, after I saved him from the soldiers?
3. **If he did not poison her glass, why did Renilde look at me in that fashion, as if to warn me?** *The girl seemed so terrified of the cocoa—why did he force her to drink it? Why did she keep apologizing to him?*
4. **Why would Terranova, after setting out to poison me, poison Renilde, instead?**

Could this be connected to Renilde's confiding in Mr. Kendrick? But she hardly told him anything! I suppose I am imagining things, and tomorrow I shall feel a great fool.

The next morning, Renilde failed to come down to breakfast.

"Where is Miss Rinaldo?" asked Arabella.

"She . . . is gone," said Osvaldo.

"Gone? Gone where?"

"What Osvaldo means," said Father Terranova, his be-ringed fingers flashing as he cut his ham, "is that Renilde is with God."

Terranova's party crossed themselves without looking up from their plates.

Arabella could scarcely believe her ears. "What are you saying? Do you mean that she has died?"

"Yes, I am afraid so," said Terranova and he sighed, as if with regret.

"What? Is she laid out, upstairs?"

"Oh, no. The body was taken away early this morning."

"Taken *away?* By whom?"

"By the sexton. It was taken away and buried."

Arabella looked around the table to see how everyone else was reacting to this. Charles, Belinda, and Mr. Kendrick sat as if turned to stone, with their eyebrows sitting straight across their faces, and their mouths slightly open. Terranova's party, on the other hand, were drinking coffee and eating breakfast as if nothing had happened, and though they kept their eyes, at least, at half-mast, no one was crying. Renilde's own *mother* was dry-eyed.

"Something is not right, here," cried Arabella.

"How very perceptive you are, *signorina,*" said the priest quietly. "But then, we are none of us very good actors. I think it is better, much better, if you do not ask questions, yes?"

She looked at him. At his heavy, square-shaped body, and colossal hands. She looked at the monks, who were also large, and also ready to do his bidding. And she prudently decided to hold her tongue, for the time being.

Chapter 19

A CLEAR CASE OF PARRICIDE

This is outrageous! Despite his general popularity, Terranova is a man of unspeakable evil! For he has surely murdered his cousin, who made the mistake of confiding her scant knowledge of the statue's whereabouts to Mr. Kendrick. Neither he nor I took much notice of what she said at the time, for we both believed she was fabricating the story in order to ensnare my worthy friend in the net of her matrimonial hopes.

Poor Renilde! I believe her now! "Please! I am sorry, cousin!" Thus she begged the monster for her life. And then he forced her, before God and all of us, to drink that fateful draught! I saw the look which passed between them then. I shall never forget it. He seemed to be saying, "Thus are you punished!" And she, courageous in her final moments, seemed to answer, "I, who am about to die, salute you!"

I am resolved to learn the details from her brother, who is currently sitting here in our parlor, making love to Bunny.

It was raining. Arabella was content to remain indoors, for the hotel was comfortable, and the inclement weather afforded her an opportunity to wear her writing turban, which resembled Madame de Staël's, but with narrower stripes. She sat at the little desk before the window, scribbling away in her CIN with a goose-quill pen, and cutting, or so she imagined, a dashing figure of singular romance.

Things were easier now, for Terranova had left the hotel temporarily, taking his monks with him. The two living Rinaldos and Signora Terranova had remained behind, but they were not much in the way. Arabella was about to make use of Osvaldo, as a matter of fact.

"It is raining, yes; but it is a *dry* rain," he said, with an expression that was probably meant to convey profundity, but merely succeeded in making him look constipated.

"And what is that supposed to mean?" asked Arabella, wiping her quill and setting it back in its stand.

"I think he means it is not the sort of rain that lurks about in damp puddles and turns things moldy," said Belinda, who was sitting next to him on the sopha and knitting a small pair of trousers from dark green wool. "After it stops, there is little sign that it was ever there, and everything dries out in half an hour."

"Good! Yes!" cried Osvaldo, grinning and pointing at her as though they were playing charades. "This is it!"

Arabella decided to take advantage of his elevated mood. "Osvaldo," she said, "tell us about Renilde's death."

He immediately fell silent, so she rose from her chair and came to sit beside him upon the sopha. Thus, flanked by Beaumont sisters, the unlucky fellow now stood no chance of escaping with his secrets intact.

"I am not supposed to speak of it," he mumbled, looking down at his hands.

"I know you are not. But no one can hear us now," said

Arabella, patting his hand. "And we should very much like to learn of this matter."

"Yes," said Belinda, linking her arm through his and pressing her thigh against his own. "Please tell us, Osvaldo, dear."

What could a man do under such circumstances?

"She fell sick," he said. "In the night. We called the doctor."

"Do you mean the doctor who lives next door?"

". . . Yes."

Arabella noted his hesitation. "So the doctor came, and then what did he do?"

"Renilde had a fever. She was screaming . . . words that made no meaning. The doctor, he could do nothing to help her, and she died, without suffering too much. We had to bury her at once, you see, because of the fever."

"Fever? I do not understand you."

"It was a *peste* . . . a *plaga* . . . the kind of sickness that spreads quickly and kills many people. We have to hide it, you see? If people find out, they might burn the hotel down. Because any one of us might have catched it from her. But you must promise that you will tell no one I have said this. My cousin told me not to tell you."

Arabella seemed suddenly to lose interest. "Yes, yes," she said wearily. "We shan't tell anyone. You had better leave us now, so that you won't be suspected of having divulged the secret."

After he'd gone, Belinda turned a stricken face toward her sister.

"My God, Bell! Mr. Kendrick was in close contact with Renilde, shortly before . . . ! Do you think he will . . . ?"

"I do not. And I do not believe that story, either."

"You don't? Why not?"

"I shall speak to the doctor, in order to make certain, but I know he was not here last night. When someone is raving with a high fever, and the doctor is called, there is much running up and down stairs. Servants are roused to change the linens, fetch water carafes, empty slop basins. There is noise, Bunny, lots of it, and you and I are both light sleepers. Yet we heard nothing at all, nor were the servants behaving this morning as if they had not slept."

Arabella ticked off the points on her fingers as she spoke: "The house was not put under quarantine, which the doctor would surely have done in the case of infectious fever. Renilde's possessions were not burned. And no one else has developed any symptoms. I shall tell you what I have been thinking, and what I am now certain of, after hearing Pear-Head's lie. Mr. Terranova is a murderer, and a very dangerous man."

Belinda gaped at her in horror. "What a dreadful business!" she cried. "Shouldn't we tell the police?"

"I do not think so. You saw those soldiers kneeling to Terranova. And he lives in Palermo, remember. He lives in Palermo, yet is instantly recognized in Resina, by Austro-Hungarians. *That* is an important man."

"What can we do, then?"

"Professor Bergamini is already inquiring after other lodgings for us in Naples. I shall tell him that it needn't be Naples now—this is an emergency, and we shall settle for anything at all."

"But what if the professor asks the reason for our rapid departure? Shall we tell him?"

"No. We shall say that we are upset over the death which occurred here—that is no more than the truth. We cannot tell them the *whole* truth, Bunny." Arabella was watching Belinda's busy hands as she spoke. "Remember, Terranova and Bergamini know one another."

"All right," said Belinda. "I, for one, shall be very glad to get away from this place. To think of that . . . *murderer* sitting next to you on the downstairs divan, and fondling Cara!"

Belinda reached down to stroke the head of her little pet. From the moment they'd met, dog and mistress had been inseparable. Their mutual devotion was only natural in two such sweet-natured, exquisite little female creatures, but it had been strange the way Terranova had seemed to dote upon her, also. The first time he had seen Cara, he had gone down on his knees, placed his head against hers, and murmured endearments. And yet, when Belinda had offered to let him take her for a walk, he had suddenly shewn extreme indifference, and claimed to be "too busy"!

Arabella fixed her eyes upon the little green trousers Belinda was creating. She was really not in a position to do anything about Terranova, for there was no one she could trust. . . . Trousers . . . perhaps she should take Mr. Kendrick into her confidence. Would he know what to do? It seemed cowardly to simply run away, leaving Renilde in an anonymous grave somewhere . . . green trousers. *Little* . . . green . . . trousers.

"Bunny!" she said in sudden alarm. "What is that you are knitting?"

"Pantaloons. Do you like the color?"

"The color is neither here nor there," Arabella replied with mounting agitation. "For whom are they intended?"

"They're for Cara." Arabella sagged with relief. "She shivers so in the draughts! Up we come, *cara mia*." Belinda lifted the dog from its sentinel post next her chair and wrestled the trousers over its hind legs, pulling the tail through a hole at the back. Then she set her pet down on the carpet.

"What do you think?"

Arabella studied the animal in the trousers, who seemed to look back at her apologetically over its shoulder, barely moving its tail.

"Hmm," she remarked judiciously. "When dogs wear

clothing, you know, the garment is usually located farther up the body, as I believe it is in their chests and stomachs that they most feel the cold."

"Oh," said Belinda. "So, more like a shell, then?"

"I would imagine so."

"How vexing! That was the last of my yarn!"

"*Signorina!* I shall bring-a you some wool for your dog-gie's jumper!"

Osvaldo had just reentered the room, with his snuff box and a paper-wrapped parcel. He probably would not have been so eager to oblige her, had he known he was offering to enhance a gift from his rival, but the poor fellow had no idea of there being anyone else. For her part, Belinda was so involved in her daydreams of Bergamini that she barely registered Osvaldo's existence. Even now as he stood aside for her, cramming his nostrils with rappee blend ("which, she's-a is a-use by my uncle, the prince regent of-a you country"), Belinda swept past him and out of the room without so much as a nod of gratitude.

Osvaldo did not follow her, though. This time, it was with Arabella that he had business.

"*Signorina*, I am sorry, but we found these," he said, hefting the parcel, "in Renilde's dresser. Aunt Simonetta said-a to burn them, rather than give them to you, but I could not do such a heartless thing to my future sister. You will be my *only* sister, when Belinda and I are married."

He unwrapped the bundle, spilling the contents across the desk. There were all the letters that Arabella had written home, and all the ones that had arrived for her and been hidden away.

"Renilde was-a keeping your post from you. I don't know why she did this," he said. "But I can-a guess. Please, *signorina*, say nothing of this downstairs. Aunt Simonetta will be so angry if she knows I gave these-a to you."

"Thank you," said Arabella, who was experiencing relief, surprise, and indignation all at once. "This was . . . this was very kind of you."

He turned to go, but she laid a hand upon his arm.

"I went to the churchyard this morning to search for Renilde's grave," she said. "There was no sign of it."

"No," he said. "The coffin was taken to her father's family, in Siena. They raised Renilde, you see? We hardly knew her. But Renilde, she was . . . she *have* a disappointment? Yes? By the man she was going to marry. So Cousin Felice asked her to join our party here, to have get away from sad times. I will leave you to read your letters. And once again, I am sorry for this."

Solace? Anger? Joy? Arabella did not quite know what she felt. The letters were full of news from home and anxious enquiries concerning her mysterious silence. But none of them so much as mentioned the scandal. On the other hand, the writers had never received her letters asking about it.

At the bottom of the pile was a letter from her protector, the Duke of Glen*deen*. His ship having stopped in some port or other, he was anxiously asking her how she did. Evidently, news of the scandal had reached *him* all the way out on the high seas! He expected to be home by New Year's, he said.

" 'Missing you dreadfully,' " she read, later, to Belinda, " 'because I have been at sea all these months, you know, and every night when I rack out, I think of you and I hoist up my nightshirt, and then I . . . ' et cetera, et cetera."

Arabella twirled her hand in a circular motion that was meant to convey what the duke had written, but in fact meant "see you later" in Italian gestural parlance.

"Still," said Belinda. "Even he does not say that everyone is talking about us. Something else must surely have happened by now to take people's minds off it."

But Arabella was far from reassured.

Encountering Renilde's mother that night in the passage,

she attempted to commiserate with the quiet little woman upon her loss.

"I am glad at least," said Arabella, "that her father's family will be able to give her a proper funeral."

Ginevra Rinaldo looked confused. "Her father's family?" she repeated. "What do you mean? My late husband was a foundling, not that it's any business of yours, and was raised in an orphanage. He never had the least idea who his people were!"

Chapter 20

THE VILLA BELVEDERE

On a wet, cold London night, a carriage, its lamps extinguished, and moving as silently as it is possible for such an equipage to move, pulled up to the Lustings gate. Its owner had attempted to trump the prevailing fashion in horseflesh by acquiring six beasts in not two, but three different colors, with lamentable results. Thus the carriage was drawn by just four horses—one each of two of the colors, and two of the third, creating a lopsided effect. In the dark, though, one didn't notice this so much.

Presently, a figure with a closed basket on its arm stepped from the carriage. It was clad in a hooded black domino, of a style in vogue some twenty years previously, creating an effect both malevolent and ridiculous. The basket, which was emitting a series of bloodcurdling shrieks, was simply terrifying.

"There, there, my darling," soothed Lady Ribbonhat. "Hush now, and Mama will give you something nice."

In her sinister raiment, she might have been taken for a priestess of the dark forces, placating an angry imp in a pot. But in any case, she was not a persuasive priestess. The yelling continued, unabated.

"In a few moments, Rosaline my precious, your own William will smell your perfume, and come to have his way with you, like always. Be patient, darling; we'll wait here whilst your scent carries on the wind."

For several years past, the two cats, Rosaline and Rooney (aka William of Orange), had shared an illicit love, one that transcended all of Lady Ribbonhat's attempts to thwart it. Rooney had managed to cover his lady love no fewer than seven times, and even when she was not in heat, he had been known to swim ditches and claw his way through hedges in order to be near her. Nor did she leave him unaffected this time. Rooney caught her scent from his promenade along the loggia railing, and quickly made his way to the front gate, which by that time had been closed and locked for several hours. But mere iron railings pose no barrier to a cat. He came right up to it . . . then paused. For he sensed, as cats will, that something was not quite right.

"There you are, William!" whispered Lady Ribbonhat from the other side of the gate. "Come on, then! Come to your own pussy!" She took Rosaline out of the basket and crouched down, manually lifting and lowering the cat's tail in order to entice Rooney to venture through the bars.

And then, all at once and from four different directions, half a hundred enthusiastic tomcats hurled themselves onto the person of Lady Ribbonhat. Some of them even leapt down from the wall above, quite submerging the unfortunate dowager. Caught as she was in that awkward crouching position, La Ribbonhat was entirely unable to bear the sudden, extra weight and fell over. For she was not a very large person, except for her head, and in this instance that was more of a hindrance than otherwise. Rosaline sprang clear and ran off down the road, with her gang of admirers in close pursuit, whilst poor Lady Ribbonhat, hopelessly entangled in the voluminous cape, rolled to the brink of a nearby drainage ditch, teetered there for a moment, and then fell in with a splash. All the while, her despicable coachman, instead of coming to her aid, sat upon the box, hugging himself and roaring with laughter.

Once again, Professor Bergamini had been a godsend. And whilst he was finalizing their new accommodations in Ravello, Arabella and her entourage had had the hotel practically to themselves. Terranova and the others had now left for good. Only Osvaldo remained behind, and he was beginning to grow on them. But Renilde's death and Arabella's near poisoning still seemed to hang in the air like the suffocating smoke from a funeral pyre. Arabella had questioned the doctor neighbor, who had corroborated Osvaldo's story as far as having been to the house to see Renilde on the night she died. He did not allude to any plague, however, and maintained that the girl had died of brain fever.

"It infuriates me," said Arabella, "the way everyone colludes with Terranova! He is getting away with murder, simply because people are in awe of his rank!"

"Perhaps they are afraid of him," said Belinda. "I mean, if he really did murder Renilde just because of what she told Mr. Kendrick, he might kill anyone who displeased him. Perhaps he has done this sort of thing before."

It was a great relief to get away from the place. And probably the landlords were no less sorry to see the last of their English guests, although they waited politely upon the steps, preparing to wave their handkerchiefs as the procession of carriages passed down the drive. Osvaldo, on the other hand, his rotund paunch pressed against the carriage as though he would topple it, was beside himself.

"You must-a be brave, my dear," he said, speaking to Belinda in an undertone, and attempting to take hold of her hand through the window. "We shall meet again, very soon. When two hearts beat as one, there is no keeping them . . . apart . . . *for long!*"

He had to shout this last bit, as the carriage was pulling away, and he was obliged to let go of the window.

"What was he saying to you just now?" Arabella asked.

"I could scarcely make him out," Belinda replied. "I think it was something about his having twice the normal complement of vital organs."

"O-ho! He was trying to impress you," said Charles, assuming an air of superior knowledge. "Italians are like that, you know. They brag to the ladies about having extra bits, in order to appear more attractive."

"Do you mean to say that the Pear-Head is typical?" asked Arabella.

"Yes, why not?"

"Is it typical for Italian men to creep into ladies' bedrooms and leave semi-literate notes beneath their pillows?"

"Did Osvaldo do that?" he asked. "How wonderfully romantic of him! What did it say?"

"I can't remember," said Arabella. "It was some time ago."

"No? Well, Belinda does, I'll wager! What did he say, Bunny?"

"Here," she said, plucking it perforce from her reticule and thrusting it at him. "Read it yourself, if you've a mind to. And then, please do me the favor of tossing it out of the window."

My dearlist Berlinda, I am overcame by love, and my need for you is keen. Yes, so very keen, that I am forced to walk doubled over sometimes. Please say you will be mine for I know you are the same. My bed she is beg enough for two but my cousin and my mother and my aunt are much in the way yes? But the three priests stay in the attic. So

*they are not in the way. Tonight
they all dine out with friends. I
shall stay here and wait for you so
we can quickly drench ourselves in
love's nectar with out fearing but
you will have to hurry so that I may
catch them up and so not miss my
supper. And if you are pignent, I
will marry you. May I know the size
of your dowry? Also your brestes.*

*Yours in need,
your dearlest Osvaldo*

"Well, isn't that sentimental! I should never have thought the fellow capable of such delicate feelings."

"Oh, do stop, Charles."

"But look, Belinda; are you not moved? He says he will marry you if you're 'pignent.' Imagine, living in wedded bliss with Osvaldo, in Holborn or someplace, and raising the results of his 'need'!"

"Speaking of that," said Arabella, "I have been meaning to talk to you for some time on the subject of your own progeny, Charles."

"Whatever for? I'm doing the best I can for them!"

"You are!"

"Yes. I'm staying out of their lives completely."

"That has been the saving of Eddie. She has a wonderful stepfather in Constable Dysart, and I shouldn't imagine she needs you in the least. But Neddy doesn't get on with his new father. He's going to the bad, I am afraid."

"Just like his sire!" said Charles proudly, turning to Kendrick for validation.

"It's nothing to boast about, Beaumont," said the rector severely. "I know it is none of my business, but when did you last see the boy?"

"I have only ever seen him one time in his life. At least, I presume it was he. About a year ago I noticed Polly, on the other side of Curzon Street, holding a peevish-looking brat by the hand. She was pointing at me and explaining something to him. So I straightened me shoulders, stuck out me chest, and stepped off the kerb . . . right into a human turd the size of a potato!"

"Life imitates art," murmured Belinda.

Kendrick grinned, in spite of himself.

"I screamed so loudly that people complained as far away as Spitalfields. Then I swore a blue streak and tried to dislodge the thing, but it had enveloped my shoe on both sides, to say nothing of the stirrup strap on my trouser! Gad, what a morning!"

"All right," said Arabella, "I suppose Neddy *is* better off without you, at that. But I do wish somebody would take an interest in him, though he is such a loathsome little stoat, that I cannot imagine who it would be."

"He wants a puppy," said Kendrick. "Perhaps I'll give him one from Dogma's next litter."

"He's had a puppy," said Arabella. "It ran out in the street, probably to get away from Neddy, and was crushed by a cart wheel. He does *not* require a dog unless we can find one that will teach him morals, manners, and a useful trade."

"Yes," said Charles, "and perhaps when this prodigy pup finishes with my boy, it can start teaching *you* a few things, as well."

This hostile remark having seemingly sprung from nowhere, Arabella assumed it would be simple to deal with.

"Don't presume to lecture me," she said, her voice flat, her manner calm. A cobra that has suddenly received the gift of

English speech might sound like this. The tone was light, the import heavy. Generally, such a voice was all that was necessary to effectively quash revolts amongst the lower orders. But not this time.

"I am afraid I must," said Charles. "Kendrick is besotted and Bunny isn't strong enough to stand up to you. Ever since we left England you've been growing steadily more high-handed. You fly into rages, insult people, use them, and take their good offices towards yourself for granted. We have all begun to find your company deuced difficult to bear, of late, and I wish to God that you would either come to your senses, or shut up!"

Bitter truth is hard on the digestion, and persons with upset stomachs are seldom inclined to be talkative. Thus, the ride to Ravello, begun on a note of such promising high spirits, ended in silence. But it was a silence with a certain meditative quality. Once her resentment cooled, Arabella considered the import of Charles's words. As for her companions, theirs was the watchful silence of witnesses to a just reprimand. They were all observing Arabella, though they did not appear to be doing so, in order to ascertain her response. Thus the party proceeded, mile after mile, with not a word spoken, whilst all four brains were as busy as could be.

When Bergamini had announced that they would be staying at a temporarily vacant house belonging to some friends of his, everyone expected to find a comfortable but slightly shabby residence, in keeping with the slightly impoverished circumstances common to academics and the circles in which they orbit. So, when the carriage pulled up before a glittering palace overlooking the sea, its occupants were speechless with amazement.

The Villa Belvedere had been constructed in high Renaissance style, and was surrounded by terraces and lawns.

Below the sea cliff, studded with bell towers and dark pine trees, lay a small beach with a dock, where brightly painted local boats bobbed at their moorings. It was beyond picturesque.

Bergamini himself met them at the door, and an exhaustive tour of the villa and grounds ensued. Charles and Mr. Kendrick soon peeled off from the group in order to try out the billiard room, though. Belinda hung happily on the arm of her aged admirer, listening, or not, according to her heart rate. But Arabella drank it all in: the fluted columns, the gilded furnishings piled with silken cushions, the painted ceilings, the grand staircases, the sea views and chandeliers. She had seen palaces aplenty in her lifetime, but possibly never one so beautifully situated, or whose situation represented such a welcome escape. The three survivors finished the tour in a romantic little sitting room overlooking the garden.

"So," said Bergamini. "Do you think this will suit you?"

"Amply," Arabella replied. "It is magnificent, Professor! You must permit me to recompense your friends for allowing us to stay here."

He was horrified. "Please! Speak no more of it! You and your party are honored guests! I do my level best, you know, but if the owners were at home, you would be treated like royalty!"

"But why? We have never met them!"

"Because you are friends of mine," he said simply, "and they are friends of mine, also. The owners and I are very close. As close as, as . . . *this!*" He seized Belinda around the waist and pulled her up against him, eliciting a little scream of joy.

"Will you be stopping here with us, Teofilo?" Belinda asked, glancing up at him through her eyelashes.

"I wish I could, *cara mia,* but I have commitments elsewhere. I shall visit often, though, while you are here." He kissed her hand and looked deeply into her eyes. "I go now, to dream of your sweet, scented limbs, and the darkly furred sections pertaining thereto."

After he had gone, Belinda held the curtain aside to watch his figure retreating down the garden path.

"Oh," she sighed. "Did you ever hear such a wonderful remark? Why is it that Englishmen never say such things?"

"Perhaps they are afraid," said Arabella, lighting a cigar.

As a rule, she only smoked outdoors, when she was fishing. But the tranquil beauty of her present surroundings had evoked a sensation not unlike her Piscean muse. And the window was open.

"Of what should they be afraid?"

"Of being considered ridiculous, or offensive, or both."

"And so they would be judged, I daresay," Belinda murmured as she let the curtain fall to. "Yet, when Italians speak thus, it only sounds beautiful. Why is that?"

"I don't know," sighed Arabella. "I suppose it's the accent."

"Bell, you know how you have always told me to follow my heart?"

"Have I? What on earth was I thinking?"

"I am serious. What would you say if I were to marry a foreigner, and live abroad?"

Arabella felt something akin to panic. "But the man hasn't a penny, Bunny!"

"He is rich in friends, and highly respected."

"How respectable will he be if he marries a courtesan? Dukes may do so, for wealth carries all. Poor scholars are another matter."

"That may be true in England, but this is Italy. I rather think Teofilo will be the more admired for it. An elderly man, with a lusty young wife: Such a match can only add to his prestige here."

"Are you certain of his intentions? Has he spoken of marriage?"

"No, but I am certain of his feelings towards me. He is a widower, and an honorable man."

"Yes, he seems to be that."

"My darling has not as yet had the opportunity of proposing. When next he drops in, I intend to provide one."

"Oh, Bunny dear, do consider! He is ancient, and cannot live long. What will you do when he dies?"

"Weep."

"No, I mean what will you live on?"

"Tears, I suppose. I am truly certain about this, Bell."

Arabella said nothing, for she plainly saw that any further expenditure of breath upon this subject would be useless, and she abhorred wasted effort.

THE FORBIDDEN ROOM

Arabella had not forgotten about the items that had mysteriously appeared in the basement of the Naples Museum, wrapped in canvas and burlap. Despite all that had happened, including Renilde's murder, the recovery of her letters, transference from one lodging to another, and Belinda's impending engagement, she had fully intended to go and see about them herself. But the museum had recently suffered an "infestation" originating from a poorly preserved mummy, and the building was closed to visitors during the general fumigation.

"Do not worry, *signorina,*" Bergamini said. "No one will be allowed access whilst the building is full of smoke. If the statues really are in the cellar, they will remain there until the museum reopens."

He promised to take her there on the very instant that that should happen, and he was as good as his word. But the mysterious things in the cellar, whatever they had been, were there no longer. The curator explained that he had investigated the day after the complaint was lodged, but had found the storeroom empty.

"We must assume that whoever installed the items there

has taken them out again," he said. "I am so, so sorry, Excellency!"

Arabella sagged with disappointment.

"Why did he call you 'Excellency'?" Belinda asked the professor.

"It's a kind of joke," Bergamini explained. "The museum sometimes takes on the qualities of a kingdom, you see. And in this kingdom, I am a prince of sorts. *Signorina*," he said, bowing to Arabella, "please allow me to express my deepest regrets for your disappointment."

But Arabella, apprehending his views on the foreign ownership of Italian artworks, suspected that his regrets were not quite so deep as all that. "Very well," she said. "You may proceed to express them."

Bergamini ignored this remark. "As long as we are here," he said, "perhaps you will permit me to show you some of my country's treasures."

And he led the way down the corridors, with Belinda on his arm. Arabella lagged behind them, partly to give the couple some privacy, but chiefly because disappointment had sapped her enthusiasm. All the same, she could not help noticing the splendid paintings that hung about her. One that particularly took her fancy depicted a herd of goats against a background of olive trees, cypresses, and the classical ruins of some once-great city. Yet the domes and spires of Naples could be clearly seen in the distance, and no other large settlement had ever existed so near it. But for that detail, and the fact that the Neapolitan structures were of Renaissance vintage, it might have been a scene straight from the days of ancient Rome. Arabella lingered before the picture, imagining herself tending the goats and thinking in Latin, while the professor strolled on ahead with Belinda and her little greyhound.

"What are these?" Belinda asked, pointing at a collection of small concrete slabs with Latin inscriptions.

"Ancient headstones," Bergamini replied, "from a burial ground for pets."

"Why," said Belinda, "we have such places, too! Do you mean to say that the Romans invented the idea?"

"Oh, by no means! All the ancient civilizations had them."

"What does this say?" She pointed with one hand to a stone etched with the head of a dog, whilst protectively caressing Cara's neck with the other.

The professor translated for her:

> *O, Helen!*
> *Thine eyes of soft brown,*
> *Will nevermore regard me*
> *From the edge of the supper table.*

Belinda tried to blink back her tears, but they were too numerous. The fat drops coursed down her cheeks and collected in a row beneath her jawbone, whereupon Bergamini pulled out his handkerchief and dabbed her face with it, in a manner most touching. Then he kissed her, and her knees gave way, so that she fell against him, quite.

Back at the goat painting, Arabella roused herself to the realization that she had completely lost track of the others. But she looked up just in time to see the professor's back disappear through a doorway at the end of the room, and she hurried after him, calling his name.

He turned round, smiling.

"Yes?" asked the gentleman pleasantly. "How may I help you?"

But it was not Bergamini! The old fellow who had looked just like the professor from behind looked very much like him from the front, also. He responded to the name she had called as if it were his own, and he and Arabella stared at one another for a few faltering heartbeats. Then the face of the impostor contracted with distress, and he scurried away.

She found the real Bergamini soon afterward, with her sister in his arms.

"You must have seen my brother," he said when she told him what had happened. "He works here, too, you know."

"Your brother?"

"Yes . . . I am a twin."

"Then why did he run away from me?"

"He is terribly shy. He runs away from everyone. Even his own brother."

But Arabella recalled that the man had not exhibited the slightest tendency toward shyness until he had actually seen who she was.

"What is his name?" she asked.

"Professor Bergamini, the same as myself."

"No, I meant his Christian name?"

"Why . . . Teof . . . I mean, Girolamo."

She deemed this significant, and removed her notebook from its bag.

"Oh, good!" said Belinda. "You have brought your CIN! May I borrow it?"

"Of course. Why? Have you found something interesting?"

"Yes, indeed! The loveliest portrait of Madame Murat, wearing the most *heavenly* court dress that ever was seen! I simply *must* copy it!"

Arabella handed over the notebook and the pencil from behind her ear. Then she stood next to Bergamini, admiring Belinda's youth, grace, and beauty. But when Arabella observed the rapt expression on the lower half of the professorial visage (for he still wore the overhanging hat and dark spectacles, even in here), she was filled with sadness.

He is going to take my Bunny away, she thought. The little sister whom I have loved and cherished for so many years. How shall I live without her?

Yet Arabella had always known such a day would come, and was determined to make the best of it. Only, she wished the child could have managed to fall in love with somebody younger and richer.

Belinda, meanwhile, was engrossed in what she was doing, and talking to herself the while: "A white silk undergown, 'broidered with gold," she muttered, sketching furiously. "With that stiff-ish frill of gold lace at the shoulders, and an overskirt of cadet-blue velvet . . ."

"I do not wish to hurry you, *cara mia,*" said Bergamini, incurring a glance from the little dog of that name, "but I have received special permission to show you a room not normally open to visitors. The few gentlemen so honored make steep donations, and ladies are never allowed in under any circumstances. An exception has been made for you, though, as my guests. We may tour the room from two to half past the hour."

"What is the time now?" she asked, her eyes tracking from painting to sketch.

"Ten minutes past two," said the professor.

"*Oh!* We had better go, then!" she cried. And so saying, she jumped up from the bench, quite forgetting Arabella's notebook in her haste.

"This room," explained the professor, unlocking a door obscurely placed next to a supply cupboard, "contains items from Pompeii and Herculaneum considered too shocking for people to see unprepared. But I think they will find acceptance with two such enlightened young ladies."

A stocky figure in a cassock approached them.

"Ah! Signorina Beaumont, Signorina Belinda, and Professor Bergamini! What a very pleasant coincidence! May I join your party?" It was Father Terranova!

At the sound of his voice, Arabella had stiffened as though she had been dipped in a tub of ice water. But the sight of her sister gone pale as milk restored her presence of mind.

"I doubt that you will wish to, Signor Terranova, when

you hear where we are going," she said. "Professor Bergamini was about to shew us a room full of objects, salacious and profane."

"Really? But that is splendid," said the priest. "I have always wanted to see the forbidden collection!"

"Then, why haven't you? It is generally available to men, I believe."

"Well, on public days . . . with the room attendants here . . . it is quite impossible, you understand."

"Do you mean that the public might deem your presence in such a room inappropriate?" she asked, thinking that he was probably more interested in avoiding the entrance fee.

"Just so. Ah! And you have brought your little dog! Your beautiful little dog!"

He repeated the demonstration of effusive delight with which he had greeted Cara's arrival at the hotel, patting her head and stroking her neck in a positive orgy of adoration. His monks gathered round him, as though they, too, were transported by the charms of the little greyhound.

Arabella wanted to say that it really *was* inappropriate for a priest to enter the forbidden room. She wondered what else he did that was inappropriate, aside from murdering Renilde, but there is a vast difference between speaking one's mind and butting in to judge others when one's opinions have not been asked for. Besides, if Terranova had murdered Renilde for knowing too much about the statue, he might try to murder Belinda and herself if he suspected that they knew he had. In all events, Arabella must keep him convinced of their ignorance.

"I have no objection to your joining us, Father," said Bergamini cordially, "provided that the ladies do not mind."

The ladies did mind. Whatever may be said on the public record, few persons actually enjoy the company of murderers. Besides, Belinda wanted to savor Bergamini's company in private, excepting for Arabella's presence, of course. Arabella, too, would have much preferred having had the place to themselves. But wisdom dictates that one should never be rude to a killer. So both sisters minded their manners, and appeared to acquiesce with good grace.

Now they were a party of seven, crowded into a set of two small rooms, where the eye, wherever it wandered, could not help but light upon a depiction of the procreative act, whether in the form of a painted vase, a sculpture, a piece of jewelry, or a household implement. Moreover, the chamber was so close, and the occupants so numerous, that one was constantly coming into physical contact with other people. It was terribly awkward, and Arabella tried to ignore it by concentrating on the artifacts.

One fresco that particularly delighted her depicted an old woman selling birdlike male genitalia to young women out of an open-work basket. The girls were having their way with these little winged marvels in the bushes, under trees, all over the landscape. It was a decidedly improper subject, by modern standards, but the style of the painting was so sweet—reminiscent of the watercolors of Arabella's friend, Tom Rowlandson—that one could scarcely take offense at it. Unless, of course, one were Father Terranova.

"What perverted minds," he muttered, standing so close to Arabella that the skin of her arm registered the heat of his body. "No wonder the Almighty saw fit to smite them with His terrible volcano: Pompeii and Ercolano were just like Sodom and Gomorrah!"

"Oh, surely," said Arabella, "Rome was much 'worse' than they were! And Naples was scarcely any better. Why did He spare those cities? The 'wicked' relics surrounding us are still here, aren't they? If it were God's aim to erase Pompeii and Ercolano from the face of the earth, why did He not destroy their artifacts, too?"

"I cannot presume to speak for the Lord," said Terranova sanctimoniously.

"But that is exactly what you did! You said in so many words that God destroyed Pompeii and Herculaneum because they were wicked. Mr. Terranova, why have you come here, may I ask?"

"I do not have to account for myself to you, *signorina*. But I will tell you that it is a priest's sacred duty to know about the things which he preaches against. Otherwise, he cannot expect to have credibility amongst his followers."

Arabella was losing her temper, and trying, above all, to keep the knowledge of Renilde's murder from shewing in her countenance.

"Sir," she said. "Would you do me the favor of continuing your tour of these premises from the other room?"

To her surprise and relief, he bowed and left her. Just in time, too. For she had spied the infamous bronze of Pan—not *her* bronze—enjoying himself with a nanny goat, and Arabella could not have endured listening to the pious hypocrisies of Terranova the murderer whilst contemplating such a wonderful piece.

The casual erotica of ancient times had been prevalent everywhere, apparently: in the temples, on the streets, in homes and public meeting places. Local businesses had used *tintinnabula*—bronze bells above the doors that jingled whenever a customer entered—whimsically cast in the shape of erect phalluses. Her favorite was a phallus fashioned like the body of an animal, with a phallus springing from between two hoofed legs and another phallus for a tail.

If only there had been replicas for sale in the museum gift shop! Public attitudes had once been so accepting, so joking and matter-of-fact. Where had it all gone wrong?

"A regrettable, dark side to an otherwise admirable culture," pronounced Terranova when they reconvened in the corridor. "I thank God for the Church! Without us, one shudders to think what would have become of mankind!"

And so saying, he left them.

"Father Terranova is an extremely pious man, is he not, Signorina Beaumont?" asked the professor, locking the door.

"He speaks as though he were," she replied. "But actions, rather than words, give the true measure of the man. The fellow is a cretin, and please spare me any jokes about his hailing from Palermo. Why does he feel it necessary to desecrate art? He neither appreciates nor understands it, and therefore would do best to avoid it."

"Yes," said Bergamini simply. "That is his job, I suppose."

Though Belinda actually realized on their way back to the villa that she had forgotten the CIN, she said nothing about it, for she was hungry, and having a row so late in the day would have resulted in a meal that was belated, indigestible, or even missed altogether. So Arabella did not in fact discover the loss until after dinner, when the resultant emotional storm was more convenient to all parties.

"Oh, Bunny!" she cried. "How could you have done that?"

Belinda had already retired for the night, and was tucked up with a naughty bedtime book. "It was entirely inadvertent, Bell. I have told you how sorry I am! But what can I possibly do about it now? What would you like me to do?"

"Tell your precious professor that you have mislaid my notebook in his beastly museum, and that I would greatly appreciate its return!"

"I already have. He has promised to look for it."

"Did you tell him that it contains things of a highly personal nature?"

"Yes. Oh, but . . . I hope you have not written anything

unflattering about *him*. Back when, you know, when I thought he was horrid . . ."

"I might have done. I don't remember. What I *do* recall is writing my suspicions concerning Renilde's sudden death, and the party to whom I ascribe the blame for it."

"Let us look at the bright side," said Belinda. "Chances are very good that it will be found and returned by someone who cannot read English. If we make up our minds that that is what will happen, it is bound to come true."

"No, it isn't, Bunny," said Arabella. "People cannot influence events merely by thinking about them, and I am probably going to agonize over that notebook until it is found. If only I had a lover! Someone to calm my nerves, and take my mind off things! Have you noticed how few playfellows we have had since coming to the most erotic nation on earth? And I thought Italians were supposed to be sex-mad!"

Belinda assumed an inebriated expression.

"You cannot be serious," said Arabella. "How many times have you and the professor actually engaged in fornication?"

"Just the once. But sex is not everything. You can see how attentive he is to me. It is only a matter of time, before . . . but if all you wish to do is fornicate with someone, that is easy enough. Men watch us and follow us wherever we go. A stranger came up behind me only yesterday, and blew on the back of my neck. He didn't say anything. He just . . . blew."

"Yes, yes; but one hesitates to do the deed with *complete* strangers."

"You had four of them in Pompeii."

"True. That was in the dark, though. It's not as satisfying in the dark."

"It was, for *me*."

"Yes, darling, but you are a freak of nature. We know this, now."

"Well . . . there is always Mr. Kendrick."

Arabella snorted. "Mr. K. would never consent to such a thing, unless I promised to marry him. Besides, it would not be fair. He would never be able to find satisfaction with any other woman, once he'd had me. This way, at least, the poor man has a sporting chance."

"Or maybe you are afraid," said Belinda. "Perhaps no other *man* would do for *you,* once you came to know Mr. Kendrick in the biblical sense."

"Oh, Bunny," said Arabella. "Now you are being absurd."

Chapter 22

DREADFUL FOOD AND
A WALTZ MACABRE

"I am quite famished!" exclaimed the rector, entering the little sitting room and flinging his hat onto the horns of a stuffed chamois. "What have we on the menu tonight?" He had just hiked up the trail from the bay, and was looking quite boyishly healthy, in a way that made Arabella suck in her breath, a little.

"*Cinghiale*—wild boar," she replied, setting down her book. "Shot in Viterbo by a friend of our hosts, and sent to us as a courtesy. Was that not kind of him?"

Charles groaned aloud. He had earlier attempted to accompany Kendrick down the hillside, but had found it necessary to turn back, and had been lying prostrate and silent upon the divan for the last quarter hour.

"You have not had this dish ever before, Charles," admonished Arabella. "How do you know you are not going to like it?"

"It is Italian," he replied, "and I am homesick. I didn't like to say so before, but there it is. I miss English food."

"Don't be silly. Italian cuisine is widely held to be the greatest of them all!"

"Well, I am *not* wide, myself," he replied, "and I don't know whether you've noticed, but I am growing less wide with every day that passes. A man can live on bread and cigars for only so long, you know."

"Let us dine out then, Bell," said Belinda, ever the peacemaker. "Perhaps the professor can suggest a good English restaurant."

"There is no such thing," said Arabella sourly.

"Why don't we compromise?" Kendrick suggested. "Let us find a place that serves fresh seafood!"

"No!" Charles cried. "What is this obsession everybody seems to have with 'fresh this' and 'sun-ripened that' . . . ? Such terms are not a part of our heritage! Where is your patriotism, Kendrick?"

"Not in my stomach," he replied acerbically.

"There must be somebody somewhere with an establishment that serves mushy peas and spotted dick," said Charles. "Ask Bergamini if he knows of such a place, would you, Bell? Good God! All these tomatoes! All this blasted macaroni!"

"The proper term is 'pasta.'"

"No, it isn't; it's *'basta!'* And *I* have had enough of it!"

Unfortunately for the others, the professor not only knew of a restaurant that served British food, but "bespoke it fair." So Arabella made him come along with them, as punishment.

It was rather a crush. They were five in a carriage designed for four persons, so Belinda was obliged to sit on the professor's lap, which was perfectly acceptable, because she was a courtesan and could behave as she liked.

"Professor," said Arabella, "have you had any news of my notebook?"

"Not yet, *signorina*. But I have alerted the staff, and we are all, as you say, keeping an eye out. I shall inform you the moment it is found."

Belinda looked contrite. "I am *so* sorry, Bell. I shall never forgive myself."

"Well. What is done is done. Besides, you did not forget it on purpose."

Charles yawned loudly. "I hope this place serves *genuine* English food," he said, "and not, you know, the sort of thing that is 'modified' for Italian tastes."

"I have never eaten there myself," Bergamini admitted, "but the atmosphere could not be more British. It is run by a Scotsman with a Welsh wife and a Manx cat, who offers English food, and occasionally Irish dancing."

He had both arms round Belinda's waist, and appeared to be quite reconciled to having a bad dinner.

"Dancing?" asked Arabella. "In a restaurant?"

"Yes. It is quite an idea, is it not? The place has rather a scandalous reputation. But as we are all persons of the world, we shall not mind that."

"No, indeed!" cried Belinda. "It sounds exciting!"

"As for me," said Charles, "I don't mind the atmosphere one way or the other. All I ask is a taste of home: a soup of foraged mutton, sprinkled with kitchen sweepings and perfectly roasted to the consistency of jack-boot leather, with mushy grace notes of fermented peas. A brace of tough and underdone pullets, with bloody, rubbery veins. An overripe grainy potato, redolent of peat bogs, a classic Yorkshire pudding, tasting of nothing at all, and a grand, bland medley of artisanal turnips and rutabagas, boiled with flour and lard!"

Kendrick caught his mood. "Might I suggest a faintly rancid flounder, boiled whole, and aromatic of unwashed stockings, in a soapy-flavored *velouté* with lard dollops?"

"I recommend a heap of partially composted cold, soft carrots," Belinda chimed in, "with an apple tart for afters, swimming in curdled cream—part dirty foam and part yellow liquid—tasting of the sweet/hot/spicy tang of flour, and liberally dusted with ashes of . . . ashes!"

"I have never cared for that sort of thing," Arabella explained to Bergamini. "Our Mrs. Moly, you know, cooks mostly French dishes."

The restaurant was lavishly decorated, as befitted a place

of unsavory reputation, with huge gilt mirrors and tapestried walls. The food was unsavory, too. In fact, it was terrible. Charles adored it, and most of the others were too hungry to be finicky, but Arabella pushed her plate away after only a few bites, and resolved to confine herself to drinking. This was not a habit with her, as she liked to have control of her mind at all times, but in the company of her family and their dear friend, she could scarcely have been safer without being at home.

"Bunny," she said, after a time, "the light is dim, and I am as drunk as a glass of bitters, so you must tell me if I am seeing aright."

"Very well," said Belinda. "To what do you refer?"

"That man over there. Is he the rarest out-and-outer to walk out of a dream, or is that just the wine talking?"

"Well, yes. He seems to be both good-looking and headed this way with the host. I don't believe he is English, though. Why do you ask?"

"Because," said Arabella. "I am shortly going to disappear, and I do not want you to worry, so I am going to tell you precisely where I shall be: safely tucked up in that gentleman's bed."

"Good evening, ladies and gents," said the host in the overly familiar manner that seemed to be the standard for expatriates abroad, "please allow me to present to you Herr Gustav Groer, of the Austrian Diplomatic."

The Beaumonts and Mr. Kendrick graciously bowed their heads in acknowledgement, and supplied their own names, except for Bergamini, who neither moved nor spoke. But the Austrian seemed to have eyes for Arabella only.

"*Fraulein*," said he, clicking his booted heels smartly together and taking her hand. "As you appear to have finished your supper, might I request the pleasure of a dance?"

And as he led her to the floor—for, naturally, she had not refused him—he asked whether she knew how to waltz.

Whenever a new fad or craze or popular entertainment cropped up, particularly if it carried a whiff of scandal, or was disapproved of by the guardians of civilized society, Arabella not only knew all about it, but also how to do it to perfection. She was thoroughly familiar with waltzes—one might almost say, *overly* familiar—yet she had never heard anything like the one Herr Groer requested of the orchestra leader. It was very dark. Very *Teutonic*. The drums beat a sinister military tattoo, and the music, though stirring, was neither easy nor merry, but grim to the point of actually making her flesh creep.

"What an interesting composition," she said as they circled the dance floor. "Is this one of your favorites?"

"It *is* my favorite," he replied. "What do you think of the tune?"

"I confess that it does not fetch me as it does you, but it is certainly . . . striking."

As she whirled round and round in the dimly lit restaurant, Arabella began to feel the drink rise to her head. And in a kind of delirium, she saw the men round her as skeletons, in veiled top hats and mourning clothes; the women as bloodless corpses in winding sheets. She dared not look at her partner's face, for he was apt to be the most frightening specter of all.

After a time, the other couples began to leave. Evidently, they had not cared for the music, either. And then, finally, it was over. The spinning room settled round her once again, and Arabella decided she was not going to be sick, after all.

"*Fraulein,*" said her partner urgently. "I must speak with you alone. I should like to take you to a place I know."

"I am not in the habit of accompanying strangers to undisclosed locations, Herr Groer."

"Forgive me. I do not wish to appear to be too much in haste, but time may be of the essence. I am an associate of Metternich's."

"Should I know who that is?"

"Oh, but surely you have heard of Klemens von Metternich! The great Austrian statesman? Of whom it is said, he has 'a finger in every pie'?"

The orchestra struck up the waltz macabre, again, for Herr Groer had requested they play it twice. He and Arabella danced once more. But there were no other couples this time, and her giddiness was beginning to dissipate.

"This statesman of yours sounds like some sort of cannibal pastry cook," she said.

"Yes, *fraulein*, he is. And I am, also. At the moment I feast my eyes only, but later I shall convince you to indulge my every appetite."

"Your English is very good, Herr Groer," said Arabella, "but it is a trifle stiff. You should simply have said, 'I want to eat you.' Or better yet, whispered it."

"Really? I should whisper so?"

"Oh, yes. Of all the sentences it is possible to construct with an English vocabulary, ladies are best pleased by that one."

"Thank you," he said. "I shall remember this."

"You know, I think the *signorina* may not be entirely safe with that fellow," said the professor quietly.

Kendrick was all attention in an instant, but Charles merely glanced up whilst pouring himself another glass of port. "I shouldn't worry about her, if I were you, Bergamini. When it comes to men, Arabella knows which end is up!"

"I did not mean unsafe in that sense," he replied, keeping his voice low. "Austrian government officials are not very popular here. Someone may try to shoot him, you see, and if the *signorina* is standing too close when it happens . . ."

"Good God!" cried Kendrick, bolting from his chair.

"There is no immediate cause for alarm, Reverend. She is in no danger here. But you would be well advised to keep an eye on her."

*   *   *

"And may I ask," Herr Groer was saying, "why you are so opposed to people discussing politics?"

"For me," said Arabella, "it is like being privy to an argument between two very dull persons, whom I neither know well nor care for. And it is an argument which never ends, you see. It is a bore."

"Let me assure you, *fraulein*," said Groer earnestly. "Boring you is the last thing I should wish to do." And he began to entertain her with snippets from Metternich's personal life.

". . . The father, so brilliant, you see, and yet the son can barely write his own name! Of course, *I* can barely write his name, either. The poor little fellow has a whale-ish appellation: Franz Karl Viktor Ernst Lothar Clemens Joseph Anton Adam von Metternich! Imagine, having to write so much, and spell it all correctly, too, when one is just learning to form one's letters!"

She laughed, and instantly perceived that he had wanted her to, that he had carefully constructed the entire conversation to achieve exactly this effect.

"His tutors are vexed at little Franz Karl Viktor's never completing an exercise, but he is probably too exhausted once he's written out his name! Besides, there is no more room left on the page!"

The Austrian laughed loudly, as if inviting her to join in, but this time Arabella only smiled. He was trying too hard now. Groer seemed to sense he was losing ground, and abruptly changed the subject. She had the impression that he had read a manual, and was mentally following:

Rule Number 9: If your partner suddenly seems less engaged, forget the chitchat, and get to the point before her interest flags completely.

"Thank you," she said. "It has been most amusing, but I must go now."

"Must you, really? I know of a place nearby," he coaxed. "Very discreet, where we can have coffee and Lauria."

"Who is she?"

"*Lieber Gott!* Have you never had Lauria?"

"I have never even *met* her," Arabella confessed, "nor am I especially interested in making her acquaintance. You see, my one requirement, for threesomes, is that the other two participants be male."

"Lauria is a drink, *fraulein!* A divine Austrian concoction of pears, pear brandy and cream. We can sip and talk, and talk and sip, yes?"

But she was no longer interested in him. "Another time, perhaps—I believe I shall make an early night of it, after all."

"You are seeking . . . a bronze statue, I believe."

He said it, just like that, out of nowhere. She turned, sharply.

"Do you know where it is?"

"We are hoping you will lead us to it."

"'We'?"

He smiled. "Oh," he said. "It's a political matter. You would not be interested. But we are willing to pay handsomely."

"For what?"

"For information leading to the capture of the persons who stole it."

"I shall bear that in mind."

Arabella suddenly had the uncomfortable feeling that everyone was watching them, with unfriendly eyes.

"Yes. We are an army of occupation, you see," he explained. "I am afraid the Austrians are rather unpopular here. This restaurant is less hostile than Italian establishments, but I think we should feel more relaxed in a German concern. I am now renewing my offer to escort you elsewhere."

"Very well," said Arabella. "But I must tell the others that I am leaving."

Mr. Kendrick opposed her plan, of course, and Belinda, too, shewed signs of alarm. The professor offered no opinion. Charles had laid his head upon the table long ago, and was snoring fitfully.

"There is no need to worry," said Herr Groer. "A military escort awaits us, just outside the door."

"It sounds as if you're arresting her," said Belinda.

"Only for private purposes, I promise you," said the Austrian, with a wolfish smile. And as he already had his arm around Arabella, who seemed quite agreeable to the idea, Belinda raised no further objection. Mr. Kendrick's reaction was rather complicated, but he kept his thoughts to himself; starting an argument with a military escort requires a degree of foolhardiness of which even he was not capable.

And so, within a phalanx of soldiers, courtesan and diplomat proceeded to the German hostelry, a place even more lavishly decorated than the restaurant they had just left, for there is no style in the civilized world so ostentatious as German Rococo. A portly hostess, all dimples and double chins, smiled a particular sort of smile as they entered.

"Is this a brothel?" Arabella asked.

"In a way," he replied, opening the door to a sumptuous bedroom. "Is that a problem?"

"No. Only, it has been so long since last I was in one."

A small table had been set up in the corner, with a bottle and two glasses. Groer pulled out a chair for her, but Arabella drifted to the window, where the street outside was strangely empty of civilians. She could see nothing but military men—Austrians, presumably—striding up and down by the light of the sputtering torches, gold helmets gleaming wickedly in the firelight. Arabella was genuinely *not* in the habit of accompanying strangers to undisclosed locations, and the folly of her decision to do so in this case was beginning to dawn on her.

"Pray, sit down," said Groer. "Come try the Lauria."

Instead, she inspected her surroundings with something like suspicion, peeking behind a screen at the bed, even parting the bed curtains to see what the coverlet and pillows were made of.

"Why so nervous, sweetheart? You are like a cat that wakes up and finds itself in a strange place."

"I do not trust you," said Arabella.

"No?" he asked, smiling. "Then why did you agree to come here?"

"Because you excite me," she replied, coming over to the table and hesitating beside it.

"Yes. And you excite me, also. Please; sit. "

Arabella had no sooner done so, however, than the chair made a curious *click-clack* noise, and a pair of steel bolts met across her diaphragm, trapping her arms against her sides and locking her in.

Herr Groer now had her at a physical disadvantage, but Arabella would not oblige him by panicking. No one, she felt, had the right to control her mind.

"What an interesting device," she observed.

"You have not seen one before?"

"None so fine as this. The bolts are usually wooden."

"*Fraulein,* you must tell me everything you know about this theft."

"Why should I? The bronze is my property."

"I do not dispute that," said Herr Groer. "You are welcome to it. I am interested only in those persons involved in its disappearance."

"If I knew who they were, I should have recovered my property by now. Anyway, what do you want with them?"

"I have told you before. It is a political matter, and one which I am not prepared to discuss with persons of minimal involvement."

"You have a strangely intense way of questioning persons of minimal involvement," said Arabella. "Why have I been clapped up in this thing?"

"Oh, this is not connected," he said, placing a hand on the chair and brushing, as if by chance, the side of her breast. "I merely wished to give you an idea of what we will be doing once I get the *official* part of the evening out of the way."

"Really?" she asked. "This forceful detention has nothing to do with the questions you are asking me?"

"Well; not necessarily."

Arabella considered this. She was familiar with manacle chairs and their playful uses with partners she trusted, but they were not such fun in the hands of strangers. With a stranger, one never knew what might happen. I am frightened, she admitted to herself. And yet, a secret tide of lust was beginning to lap at her loins.

"Very well, then," she said. "It would seem I have little choice. Some time ago, I bought a slightly larger-than-life-sized statue of Pan with two *schwanzes* from a dealer in such things who came recommended by a friend. It was stolen from this person by someone who wanted it badly enough to kill him for it. After that, I hear it was taken to Naples by ox-cart. That is all the information which I possess at the moment. If you know any more, I wish you would share it with me."

The diplomat stretched his hands before him, palms outward, fingers interlaced, and cracked his knuckles.

"Fraulein Beaumont," said he, "it would seem that you have failed to appreciate our respective positions. *You* are the one in the manacle chair. *I* am the one eliciting information."

From a small tray of fruit and pretzels, he picked up a sharp little cheese knife and touched its point to a spot beneath her jawbone, where the pulse was.

"You see, you are quite helpless at this moment. Your arms are bound to your sides. You cannot get up and your friends do not know where you are. You could scream for help, I suppose, but no one would come, and even if they did, they should arrive too late to save you." He trailed the knife point lightly down her throat. "It would be inadvisable to hide the identity of . . . thieves, or . . . masterminds, or . . . other involved persons from me," he said, punctuating his remarks with light pricks against her skin. "Because we will ultimately discover their identities, with or without your assistance. And if I find that you knew who they were and omitted to inform me, well . . ."

He spoke in a light conversational tone that was more horrible than actual physical violence. It seemed to imply a vast world of refined tortures, with which he was quite at home, and to which he might decide to introduce her in the very near future.

Earlier in the evening, Arabella had decided that Herr Groer, though handsome, was dull, and had almost dismissed him. Now, however, she found herself overwhelmingly attracted, and it was an effort to keep from throwing herself at him. In this respect, at least, the manacle chair was her ally.

"But, as a matter of fact," Herr Groer was saying, "I do not think you know anything that we do not know already," and he set the knife down again. "Besides," he added with a wink, whilst filling their glasses, "it would hardly be politic to disfigure the mistress of the future king of England. He might resent it. If you do hear anything, though, we would appreciate your informing us." He twisted a knob on the back of her chair, and the bolts were withdrawn.

So, thought Arabella, rubbing her arms where the bolts had pressed against them, the Austrians also believed this "mistress to the regent" nonsense! Well, *she* certainly was not going to be the one to enlighten them, especially if it meant the difference between a disfigured face and the one that she now had.

"Do you really suppose that I am likely to volunteer such information, after you threatened me with bodily harm?" she asked, pretending to take a sip from her glass. The liquor smelt delicious, but she needed to keep her wits about her.

"My dear Miss Beaumont! I have not threatened you! No; I have simply *warned* you, as a friend. And yes, I do think you will help us. Because we are watching you. Not all the time, but we are keeping, as you say, an eye out."

Arabella started. Bergamini had used that very phrase in the carriage on their way to the restaurant. Was Groer trying to show her that his spies were everywhere? Or was it merely a coincidence?

"The moment we suspect that you are up to something," he said, "you will be brought to me, in a place much less comfortable than this one."

"Rubbish! If you harass me, I shall go to the police!"

He grinned. "Here, *fraulein,* we *are* the police. You know, you really should pay more attention to politics."

Arabella nibbled a pretzel, considering: There was no reason she *shouldn't* tell the Austrians what she was doing; they might lead her to her statue, and Terranova fully deserved to die. On the other hand, exposing him might lead to other arrests. Bergamini's, for example. And Pietro's. Arabella had sufficient sense to avoid anything that smacked of political machinations. Involvement with causes of which she was ignorant tended to work to her disadvantage and make her look stupid.

She decided to appear to be cooperating with Herr Groer, and to add the threatening parts of this interview to her mental list of Things Not to Tell Bunny.

"If I find out any more," she said, "I shall have no objection to telling you."

"Good," he replied, handing her his card. "I promise to make it worth your while." He rose from his chair and parted the heavy bed curtains. "And now that the business portion of our evening has concluded, if you will permit me, I should like to show you something interesting."

Arabella had cause to be glad that she always carried prophylactics in a variety of sizes, for the Austrian did indeed have something interesting to shew her. And although the dimensions of the condom required was initially in some doubt, Herr Groer was the sort of man who perfectly fitted his name.

Chapter 23

TOO DEAR A PRICE

"Do you see?" asked Belinda, offering up her handi-work for inspection. "The heels are supposed to be the scrotal sacs, and the toes are the . . ."

"Yes, I see," Arabella replied. "But do you really think this an appropriate gift for an elderly academic?"

Belinda blinked. "Certainly," she said, a slight frown creasing the top of her nose. "Older people can suffer terribly from cold feet, can't they? These are *bed* socks, you know; they aren't meant to be worn with shoes. And it is winter just now, and these will be ever so warm. I am going to work in some black frizzled feathers around the heels, to look like hair. Why wouldn't they be appropriate?"

"Oh, no reason. I expect I was just being querulous."

The four of them had gathered together, in a manner of speaking, in the grand salon, a room roughly the size of the Colosseum.

"Not as large as *that*," said Arabella.

"Well," Charles amended, "as large as a life-sized model, then."

He and Kendrick were seated at a desk on the salon's far side, entering Charles's winnings in an account book. Beaumont was taking every pot he played for now, and Kendrick had persuaded him to start keeping track of it.

"I'm afraid there's no escape, old sport," said Kendrick. "With riches come responsibility."

"Here's to the three *R*s," Charles replied, lifting his glass. "Riches, responsibility, and retchedness!"

Oddly enough, he really was rather wretched. The thrill of wondering whether he would win a particular hand had completely gone, now that he knew he was bound to. So there was that, in addition to having, after all these years, to think about maths again.

On the other side of the room, Arabella was perusing a folio of Italian architectural engravings that she'd found in the library.

"Say what you will," said she, "nobody builds like the Italians. Who, of course, got all *their* architectural ideas from the ancient Romans."

"Who got all *their* architectural ideas from the ancient Greeks," appended Belinda.

"I suppose so. But the Romans improved on the Greeks' ideas."

This really was becoming too much for Charles: maths *and* ancient history, simultaneously, in a glamorous palace in idyllic surroundings. It was like a nightmare, of the annoying variety, rather than the terrifying kind, and Charles was determined to prevent its further development.

"Rather like the Americans' adaptation of British constitutional precepts," he said, hazarding the notion that Arabella would leave at the first mention of government structure and things political.

He was right. (Of course he was! Because it was a kind of bet.) His sister fled to the library where, on returning her book to its shelf, she discovered another she liked even better: *I Modi*, in English, complete with salacious engravings. Bearing away her prize to the terrace room, Arabella dropped onto the nearest sopha, and began to search for pictures of the positions she had lately enjoyed with the Austrian.

A pair of gunshots ripped through the night, followed almost immediately by a terrible scream. And this was not the scream of some hapless rabbit, caught in the talons of an owl, nor even of a wild cat, whose cry is the most horrible of all; it was the shriek that issues from the throat of a man who knows it is the last sound he will ever make.

Arabella started, violently, and the book dropped to the floor. And then Kendrick was running into the room, demanding to know whether she was all right. Belinda was close on his heels, accompanied by the frantically barking Cara. And somewhat later, Charles appeared, as well.

"It seemed to come from right outside this room!" Belinda exclaimed.

Arabella picked up the book and placed it on the table before trying to open the double French doors that led onto the terrace. But that proved difficult, owing to something that leant against them from the other side. After a while, she stopped pushing and stood there, observing this something, which lay at her feet without moving.

"Oh," she said tonelessly. "I see what it is. A man has been shot."

Arabella swayed, clutching at the drapery, and Kendrick caught her before she slid from there to the floor. Belinda was not so fortunate. She fainted clean away, and collapsed on the carpet like a crumpled handkerchief.

Charles used his weight to push the body clear of the door, and he and Kendrick went outside. Given our knowledge of Charles's character, this might seem an unlikely scenario, and I cannot account for it. But people will frequently behave in unexpected ways during a crisis.

As Arabella helped her sister onto a sopha, the servants began to stumble sleepily into the room, the household having retired some hours previously. Arabella followed them onto the terrace, where the watchmen had just arrived. The group of persons thus assembled gave the appearance of a weird masquerade, with some of the revelers clothed as huntsmen in cloaks and boots, some appareled for a casual evening at home, and everyone else dressed as madhouse inmates.

"*Signorina,*" said one of the watchmen. "These man, we see heem on-a the *terrazzo,* watching you through the window! Giovanni shouted at heem, and he ran to the door. To force his way inside, we think. And so we shoot, just to fritten heem. But . . . one of us missed."

The other watchman squatted down and turned the corpse over on its back. By the light from the windows, Arabella could now see its face, and she recognized the smuggler she had interviewed, the man who had told her nothing.

"Look, Kendrick," said Charles. "It's that chap who cursed me at the cock fight!"

But Kendrick was inside, ministering to Belinda, so Charles went in, too, though it is doubtful whether he was any help. Arabella sent the servants back to bed, and remained on the terrace alone as the watchmen bore away the corpse.

"*Signorina!*"

The hoarse young voice that issued from the shadows made her jump. She had not expected to see Pietro again, now that she had come to Naples, and she felt ashamed when she remembered their last meeting.

"You should not be here!" she hissed. "A man has just been shot! It might have been you!"

"No," he said, stepping into the light. "I am too clever for that! But I have news, *signorina!* I have found your statue!"

"You *have?*" She pulled him over to a small table at the back of the terrace, tucked beneath the overhanging first floor. "What are you doing here?" she asked.

"I came with you, beneath your carriage! Holding tight the whole way!"

"But . . . why? Do you even know anyone in Naples? Where are you staying?"

"There are many *orfani* like me, *signorina*. We live everywhere. I find the ones who live here, and I tell them what I am looking for. Then I give them some money. It is quite simple! The statues are in a hut near the harbor."

"A hut? Whose hut?"

"No one lives there. It is old. A ruin."

"Do you mean that my bronze has been taken out of one ruin, only to be placed in another? That does not make sense."

"Yes. It makes too much sense! They say the hut is cursed, that it is haunted. No one goes near it, so it is used by smugglers to hide their goods until they can be shipped out of the country."

"Oh, dear! And are you certain that the statue is still there? Have you seen it yourself? What am I saying? You do not even know what it looks like, do you?"

"No, *signorina*. But there are many statues in this place. Maybe yours, too, is there. Maybe not. The hut, she is guarded most of the time, but at midnight, the guards go home and new ones take their place. There is . . . an empty time, half an hour, when we can go in and get out again and no one will see us."

"You have done well, Pietro! You will get a bonus for this!"

"Thank you, *signorina*! Tomorrow at ten minutes to midnight, you will find me where your drive meets the main road. The hut, she is very close to here, but I will draw for you a map, in case I am prevented from coming."

Arabella took Pietro into the library and handed him a map of Ravello. "Here," she said. "We can mark this one—I have another."

Since her initial visit to Ercolano, when she had become so dangerously lost, Arabella had taken care to procure a map from each place she visited: Resina, Herculaneum, Pompeii, the Naples Museum, and Naples itself. These would make nice souvenirs, once she was home. More importantly, though, they could be used as tedious conversation pieces, to aid her in ridding the house of superfluous guests.

"We walked along this road," Arabella could say, "and down this little street here—more of an alley, really—to this square, where Bunny made us stop because she had a stone in her shoe."

And Belinda, well skilled in the drill, might say, "Not at all! I had an eyelash in my eye! The street where I got the stone in my shoe was up here . . ."

They should be able to carry on in this fashion for as long as was necessary, and if the unwanted visitor still refused to take the hint, they could bring out the next map, and repeat the process. Once in a great while, a gentleman might be so intent upon his objective that he would sit through all the map discussions in order to achieve it. Such persistence was deserving of more drastic discouragement. But occurrences of this type would be rare: Lustings invitees tended to be astute, discreet, and beautifully mannered.

After orienting Pietro, who could not read, to the location of familiar landmarks, Arabella gave him her pencil to mark the route for her. Then she begged him to be careful, and saw him safely vanish into the darkness beyond the outbuildings.

Belinda had been moved back into the grand salon, where Arabella found her quietly drinking a glass of water.

"Are you quite all right, my love?"

"Yes, I think so. But I feel so silly!"

"Not at all," said Kendrick. "You could hardly have been expecting to encounter a dead body in the course of knitting stockings— Oh, I say," he broke off, staring at the knitting she had left on a chair. "What unusual-looking socks! Is this some new 'fad' or other?"

"Yes," said Belinda. "They're Italian."

"Bless my soul! I've never seen anything like them! And yet . . . they look somewhat familiar . . ."

"Getting back to the matter at hand," said Arabella, "I must say I find this whole affair extremely unfortunate."

"That is a strange choice of words," Charles observed from the corner. He had collapsed sideways onto a chair in order to study the book Arabella had been reading in the terrace room. " 'Unfortunate' is not the first term that springs to *my* mind!"

"I meant it was unfortunate that the poor man should have been mistaken for a burglar whilst bringing me a message."

"But you cannot know that," said Charles. "The fellow might have been set up by his own people, and been executed intentionally. As a matter of fact, though, I think he was coming here to kill *me*."

"Oh, don't be silly!"

"It isn't silly," said Kendrick. "We've seen the fellow before. His cock was killed by the bird your brother backed, and he cursed Charles. But he might just as easily have come here to kill *you*."

"Why ever should he want to do that?" asked Arabella, putting a hand to her neck.

Charles shrugged. "Kendrick didn't say the fellow *did* come here to kill you; only that he *could* have."

"What I mean is," said the rector, "it is possible that you have got hold of the tail end of something . . . well, much bigger than a cat, for example."

"Mr. Kendrick is right, Bell," said Belinda. "There might be some sort of criminal conspiracy behind this art theft. Your life could very well be in danger!"

"Not to mention *mine*," Charles said.

*   *   *

Arabella had intended to tell Belinda of her plans, but the next day was so full of soldiers—the primary police in this part of the world—asking questions and requiring reenactments and measuring out distances between this point and that one, that half-past eleven at night found her lying awake in the darkness, waiting to meet Pietro and having told no one. Perhaps it was better this way. Family could be such a hindrance!

And she began to think about the smuggler's wife. What would the poor woman do, now that her husband was dead? Had he left her well-off, or gambled everything away on his cock? She could not remember having seen any youngsters about the place, but peasants were always having children, weren't they? There were bound to be some offspring, somewhere. Perhaps they had all been inserted headfirst down rat holes on the day she'd visited, or yoked to a plow in some distant field. If so, how would they live now, without their father? Their father, who had died trying to get a message to her. Perhaps.

As she checked the bedside clock for the hundredth time, Arabella realized that Belinda, finding her gone, was likely to rouse the household and organize a search party. A note was in order. But first she drew out her burgling kit from beneath the bed, and donned her warmest pelisse, and Belinda entered as she was on the point of scribbling an explanation. Arabella quickly told her everything, and naturally, Belinda was opposed to the plan.

"Of the inconveniences and discomforts which we have all been obliged to suffer up to this point, I shall not speak," said Belinda. "We knew there would be difficulties, and each of us has agreed, for various reasons, to undergo them so that you might try to find your statue. But it is not worth people getting killed."

"I agree!" said Arabella, lacing up her boots. "But the

smuggler wasn't murdered, Bunny. His death was an accident. As for the art dealer, if I ever discover his killer, I shall see that justice is done!"

"I do not believe that you care so much about the deaths."

"Of course I care! The smuggler's demise will be forever on my conscience! Not the dealer's, though. That was not my fault."

"And Renilde's? According to you, Terranova would not have murdered her, had she not spoken to Mr. Kendrick about her cousin's part in this affair."

Arabella paused. "Yes. Poor Renilde! I shall always regret that I did not intervene there, when I had the chance. I owe her my life!"

"I very much doubt that. She hated you. She stole your letters. And you didn't like her, either. But it does look as if she died for revealing what she shouldn't have about that stupid statue. And regardless of our personal feelings for the girl, she did not deserve to die for this! I think you should just forget about it."

"But I am going to find the statue tonight, Bunny! I can *feel* it! And then we shall sail for England, the moment you are packed!"

"I cannot let you do this alone, Bell," said Belinda firmly. "It is too dangerous! Why not take Charles and Mr. Kendrick along?"

"Because Charles would be of no use at all, and the rector tends to act rashly when he thinks he is protecting me. You must not mention this to either of them."

"What, even if you never come back?"

Arabella gazed into her sister's eyes.

"I'll come back, Bunny."

"But you cannot *know* that."

"I shan't be in any danger. No one will be there. I am just going to ascertain that the statue has not left the country, and then tomorrow I shall go find the smugglers, and make them a handsome offer for it. Shopping is one of the safest activities there is! People are almost never killed whilst trying to buy something. Here. If it will make you feel any better, I shall leave this with you." She handed the map to Belinda. "That is where I shall be. It is not far from here, and you can look at it if you find yourself in need of reassurance."

"But *you* will need it, won't you?"

"I'll have Pietro."

"You must be insane," Belinda whispered, "to do a thing like this. You would risk your life, and the boy's, merely to recover your investment!"

"Oh, darling! This isn't about the money," said Arabella. "I am in thrall to the beauty and the history of the piece itself. Only think, dear, my statue was fashioned by a master artist, nearly two thousand years ago! A genius, who, if he had signed his work, would be as famous today as Leonardo or Michelangelo! Imagine owning the *David,* Bunny!

"My statue was sculpted before the concept of 'sin' had even been thought of! It represents a single thread in the history of human consciousness, unbroken from the dawn of man until now. It is the part of our hearts that has always embraced life, despite repressive doctrines and excessive moral philosophies, and which will always do so—the part of human nature which loves the beautiful and laughs at the ridiculous, especially if it is lewd."

"How much do you think it is worth, then?" Belinda asked.

"A lot more than I have paid for it! And I do not intend to simply let it go until I have exhausted all the possibilities!"

Pietro was waiting for her in the road, just as he said he would be.

DYING FOR ONE'S ART PIECE

Nature was against them. It had recently rained, and now a cold wind was driving in from the sea, beating against everything that stood upright with a steady barrage of penetrating cold. There was a new moon, and thick clouds clotted the sky, so they did not even have starlight by which to see. But Pietro had learned the lay of this new city very quickly, and he led his patroness unerringly down a crooked backstreet (more of an alley, really) to an open space just above the shore, containing a derelict hut. In a city so crowded that its buildings seemed almost to be growing into and out of one another like forest mushrooms, this hut stood by itself, with nothing close around it but weeds. Arabella instinctively drew back when she saw it.

"Pietro . . . do you know why this place has been abandoned?"

"It is *maledetto*," he said simply. "You know, cursed. Quickly, *signorina!* The guards have gone. We have an only little bit of time!"

There was nothing to do but forge ahead. Arabella walked up to the hut and began fishing about in her burgling kit for the glass cutter. "The things I do for art," she sighed, carefully shearing and lifting out the windowpane. "Now, for heaven's sake, be careful, Pietro."

The boy scrambled through the opening, and then, feeling his way to the door, admitted Arabella, who handed him two candles from her bag. She struck a spark from her steel and flint, and lit the first one. Pietro touched their wicks together to light the second. The candles failed to produce much light, but it was better than nothing.

In the first of the hut's three rooms, a long table and a profusion of chairs filled most of the space. Evidently, this place was used for meetings. The second chamber contained a number of large, sheeted objects, and Arabella felt her heart quicken with excitement, but it was only furniture. Handsome furniture, to be sure, and likely to bring its thieves a good price, but the collection was not ancient, and not even slightly erotic. The third and largest room contained more covered forms. Some of these had the appearance of upright, human shapes. Arabella lifted a sheet at random, hardly daring to hope. Underneath it was a statue.

"Quickly!" she whispered. "We must pull all these sheets off!"

Exquisite white shapes blossomed one by one amidst the gloom, and soon the chamber was full of sculpted beauty. She trailed a loving hand along a life-sized marble Cleopatra, reclining on a couch and holding a snake to her breast.

"Oh," breathed Arabella. "Did you ever see anything so exquisite?"

"I live in Ercolano," Pietro replied with a shrug. "I always see these things."

It did not take long to examine the collection. Apart from Cleopatra, and a group of tigers bringing down a black buck, they all seemed to be portrait statues of contemporary people. The men wore frock coats, and there were a number of busts of Napoleon, in his cocked hat. The provenance of the female figures was more difficult to ascertain, given the current fad for ancient Greco-Roman fashions. In any event, Arabella's doubly priapic god was not among these. In fact, there were no bronzes at all; everything was marble, or imitation marble, and all were quite new.

"*Signorina,*" said Pietro. "If your statue is not here, we should go, before . . ."

The crunch of approaching footsteps sounded on the shale outside, and he quickly blew out his candle. Arabella blew hers out, too. "Hide!" she said, keeping her voice low, and ducking behind Cleopatra.

"No," he whispered back. "You stay here. I will go and see."

A moment later, he crawled to her side.

"There are two guards. And more men on the road, headed this way. I am afraid we are . . . how you say? Trapped like the rats."

Now they could hear wooden clogs and boots stomping on the floors, and rough voices, coughing and speaking together. But the men stayed in the first room, where the table was. Perhaps they would just have their meeting and leave. Then, Arabella thought, she could help Pietro to escape out the paneless window, and he could goad the guards into chasing him, so that she might escape through the door. But the meeting could take hours, by which time Belinda would have decided to tell Charles and Kendrick where she was. They would come looking for her then, and walk right into this den of thieves. But perhaps it would only be a short meeting.

And then, Arabella, who was crouching in an uncomfortable position, attempted to ease a cramp in her leg, and inadvertently kicked over the housebreaking kit. The sound of the striking steel, the pocketknife and the crowbar, knocking against one another as they hit the floor, was as loud as it was alarming. And almost before the reverberations had died away, the room was filled with men and lanterns.

*   *   *

"*Carte blanche,*" said Charles, displaying his hand. Kendrick had run out of money, so they were now playing piquet for buttons.

"It's no use, Beaumont. You always win. I am rather tired of this, if you want the truth."

"I don't," said Charles from around his cigar. "Give me cozy lies over uncomfortable truths any day."

Belinda entered the room, looking aggrieved.

"Charles," she said. "I promised not to tell you this, but I believe I must." She regarded her brother for a moment. Then she turned to Kendrick. "No, it makes more sense to tell *you*, doesn't it?"

"What has happened?" asked the rector, mild concern contracting his brow. "Has your sister's headache worsened?"

"She doesn't have a headache," said Belinda. "She has gone out to find her statue with that orphan child from Ercolano!"

While Pietro and Arabella lay trussed like chickens on the floor in the meeting room, their captors—Arabella counted twelve of them—began to argue, with animated gestures.

"What are they saying?" she murmured.

The boy turned a stricken face toward her and shook his head. "Please, *signorina,* do not ask me to tell you this."

"I must! I am certain it is not the sort of thing that you should have to bear alone, Pietro. Besides, if I know what is coming, I shall at least be able to compose myself and face it bravely. If not, the strain of uncertainty, and the shock of not finding out what they're going to do until they actually do it, will be much worse."

"They are going to kill us, *signorina,*" he said gently. "And they are trying to decide how."

"I see. What are the choices?"

"To throw us into the sea . . . or to slit our throats first, and *then* throw us into the sea . . . or to tear down part of a wall in this place, seal us up inside, and leave us to die. That way, the bald man is saying, we will die slowly in the dark, and no one will ever discover what became of us. . . . Now the one with the big mustache is saying that we should be killed at once. That is what they are discussing."

"Oh."

"Yes. But they will wait for 'Il Duce' to make the final decision."

"For whom?"

"'Il Duce.' The leader. They cannot act without his orders."

Suddenly, one of the men pushed back his chair and stood up, shouting and pointing at the captives. Pietro and Arabella were roughly hauled to their feet, although, with their ankles tied, they could not walk.

"What is this?" asked Arabella, her voice trembling. "Have they decided not to wait for the leader after all, then?"

"No," said Pietro. "We are being moved to another room, because we talk too much."

They were carried out like sacks of corn, over the shoulders of two of the men, and taken to the room with the sheeted furniture. At least, in here, there would be some chairs.

The two men remained in the room, and one of them addressed a remark to Arabella in Italian.

"I don't speak your language, I'm afraid."

"Ha!" he said in English. "What kind of spy can you be if you cannot even understand what we talk about?"

"I am not a spy. I am an Englishwoman."

"Yes. You have said that before. But you are lying."

The other guard took a bread roll from his pocket and began to chew it, appraising her body with his eyes.

"Stop and think a moment," said Arabella. "Would a

woman spy come out on such a bitter night, with a child? Just to hide in a filthy fisherman's hut? Even if I did speak Italian, I could not have heard what was being said from two rooms away. It does not make sense. No; a female spy would stay in a warm hotel, making love to her enemy, and getting him to tell her his secrets in bed."

She had begun to shift her body sinuously whilst she spoke, as though to ease the strain of her bonds. But the action was deliberately provocative, and the jaws of the bread-eating guard went slack.

"You should have come to me at once!" cried Kendrick, hastily pulling on his coat as he ran down the stairs.

"Bell told me not to!" cried Belinda. She was right on his heels, and Charles not far behind, when they emerged into the great medieval hall. Kendrick made unhesitatingly for the crossed heirloom swords, and liberated one of them from its place on the wall.

"Take up the other, Beaumont!"

"Me? Handle that cheese toaster? I should be no earthly use in a fracas! But I shall act as your second, should you require one."

Fortunately, at that point, another member of the household ran up behind them and snatched down the remaining sword.

"I'll come with you, sir!" he declared.

And thus the four of them, two fighters and two onlookers, proceeded in a body toward the fishing hut, where the long-awaited leader had just arrived.

The five members of Lustings's domestic staff were gathered in the kitchen, earnestly regarding something that they could not, in fact, see: There was an offer on the table.

" 'Tis a powerful lot of money," said Doyle softly.

"I know it is," replied Mrs. Janks.

"And it's not like we couldn't all of us use a few extra thickers," said Fielding. "We don't exactly *need* it, I guess; the mistress pays us more than enough, but think what we could do with that kind of push!"

"Oh, but we could not theenk of spending any of eet until we 'ave told Mees Beaumont!" said Mrs. Moly. "Aftair all, eet ees her cat, even if she does not want eet."

"How d'you figure that?" asked Fielding.

"Well, it come in through 'er window," said Mrs. Janks, "which she had to pay to replace, and we caught him in 'er house. By rights, it's 'er cat *and* 'er money, though I'm fairly certain she'll let us split the take and welcome. We'll still need to tell the missus what we're up to; it's only right."

"*Noooooooooo!*" wailed Tilda. "You can't sell Rooney! He b'longs to us!"

"Buck up, Tilda," said Doyle. " 'Twill all work out for the best. You'll see."

But the scullery maid refused to be consoled, and ran from the room, weeping, as heavy footsteps trudged down the service stairs outside, and a fist pounded on the kitchen door. The four women looked at each other.

"I'll go," said Mrs. Janks.

"No! I'll do it!" said Mrs. Molyneux, picking up the sack.

"Have ye got it firmly tied round the top?"

"*Oui.* I have used ze very hard knots."

Il Duce cut a sinister figure in his long black cape, and he wore his cocked hat sideways, like Napoleon's. Once he had shaken off the rain, the assemblage observed a lengthy, formalized, fraternal greeting ritual, fraught, no doubt, with mystic symbolism and secret signs. But Arabella could only see such portions of it as were visible through the doorway, and to tell the truth, she wasn't really very interested. Terror had taken up most of her mind. Suddenly, her ears caught the clang of steel against steel, and she observed the men in the next room, running to the window. A sword fight was evidently taking place outside. It was Kendrick, of course, come to save her. And he could have no idea how vastly outnumbered he was. Arabella moaned with despair. This was all her fault. Her obsession with art was going to get them all killed: Mr. Kendrick, Pietro, and herself.

A voice reached her from the other side of the window: "We're here, Bell! Can you hear me? We've come to save you!"

Dear God! That was Belinda! Well, of course it was! Her plucky sister would not have permitted Mr. Kendrick to come alone. So Bunny would die, too. And all because she, Arabella, had stubbornly refused to back down. She had to have what she had to have, whatever the cost.

Inside the other room, one of the men asked his leader a question.

"No," he replied in English. "They are fighting honorably, two against two. Let them alone, for the time being."

Two against two? Was *Belinda* fighting? As incongruous as that seemed, it was easier to picture than Charles with a sword. Please, thought Arabella, to the universe at large; if we come out of this alive, I shall give up this mad quest. And if, by some miracle I should still manage to find the statue, I shall return it to Italy.

At this point, the guards came over to untie their legs, and Arabella and Pietro were frog-marched into the presence of the leader. All she could see of him was his broad back, though, for he was peering through the window at the battle raging just outside.

"Look out, Kendrick!" someone shouted, and she recognized the voice of Charles. Charles was here, too? Arabella moaned again, as she realized that the entire adult generation of her family was about to be massacred, for a bronze statue that she had never seen, never touched, never been able to own.

The two Beaumont siblings who were still at liberty stood

outside in the darkness, watching the fighting from a safe distance.

"It may seem to you that I have behaved in a somewhat equivocal manner," Charles drawled, his voice bored, his manner self-satisfied. "But believe me, Bunny; they also serve, who only stand and wait for it to be over."

"Charles," said Belinda, "the esteem in which I currently hold you is the lowest I have ever had for any mortal born of woman! You, sir, are a cad and a coward, and you will greatly oblige me by shutting up!"

Belinda had never spoken like this to anyone in her life, and Charles was shocked to the core. It was a shame that the other sister could not be there to hear it, too. Well, she couldn't, of course, but she did hear the scream that rent the air a moment later. And Arabella screamed, too. For she knew, without knowing how she knew, that the Reverend Kendrick had fallen in combat.

Il Duce whirled round from the window. And in the guttering light from the candles, Arabella recognized the pointed beard and steel pince-nez of Father Terranova.

Chapter 25

BURNING BRIDGES, COME HOME TO ROOST

Mrs. Molyneux opened the door to Lady Ribbonhat's groom, the same one who had originally introduced Rooney to the aviatory. He, too, bore a sack, also tied at the top with difficult knots. The parties eyed one another suspiciously for a moment. Then each tried to grab the sack of the other before letting go of his own. For a time, they played an awkward little game of reach-out, pull-back upon the doorstep, until they finally managed to synchronize the snatch/release operation to occur at precisely the same instant. The groom then carried the prize to his employer, waiting impatiently in the carriage, Mrs. Molyneux having already withdrawn into the house and loudly slammed the door.

"Good-bye, Rooney!" wailed Tilda, waving a dish clout from the scullery window.

"Hell-o, dash!" breathed Fielding as she and the others stood regarding the offer that was at last tangibly present upon the kitchen table.

"Ah!" cried Terranova in mock delight. "Good evening, signorina! I was hoping we should meet again, so that I might return your property to you. Although I am afraid you will not be able to enjoy it for very long." He took her CIN from his satchel, and placed it upon the table. "One of the monks picked it up after our tour of the forbidden room. Apparently you left it on the bench outside. Do you know what I think? I think that you wanted me to find it."

"I didn't," she replied, her voice so choked with fear that it was almost a whisper. "My sister left it there."

He shrugged. The details were of little import.

"How clever you were, to deduce that I had murdered my cousin in order to keep her quiet! Too clever, in fact. And too inquisitive, also." He shook his head regretfully. "I am afraid that you and this little boy will have to be permanently silenced."

"The child knows nothing," she said quickly. "He's merely my interpreter."

"But he arranged for you to be taken to the man who drove the cart which transported the artworks, did he not? I wonder how he knew that?"

"I am not afraid to die, *signorina*," said Pietro. "Street children cannot expect to live long, in any case."

"So," said Terranova. "Now that we have the boy's permission—not really necessary, but nice, all the same—we shall dispose of you both in some . . . suitable manner." He smiled, and picked up a bottle from the conference table. "Despite your poor opinion of me, Signorina Beaumont, I am a civilized soul, underneath. So we shall first enjoy a bottle of this wonderful wine, and then I shall stand ready to hear your confession and baptize you to the true church before I kill you."

As absurd as this was—a priest offering absolution to his intended murder victim—an even more preposterous event had just taken place outside.

When John Kendrick had received a slash wound to his fighting hand and dropped his sword, Belinda had screamed. At least, everyone assumed it was she. Later, Belinda would claim that the scream had actually come from Charles, but who would believe *that?* At any rate, following the scream, whose ever it was, Kendrick's comrade-in-arms had simply called a halt to the proceedings. Then he had stepped into the light, and the guards had bowed to him! What was more, the man from whom Kendrick had received his wound apologized, and bound up the cut with his own handkerchief!

Whilst Arabella's would-be rescuers stood speechless with wonder, the stranger nodded toward the hut and smiled. "Shall we go in?" he asked. "I believe they are about to start serving the wine."

Chapter 26

OUT OF THE BAG

Lady Ribbonhat put her head out of the carriage window. "Did you get him?" she asked, extending both arms out, as well. "Give him to me!" After fumbling ineffectually at the knots for a few moments, she contented herself with cradling the sack upon her lap. "Welcome back, husband," she murmured. "I am sorry that I cannot let you out until we get home, but I shall endeavor to make you as comfortable as possible in the meantime."

A passing familiarity with Lady Ribbonhat may engender doubt that anyone so ruthless toward her adversaries, and so imperious in general, could ever be soft-spoken and considerate to a mere cat. She certainly had never addressed her husband thus when he was alive and housed in a human body, but then, he had always treated her with equal contempt.

The explanation is a simple one: Lady Ribbonhat, like many another cruel woman before her, had the habit of talking baby talk to her pets. The orange tomcat was not a pet, strictly speaking, or she would never have had him put through her enemy's window in the first place. But now that he possessed the metaphorical key to Lustings, he was her own precious widdow peegie weegie, washn't him?

"You said something, my lady?" enquired the coachman.

"Not to *you*, I didn't!" she replied sharply. "Mind your driving!" and to the sack she said, very quietly, "Do not worry, beloved; the soothsayer has told me everything. You may lead me to those letters as soon as ever you like." William of Orange made no response. "Have you gone to sleep, my precious? That's right, then. We'll soon be home."

And soon they were, where Lady Ribbonhat assigned her butler the task of opening the bag. Two of the footmen tried to help him, but at length they simply gave up and severed the rope with a knife. Whereupon their mistress snatched the sack from them and peered inside, cooing reassuringly to the orange fur she glimpsed through the opening.

"Come out, William," she said, reaching in. "Come to your own . . ." But at that point in her monologue, Lady Ribbonhat withdrew a dead hare, wrapped in the ratty orange boa that Arabella had given to Doyle two or three seasons previously.

"The hour grows late, and we are all too overwrought for explanations tonight," said Terranova, pouring wine for the entire assemblage. (They were twenty-one, including the guards, but fortunately, the priest had several more bottles tucked away.) "So I propose to call upon you tomorrow, *signorina,* or today, I suppose, at the villa at around midday. You may then give me luncheon, and I shall give you answers."

It was most bizarre. Like a dream one dreams upon the drawing room sopha after a dinner of suspect seafood. Charles and Belinda, and Mr. Kendrick with his bandaged hand, were standing about clinking glasses and chatting with men who, not ten minutes ago, had been discussing methods of killing her. To be fair, some of these men seemed to be just as confused as Arabella was.

"But . . . she is a spy!" insisted the one who had first called her that. "How can we let her go?"

"This is no spy, Hilario," Terranova replied. "Signorina Beaumont is a famous English courtesan! An inamorata of the regent's! A fine impression that would make, eh? To murder his mistress and then request his help?"

A lover of the regent's? Why did everyone think that?

"If the woman is not a spy," said one of the guards, "then why has she broken into this house?"

"There is somewhere a mistake, I think," said Terranova. "The *signorina* could never have done such a thing! . . . Did you?"

Arabella cleared her throat. She was now fairly certain that she would not be killed, as she and Pietro had been freed from their bonds and her friend and family were now present, but it was all so odd that she could not be absolutely certain about anything.

"Well, in a way," she said cautiously, "I suppose I did. But you broke into my hotel room, against my expressed wishes. Now that I have entered your . . . hovel, equally uninvited, I suppose we are quits."

Terranova grew stern. "No," he said. "We are not. I have behaved in an unorthodox manner for the sake of a noble cause. You have acted solely for yourself and broken the law, in pursuit of a thing that was not yours to begin with. At least, I assume that is what you were doing."

She nodded mutely.

"Well, the statue is not here," he said, his fists on his hips. "You are hounding up the wrong tree bark, *signorina!* Now, go home! We shall talk this over tomorrow, yes?"

A part of her hated herself for slinking off like a whipped cur, but the part of her that was practically hysterical with relief didn't care a bean for the other part. Arabella decided that she had never in her life been so glad to see a person for whom she cared so little.

"*Signorina,*" said Terranova as she turned to go. "Don't forget your notebook."

*   *   *

"Do you reckon we're rich, Mrs. J.?" asked Tilda, standing a little back from the crowd round the table, with Rooney in her arms.

"Yes, Tilda; I reckon so," the housekeeper replied. "Mrs. Molyneux, would you do the honors?"

"*Avec plaisir,* madame," said the cook, slicing through the twine and reaching inside the bag. "Een goes zee hand, and out comes . . ."

> . . . *writing paper, miss! Lady Ribbonhat's own personal stationery, with her family crest and curly initials. I've saved it for you in the drar of your boodwar desk, thinking as how it might come in useful-like. But we are dissappoinnted not to have the money, seeing as how you told us it was all right to keep it.*
>
> *We're all of us very glad to hear that your gettin' your post again, now that the thief what took them is dead. She must not've been right in the head. My husband-that-was had a sister just the same.*

Chapter 27

REVELATIONS

The next day was fine, but everyone got up late and was out of sorts with each other. Belinda brightened considerably when the professor dropped in, and immediately whisked him off for a tête-à-tête in the small sitting room.

Arabella was vexed with Belinda anyway, for having revealed her whereabouts to Mr. Kendrick on the previous evening, explicit instructions to the contrary. And now Kendrick seemed to be angry with *her,* probably because he had hurt his hand, which was hardly her fault. It was all a great muddle, and she would have taken it out on Charles, but her brother had wisely decided to spend the day in bed.

Mr. Kendrick lay pale and silent upon the sopha in the terrace room. His hand was expertly bandaged now, and his arm was in a sling, which secretly pleased him. He was not pleased overall, though, and to Arabella's occasional chatty remarks, he turned his head away and remained obstinately mute.

Eventually, Belinda returned to them in the highest of spirits, her hand in Bergamini's.

"Let us all go out on the terrace," she said. "You and I should take our easels, Bell; we have yet to paint a single picture here, and you know we shall be sorry not to have any when we get home. Mr. Kendrick, you can lie upon the chaise outside and rest your hand, while Bergamini reads to us from this volume of love poems."

She handed a book to the professor, and Arabella regarded her sibling with thoughtful speculation. Usually, it was her own prerogative, as the elder sister, to stage-manage the men. But the usual hierarchy was let to go hang in favor of a betrothed woman, regardless of birth order.

"These are hardly what I would call love poems, *cara mia*," said Bergamini, flipping through the book that Belinda had given him.

"What would you call them, then?"

"I do not know the English term, if there is one. But these are like print versions of the items which I showed you in the Naples Museum."

"Perhaps I had better stay where I am, then," said Kendrick, who, in any case, had no wish to be a part of any company that included Arabella.

"I beg that you will oblige me by coming with us, Kendrick," said the professor. "I shall not read from Belinda's book, but I have an announcement to make before Father Terranova arrives, and I should like you all to be present for it."

"What about Charles?" Belinda asked. "Shall I send someone to fetch him?"

"No, do not bother. His presence is of no consequence."

Arabella bristled at this! Charles may have been a cad and a bounder, but he was a part of the family and Bergamini wasn't; not yet. He had no right to disrespect her brother. And although she was too exhausted to castigate him then and there, she nevertheless made Bergamini hold back his pronouncement until Charles could be summoned, yawning and grumbling, from his room.

The cliff terrace at the Villa Belvedere commanded the most beautiful vista on the Amalfi Coast. This sounds like an outrageous claim, but it is quite true, nevertheless. Overlooking the sea and surmounted by trellises covered in bougainvillea, the terrazzo was both sunny and shaded, exposed and secluded, and the graceful balustrade of pale pink stone lent it a summery air, even in winter. It certainly didn't *feel* like winter today; the sun was warm upon their faces as the women set up their easels, and Bergamini, who kept to the shade, poured out a cool drink for the gallant Rector of Effing.

Even though Arabella's heart had sunk at the thought of the professor's announcement, she could not help but be a little cheered by this wonderful weather, and by the beauty that surrounded her on all sides. She had always known that Belinda would marry one day. It was what she (Belinda, that is) had always wanted. But Arabella had never imagined that her sister might be living abroad. They would seldom see one another, and that was going to be hard to bear.

The professor cleared his throat. "First of all, I would like to congratulate everybody for managing to stay alive long enough to see this beautiful day," he said. "Signorina Beaumont, I shudder when I think of the fate which might have been yours last night, had the director of our local Carbonari chapter been anyone other than Father Terranova. I am reminded of your refusal to eat the Figpeckers. Being already acquainted with them in a social sense, you could not bear to take part in their destruction. Apparently, the good father has the same sort of feelings about you."

Arabella shot him a veiled glance from beneath her sun hat, whilst continuing to paint the light on the sea.

"And Reverend Kendrick. I have been given to understand that you fought off those two sentries with courage and finesse."

"Well, I wasn't alone, you know," said the rector modestly. "I had a confederate."

"Had you? And who was that?"

"Well . . . I don't know who he was, as a matter of fact. I

had never seen him before. But he was a most valiant fighter! He met us in the hall, and took the second sword off the wall there. I assume he is attached to the villa in some way."

"Is he?" asked the professor in some surprise. "I am an intimate of this household, as you know, but I have not heard that any of its members were engaged in combat last night. Can you describe this fellow?"

"I am afraid I did not get a very good look at him. It was dark, and everything was happening so quickly. He was about my height and build. Thirty-two, or thereabouts. Dark-ish. Handsome."

"Would you say that he looked like me?"

Kendrick was nonplussed by the question.

"No," he said at last. "No; not really."

"Would you say that he looked like me, *now?*"

And so saying, Bergamini removed his tinted spectacles, the gray wig and bald pate, and rubbed off his wrinkles with a pocket handkerchief!

The effect was electric. Belinda gave a cry and jumped from the stool, nearly knocking her easel into the sea. Kendrick spilt his drink all down the front of himself, and Arabella sat frozen with astonishment. Charles only yawned and scratched the back of his head. But then again, as Bergamini had astutely observed, his presence there was of no consequence.

"I hope that you will all forgive me for perpetrating this deception," said the speaker, "but I assure you, it was quite necessary. When the real professor Bergamini received a letter from John Soane, informing him of your impending arrival, he quite properly brought the matter to me, and we decided that I should take his place. You see, Bergamini rarely leaves his office at the museum. He was on his way to one of the storerooms on the day that you hailed him, *signorina,* and he realized at once who you were; so he quite understandably ran away, lest you should discover the truth."

"But why have you done this?" asked Arabella.

"Because you were coming to look for the bronze Pan. We doubted you would find it, but a highly visible foreign courtesan nosing about and asking questions might have easily upset the rather delicate arrangements we were making with regard to its disposal."

"We! To whom do you refer, *signor?*"

"The Carbonari. An organization to which I have the great honor to belong."

"But I do not understand this," said Belinda plaintively. "Why would Professor Bergamini bring John Soane's letter to *you?*"

"Because I am the patron of his museum."

"You are? Who are you?"

"Prince Benedetto Gandini-Palmadessola, at your service!" he replied with a bow. "This villa is my principal residence, though I also possess several others. Ah," he said, looking past her toward the door. "And here is Father Terranova, punctual to the minute! We shall now take this opportunity to enlighten you all more fully."

The prelate greeted the members of the astonished company with jovial cordiality, whilst servants appeared with chairs and a dining table, and proceeded to set up for luncheon. The prince slipped away for a time, to finish removing the adhesive remnants of Bergamini, and emerged looking quite wonderful. Throughout the ensuing meal, the English guests sat in a kind of daze, though in Charles's case, this was due entirely to insufficient sleep and a surfeit of alcohol, and the servants went quietly in and out, replenishing water goblets, bringing little dishes of lemons and lemon forks for the seafood, and seeing to everything with crisp efficiency. Arabella thought, fleetingly, of the servants who had attended to her needs so assiduously on that torrid afternoon in Pompeii; one or two of these fellows looked (and acted) rather familiar.

"First of all," said Father Terranova, who really *was* a priest, "I should like to acquit myself of the charge leveled against me in your notebook, *signorina*. I have *not* murdered my cousin."

In such a place, on such a day, the subject seemed absurdly inappropriate, and Arabella had to struggle to recollect her sense of outrage from the corner of her mind, where she had swept it.

"It does not signify what you call it," she said. "I suppose you are going to tell us it was a mercy killing, or that Renilde died a martyr for your noble political cause. But taking a life is always wrong, except to save that of another."

"Ah!" said Terranova. "But that exception *applied,* you see."

"Inventing justifications after the fact will not fool me," said Arabella severely. "The way in which you casually announced that Renilde was with God, and then forbade further discussion about it, as though we had been arguing over a disproportionate wine bill, displayed a coldness of heart and a wanton disrespect for decency, *signor!* Renilde was a human being! And you did not even give her a funeral!"

"That is true, *signorina*. There was no funeral for Renilde, because Renilde is not dead. I will give you her address, if you like, though I cannot be held responsible for the reception she is likely to give you, if you visit her. You are not exactly a favorite of hers.

"We have always known the girl was unbalanced, you see," he explained, addressing himself to Mr. Kendrick, "and we believed, in our ignorance—my mother, my aunt, and myself—that if we kept her close to us and spared her any agitation she would be all right. But we were wrong, and the consequence of our mistake was nearly fatal. Renilde became obsessed with you, Reverend Kendrick. Something of the sort had happened before, and we hoped that one day, a kind man would marry her and take her off to a calm and quiet life in the countryside. We were trying to avoid the alternative, you see. None of us had the heart to send poor Renilde to the madhouse."

"Stealing letters is antisocial, certainly," said Arabella, recovering from the surprise of learning that Renilde was alive, "but hardly abnormal to the point of institutionalization."

"Unfortunately, there was more to it than that, *signorina*. I am thankful that you were unable to read that curse scroll which she nailed over your bed."

"Was that Renilde's doing?"

"Without doubt. She has the singular habit of dotting her *I*'s with little squares."

"What did it say?"

"Please, *signorina;* I have been doing my best to forget what I read there. I shall not, under any circumstances, utter the words aloud. They were meant to frighten you away, of course. Renilde saw you as the main obstacle between herself and Reverend Kendrick. But even so, they were terrible. The awful ravings of an unhinged mind."

"Nevertheless," said Arabella, "it was only a threat, however vile. That is not the same as attempted murder."

"Of course not. But in the last few years, Renilde's condition has steadily worsened. On the night the soldiers came to the hotel, she tried to kill you, *signorina,* and but for my interference, she might have succeeded. You see," he said, "she poisoned your cocoa whilst the rest of us spoke to the soldiers in the hall. I had observed Renilde's agitation earlier in the evening, so I stepped aside as everyone else was filing out of the coffee room, and watched from the shadows while she emptied the contents of a vial into your distinctive wine goblet. When the soldiers left, the cat knocked over one of the ordinary glasses, and the landlady, fearing for her costly piece, unknowingly transferred the poisoned contents to a glass identical to all the others. So, carefully noting its position, I rotated the platter to confound Renilde. When I saw that she had completely lost track of its whereabouts, I took it for myself."

"*You* took it?" Arabella exclaimed.

"*Si*. I did not drink it, of course. And after Renilde went up to bed, we called in the doctor from next door and arranged to have her sent away. It's not a bad place," he said sadly, "as such places go. The attendants there are very kind, and poor Renilde responds to kindness. Well, usually, she does.

"We had to keep this matter secret. I hold a vital position in the Carbonari—which I will explain to you in a moment, if you can bear to sit through a political discussion—and I cannot afford to have the slightest whiff of scandal crop up now. I must avoid attracting attention at all costs. Our family council decided it would be better if we said that Renilde had died.

"You were right, in your diary, about one thing," he added. "She *did* tell Mr. Kendrick the truth that evening: I *am* the person responsible for the theft of the Pan statue."

Arabella swallowed. "Do you know where it is?" she asked.

"Roughly."

A pair of pelicans sailed past the cliffs, their shadows sweeping the terrace like a memory of prehistoric mosquitoes.

"On the day we went to Pompeii," said the prince, "you witnessed an argument between myself and the good father here. Later on, you probably suspected me of conspiring to keep you away from the hotel for the afternoon."

"The thought had occurred to me."

"But that was not the subject of our discussion. I had only just learned that Terranova was behind the Herculaneum theft. And I was threatening him with legal action. I did not then know that he was Carbonari, and because I was not yet a member, he could not reveal himself to me. By the way," he added with a smile, "one should never threaten a suspicious person with legal action. It cannot possibly help you to let the suspect know what you are going to do, and if he is desperate enough, it might just convince him that he needs to kill you."

Arabella made a mental note to make an actual note of this in her CIN.

"Father Terranova recognized my ring," the prince continued. "He knew that I was not Bergamini. And as soon as it was practical, he approached me with an appeal to join his organization, which I wholeheartedly accepted."

Kendrick had been listening to all this with his good elbow upon the table, his chin in his hand. Now he spoke up for the first time. "Why then," he said, turning to Terranova in some surprise, "*you* must be responsible for the art dealer's murder!"

The priest lifted his hands in protest. "I am opposed to violence on principle," he said, "but our brotherhood is sworn to promote the goals of the organization. And if one wishes to make a frittata, one must break a few eggs. It is true; the appropriation of the Herculaneum artworks was originally one of our projects, and the Englishman, this so-called art dealer, a Carbonari gone to the bad, seized the chance to cut in ahead of schedule and take the items for his personal profit. It was a bold plan, and would probably have succeeded, had his workmen not maintained their loyalty to the cause.

"I never said 'kill him' in so many words. But I gave the order to prevent the unlawful removal of those art pieces by whatever means necessary. If it helps you any, Reverend, the death was an accident. The men told me they only meant to render him unconscious, and deliver him up to a tribunal."

"But why should the Carbonari be interested in art smuggling?" asked Arabella. "Aren't you supposed to be fighting for Italian independence?"

"For *unification, signorina*. Just at present, Italy is a disconnected mess of kingdoms and principalities ruled over by foreigners. We cannot hope to win our purpose without the support of powerful nations like your own, particularly those with strong commercial connections in the Mediterranean. So . . . we give Britain priceless artworks for her museums, and Britain in turn lends her support to our cause."

"I was frankly quite worried," said the prince, "when you left us, in the company of that inquisitive Austrian diplomat. Without realizing it, you might have implicated either Father Terranova or myself, which would have implicated others, which would have set the cause back months or even years and resulted in the executions of brave and dedicated people whom you have never met."

"That is why we went to all this trouble," said the priest. "We wanted you to give up and go home, before you could do any damage, but you are rather stubborn. In fact, you are intractable!"

"But how did you know that I was coming to the hut?" asked Arabella.

"Because we told Pietro to take you there," said the prince.

"Pietro!"

". . . works for us; yes. He is one of our most valuable spies."

"You mean, he is *not* really an orphan of the ruins?"

"Oh, he lives in the ruins, right enough. But that is his choice. And he is much more effective working from there. Street children are virtually invisible."

"Then not one person I have met here was the person he appeared to be!"

"Under such oppressive conditions as we have," said Terranova, "it is simpler to assume disguises."

"Hmm . . ." said Arabella. "I should have thought that would complicate things. So, the blessing you dispensed from my balcony . . . that was not actually what you were doing, was it? You were not serious about baptizing the Herculaneans?"

Terranova appeared offended by the suggestion. *"Signorina!* How could you think that would be a good idea? Nobody would benefit! The Christian souls would of course be bound to welcome their persecutors to paradise, but I doubt whether they should be happy about it. And the pagan souls would be miserable in a Christian heaven. I am hurt that you could think I would willingly cause such misery!"

Belinda excused herself to answer a call of nature, and in her absence, the prince explained about those supposed "gifts" from Charles.

"The dog's collar," he explained quietly, "is split on the inside surface, an ideal place for hiding messages. After your . . . er, dance, with the Austrian, the watch they posted on your party was increased, and it was not safe for me to meet with Father Terranova directly. So I used the dog. She has had courier training, you see, and I knew that Father Terranova would recognize her. On the day that Charles presented the dog to your sister, the collar contained a warning to the good father to flee at the first opportunity."

"So, that's why you were so attentive to the dog?" Arabella asked.

Terranova smiled, bowing his head in assent. "And then again, at the museum," he said. "My meeting you there was no accident. His Highness had placed specific information for me inside the collar."

"That is why I invented the story of the statues in the storeroom," the prince admitted. "I had to get you, your sister, and her dog to the museum, so that Father Terranova might retrieve the document which I had hidden in the collar. We were watched, even there."

"Yes," said the priest. "And when Signorina Belinda left your notebook upon the bench, we thought that she was working for the enemy! One of my monks retrieved it just in time; two other men were making towards it in all haste. You wrote some things in there, *signorina,* whose import you could not possibly guess, but which would have been all too clear to certain other parties, and deadly for us."

Arabella looked at her hands. "I . . . I am so sorry . . ." she began.

"Tut-tut!" said Terranova. "Do not mention it! Everything has worked out for the best, as you see!"

"But I beg you will not mention this—about the dog—to your sister," said the prince. "She believes her to be a gift from her brother, and she is very happy in that belief."

Charles opened his mouth, as if to speak, but he shut it again. The truth was, he had found the act of giving most agreeable. The gratitude bestowed upon him with such heart-felt delight by his sisters had made him feel extraordinarily good, and he resolved to do a *genuine* good deed for some-body someday, to see whether the sensation were repro-ducible.

"Where is my statue now?" asked Arabella as Belinda re-turned to the table.

"I wish you would not keep referring to it as 'your' statue, *signorina,*" said the prince. "Each time an excavated treasure leaves the country, Italy is impoverished. The Pan statue, and the other items taken from Pompeii and Herculaneum, are part of our heritage. They are what makes us who we are."

"And where is it now, did you say?"

"I didn't, but it is in London, at the moment."

"*What?*"

"Yes; despite what I have just told you, in this case, we have judiciously sacrificed a few pieces of our heritage in order to purchase our future. One day, perhaps, we will be in a position to buy them back."

"Where in London?"

"The collection sailed over some weeks ago, bound for the British Museum."

"And did it make the trip," asked Kendrick, "in the *Sea Lion,* perchance? A xebec? With red sails?"

"How did you know that?" asked Terranova.

Arabella rested her forehead against her hand.

"I was so *close*," she groaned.

"Take heart, *signorina*," said the prince. "When you return, you may go to see 'your' statue at the museum, on public days."

"Ha!" she said. "How little you apprehend my countrymen, Your Excellency! They would *never* place a double-horned statue on public display! It will be hidden from view; locked away in some closet, I'll be bound. As things stand now, it might as well be lying at the bottom of the Aegean!"

Terranova shrugged. "Perhaps. But it will have served its purpose. Besides, how many people would have seen it, I wonder, had it occupied a room in your house?"

"More than will see it at the museum! Why have you allowed me to waste my time in this fruitless fashion?"

"By the time you arrived, the bronze was safely on its way to England, and your government had generously responded with money and weapons for our cause. But you were so interesting. So very entertaining, that we wanted to play a little with you, and let you have the fun of thinking you were solving a mystery," said Terranova. "However, as His Highness has said, we did become concerned when the Austrians became involved. They tend to execute first, and ask questions later. Which rather defeats the purpose."

"And why have you told us all this? Isn't it supposed to be a state secret?"

"Yes," said the priest. "So now, if you have quite finished your lunch, we are going to have you all thrown from the cliffs."

"Pay no attention to him," said the prince with a smile.

"I hope that you will have the goodness to keep what we have told you today to yourselves," said Terranova. "But there is really not much danger of your informing our enemies, for they are England's enemies, also. That is all there is to know. Now will you *please* go home?"

"Certainly," said Arabella. "There is no point in staying, since the statue is gone to England."

As Terranova got up from the table, his three monks, who had dined in the servants' quarters, emerged from the palazzo to surround him once again, and the party moved off.

"I suppose those men are not really monks," said Arabella, watching them go.

"They are, actually," said the prince. "But they also function as bodyguards. Beneath their coarse robes you would find the honed bodies of athletes."

Arabella struggled to retrieve her wicked mind from under those rough robes, whence it had flown. As to which were the coarser, the garments or her thoughts, there was no reliable way to judge.

Charles and Kendrick having seen the pious retinue to the door, Arabella and Belinda found themselves alone on the terrace, in the glow of the sunset, with their prince and host, Benedetto Gandini-Palmadessola. The odor of ancient seas was borne in to them on the wind. And then Belinda, who had been very quiet all afternoon, gathered her dog onto her lap and spoke up at last.

"Are you really a widower?" she asked timidly.

"No," he replied, smiling down at his wedding ring. "I have a wonderful wife, and three beautiful children."

"Oh," she said. "I thought perhaps you . . . I mean, the way we've been, together, and, well, at that luncheon . . . in Pompeii . . ."

The prince regarded her with mild amusement. "I am a man," he said. "Not a lap dog."

Observing her sister's desolate expression, Arabella forgot their host's extreme generosity, forgot her own position, forgot everything, in fact, in the searing heat of her all-consuming anger.

"No?" she lashed out. "Our mistake, then! You must have spent three quarters of an hour in Belinda's lap that day, having spent the previous quarter of an hour lapping *at* her lap. And you most certainly *are* a dog, sir!"

He smiled again and shook his head. "You do not understand, because you are Protestants."

"Actually, we are not," said Belinda quietly.

"But you live in a Protestant country, so you *think* like Protestants. I am sorry if I have hurt your feelings," he told her, "but you see, we are different. Protestants must behave themselves at all times, while Catholics may do anything, *anything,* as long as they tell a priest about it afterwards. If we break the law, we are subject to legal punishment, of course. Otherwise we go home to our families with clean consciences."

"That's a neat system!"

"We like it."

At that moment, all the church bells began to ring for Vespers.

"If you will excuse me," said the prince, rising and kissing Belinda's hand in farewell, "I must attend confession."

NO PLACE LIKE ACKERMANN'S

A light snow, the first of the season, had sprinkled itself over the iron railings and gray stone doorsteps of Regency London. Arabella and Belinda had risen early (for them) and run out of the house, in order to lose no time in applying for news of the family scandal.

"I shall take the left side of the window," said Arabella, "and you take the right. Then we can work our way towards the middle without missing anything."

But in its reportage of the ways of the world, Ackermann's window, like great literature, is both highly instructive and "monstrous entertaining." So, despite their single-minded purpose, Arabella and Belinda soon found themselves diverted by a plethora of non-essential information: Napoleon had suffered heavy losses and been defeated at Moscau. Arabella had actually heard about this, because people had talked of little else wherever she went. But of course, she had not actually *seen* Napoleon, as she did here, clad as an infant in a cockade and diaper, weeping floods of tears and leading an army of human and horse skeletons through a blinding snowstorm.

Next to this was a picture of British soldiers and Hessian

mercenaries in America, setting fire to things and generally misbehaving themselves. It was most gratifying to find the princess regent, Belinda's particular enemy, presented as a fat, tantrum-throwing hussy. Of course, the regent himself was *always* depicted as bloated and repulsive, but Arabella never tired of seeing his caricature. It made her laugh, every time. And here was Lady Ribbonhat, too, with her enormous head and dwarfish physique, embroiled in some sort of contretemps concerning a mud puddle, a London constable, and a lot of cats.

The sisters reached the center of the window at the same moment, and found themselves looking at a double Beaumont family portrait. In the left frame, Arabella and Belinda were shewn, out of doors, this time, and with their clothes on, demurely walking along the street on either side of Charles. His arms were spread protectively behind them, in a pose vaguely reminiscent of that sketch of the Pan statue. But the frame on the right shewed the same scene from the rear, with Charles's hands lasciviously fondling his sisters' respective rumps. The caption read "Sibling Ribaldry."

Belinda groaned and clutched her muff to her breast. "Whatever shall we—"

"Ladies! Welcome home at last!"

Lord Egremont tipped his hat and smiled at them, as he rode past on his gleaming chestnut mount. Farther up the street, Lord Alvanley could be seen approaching on foot.

"Miss Beaumont! Miss Belinda! London has not been the same without you!" he cried. And he shook them each by the hand with evident satisfaction.

"Alleluia! The Miss Beaumonts have returned!" shouted the eccentric Mr. Beckford, waving from the window of his ornate carriage. "We'll have a house party at Fonthill in your honor!"

They were hailed by nearly a dozen well-known worthies in the space of five minutes. Nobody seemed to be taking the scandal very seriously. As the sisters proceeded from one establishment to another, the shopkeepers served them with as great a pleasure as ever, and Arabella finally professed herself glad to be home.

"Apparently, it was not a problem, then," she said as the carriage made its way back to Brompton Park. "We need not have taken the men with us after all."

"No; and Mr. Kendrick need not have risked his own life in fighting to save yours," Belinda replied . . . somewhat spitefully, Arabella thought.

"I am not saying I *wish* I had not taken them. I am merely observing that an overhasty misjudgment may produce unnecessary expenditure."

It was the last remark spoken by either of them until the carriage rolled in at the gate, where they encountered the rector's horse in their stable, and its owner in their smoking room, sharing the proverbial feedbag with Charles. The gentlemen were enjoying Mrs. Moly's *bredela,* small, Alsatian Christmas cakes, of which Arabella was particularly fond. But if Kendrick was slow to rise when his hostess made her entrance, she hardly remarked it.

"Bunny, my love," said Arabella, removing her gloves, "ring for more *bredela* and two more plates."

It was scarcely gone two hours since breakfast. But this was the orange and cinnamon variety and it was nearly Christmas and Mrs. Moly only made it once a year and, after all, 'twas the season.

"It is good to see you, Mr. Kendrick," said Arabella, "although I should have thought you would want to go home to Effing after such a long absence from it."

"I spent last night at my club," he said quietly, "in order to do some snooping. And I shall go home, presently, for I daresay you are sick of the sight of me. But I have some news about your bronze, that I thought you might be glad of."

Kendrick had traced the Herculaneum artifacts, listed at

the shipping office as "unspecified cargo," from the docks to a removal van, and from said van to their present location.

"Yes. I know," said Arabella, removing her bonnet and patting her hair in the large looking glass. "They have been locked away forever in the bowels of the British Museum." She dropped into a chair, with the force of conviction.

"Well, no, as a matter of fact. That was what *I* supposed, too, but I wanted to make certain. And I am glad that I checked, because your bronze, and all the other treasures, are currently reposing at Carlton House!"

"Oh, no!" she groaned. "I had nearly become reconciled to the failure of my endeavors. Eventually I might even have come to acknowledge some kind of lesson from this. But," she said, through gritted teeth, "that my wonderful statue should end up with the Great Git, at *Carlton House? This* is simply not to be borne!"

"Oh, that reminds me," said Charles, heedless of the emotional turbulence boiling up before him, "the incest scandal which you predicted with such dire forebodings has completely blown over. If you ask me, it never was a problem in the first place! Kendrick and I could have remained ensconced here at Lustings the whole time you were gone, eating whatchamacallems and staying safely out of harm's way! Of course, I shouldn't have found my Fortuna figurine," he admitted. "In any case, though, the scandal is quite over; everyone has forgotten about it."

"Not everyone," said Arabella, pouring out tea for Mr. Kendrick. "Bunny and I have just seen another cartoon about our family in Ackermann's window."

"Everyone who *matters,* I meant. *En garde!*"

He thrust a pasteboard rectangle under her nose, so close to her eyes that she could not read it at first.

"What is it?" she asked, pushing his hand away.

"Exactly what it looks like: an invitation to the snow ball."

"The what?"

"The regent's winder ball. D'you think I'd have had an invitation to that, if I had been judged a social leper? I am not going, of course."

"Oh!" said Belinda. "The *winter* ball, you mean!"

Upon the instant, Arabella felt a fountain of renewed hope and energy surging through her, expanding upward and outward in all directions, like the contents of a champagne bottle that is uncorked at a picnic, after a rough journey in a hackney carriage.

"Yes, Charles," she said. "You *will* go to the ball, and furthermore I shall go, too, with you as my escort!"

"But won't that revive the scandal?" asked Belinda, gnawing her nether lip.

"I shall be in disguise!"

"That is what you always say, and yet everyone always knows who you are."

"Oh, nonsense. You should come too, Bunny. The invitation says 'Charles Beaumont *and guests*.' A ball is just what you need, dear, to restore the pink to those adorable cheeks!"

It did not occur to her to include Reverend Kendrick in their party. Perhaps this was owing to the fact that he was sitting in the shadow cast by one of the bookcases, but the fact was, she had quite forgotten he was in the room at all.

Chapter 29

HIGH STAKES

Such a business over what to wear! Arabella, after much debate both inward and outward, decided upon the blue domino and Venetian *Carnivale* mask given her by Charles, via Prince Palmadessola. Underneath this, she styled herself a well-upholstered, matronly female, with a wild attitude and gray hair, for the regent was partial to such women. Belinda, from the notes and sketches she had made in Arabella's CIN, was stunning as Madame Murat, Queen of Naples. Charles flatly refused to wear any type of costume other than that of an elegant man about town paying a call upon his sovereign, for he planned on spending the evening at the gaming tables ... "And who, pray, is going to take a large blue rabbit for a serious opponent?"

The siblings had themselves announced as "the three graces," rather than use their proper names, and succeeded in descending the staircase and passing through the reception line without detection. But they had no sooner cleared the gauntlet than Belinda gave a strangled cry and fled from the room. Arabella was unable to discover the cause, despite craning her neck and attempting to see through eyeholes not designed for the purpose, until she was herself caught by the elbow.

"Hello, Miss Beaumont!" lisped Osvaldo, loud enough for half the room to hear him. "You see? I am as good as my word! I said I would find you again, and here I come! Where has your sister gone? I just catched a glimpse of her on the staircase, and now I cannot find her anywhere! She looks, how do you say, heavenward, tonight!"

"Do you know," said Arabella, "I believe I saw her leave through there," and with her fan she indicated a portal on the opposite side of the room from the door through which Belinda had actually gone.

Osvaldo took hasty leave and ran off, a hunter in quest of a Bunny. Charles, of course, had drifted away to the delights afforded by the card room, and Arabella was now alone, in hostile territory. If the regent should suspect who she really was . . . but he wouldn't. She peered with curiosity through her slanted eyeholes at the room in which she found herself, for Arabella had often heard about this chamber. It was the infamous Crimson Saloon, an interior space so relentlessly saturated with that color that the eye wearied of it almost at once.

The furnishings were upholstered in crimson damask. There were crimson draperies at the windows, crimson carpets on the floor, and the walls were covered in crimson velvet. The crimson chairs and sophas having been pushed back against the crimson walls for the occasion, people were dancing in the crimson void thus created. Gigantic pier glasses and gargantuan crystal chandeliers reflected and multiplied the effect of the crimson atmosphere, producing a feeling of faint queasiness in some; acute nausea in others.

Some relief could be found in staring up at the Florentine ceiling, which was decorated with mythical Florentine beasts in soothing tones of blue, orange, and yellow, and when the neck tired of straining upward, one might gaze at tables, supported by richly gilt griffin legs, and at the bric-a-brac that covered their surfaces. But these collections included vases, and sadly, many of these were . . . crimson.

Arabella, who much preferred a simple interior to a fussy one, soon found her senses overwhelmed. Hence, she failed to notice the elegant maharajah who stood before her, camouflaged as he was in crimson-colored silk, until he bowed.

"Thank you," she said, accepting the cup of crimson punch that he offered her. Then she lifted her eyes to his, and felt her heart fly into her mouth.

I can assure those readers unacquainted with this feeling that it is most uncomfortable at the best of times, but if it happens while one is drinking, it is also uncouth. Arabella choked, splattering crimson punch all over her exquisite gown of golden jacquard. (It had not, thankfully, spurted from her nose.) The rajah gave her his handkerchief to mop up, during which procedure she took the opportunity to glance at him again. His beard was false, his visage darkened with walnut oil, but he was a stunningly handsome creature all the same. At the third glance, she read the man's very soul in his eyes, and realized that he was reading her own just as clearly.

"Thank you," she breathed, handing back the handkerchief.

He touched his forehead, his lips, and his heart: Evidently he could not, or would not, speak. Then he bowed again and retreated backward, holding her with his gaze until he disappeared into the crowd.

Extraordinary! thought Arabella. Who *was* that fellow? And after a time she realized that the crimson color with which she was surrounded was starting to give her a headache.

Usually, when the great courtesan attended parties like this, she had a knot of admirers simpering about her, begging for a dance or for some small commission, such as fetching a bottle of *sal volatile* for her headache. But not this time. Perhaps her grandmotherly disguise had put them all off. Yes, surely that was it, for nobody knew who she was.

"Miss Beaumont! How delightful to see you again!"

It was Cecil Elliot, dressed as a cavalier. He had approached unseen, but now made her a most courteous bow, sweeping off his plumed hat with a flourish that would have done Charles I proud. Fortunately, this was executed within the limited range of her eyeholes, for it was a most magnificent bow, and not to be missed.

"How do you do," returned Arabella coldly. "If you will excuse me, I had rather not speak to you."

"Oh, dear! . . . But why ever not?"

"Because, Mr. Elliot, after you left the *Perseverance*, claiming you had been recalled to London, the captain informed us that you had requested the transfer yourself!"

"True enough."

"Well. I do not entertain the company of liars, if I can help it. Nor do I encourage the addresses of gentlemen who abandon their acquaintances in mid-ocean, without informing them of impending danger."

"Impending danger? To what do you refer?"

"I do not know what the danger was. Luckily, we escaped from it. But I naturally concluded there was something frightful in the offing, or you would not have left us as you did."

"Oh, Miss Beaumont! My darling Miss Beaumont! If I'd had reason to suspect that your safety was in any way compromised, please believe that I would not only have apprised you of it, but seen you personally delivered out of danger. That you should think me a coward is unendurable, and unjust in the extreme. I pray that you will allow me to acquit myself to you."

"Very well. I am listening."

"Not here. I am afraid that the details require complete privacy."

"Well, I cannot leave this place till I have got what I came for. Once that has been accomplished, I shall see what can be arranged."

"You are too good," he murmured, taking her hand and kissing it.

"How did you know it was me?" she asked, trying to hide her vexation.

"I should know you anywhere! Your voice, your walk, your carriage . . ."

"I came in a *hired* carriage on purpose, so as not to be recognized!"

"No," he said. "I was referring to the manner in which you carry yourself."

"Oh. Oh, dear; do you think the regent will recognize me, too?"

"Probably not—he has already had a skin full. I doubt he would recognize his own grandmother, by now."

"I am told that I resemble her, in this costume," said Arabella.

"I couldn't say. But you resemble *somebody's* grandmother, certainly. I hope your journey to Italy was a delightful one. Was your purpose achieved?"

"No, Mr. Elliot. I regret to say that it was not. Are you, perchance, familiar with the disposition of the regent's treasure cave?"

"If you are asking whether I know its location, yes."

"Ah! And would you be so good as to escort me thither?"

"Well, I *could,* but the room is locked and surmounted by an armed guard. I would therefore recommend you seek out the regent and request a personal tour."

As things turned out, she didn't need to seek very far. "Prinny," the great, fat git himself, walked unsteadily up to her as she was helping herself to lobster salad. He was merely complimentary at first, but rapidly proceeded from there to flagrant flirtation, and finally to an all-out amorous assault.

"Your Majesty," she said, fending him off with her fan.

"Like yourself, I am a great lover—" Here she had to turn her face away in order to avoid direct contact with his greasy lips.

"I was certain you would be, the moment I laid eyes upon you!" he gasped.

"No, no, sir! You mistake me! I was about to say, I am a great lover of *art!*"

"Really?" he asked, ceasing in his attempts to grope her. "I am, too!"

"So I have heard. I have also heard that you keep a most remarkable collection of antiquities, some of them decidedly . . ." and here she put her mouth against his ear and whispered *"improper!"*

"You have heard correctly, madam! Should you like to see them?"

"Oh, but I could not ask you to leave your guests!"

"Yes, you could. They can get on without me for a quarter of an hour. Elliot!"

Mr. Elliot glided over, a difficult trick when one is wearing cavalier boots, but he was what is popularly known as "a smooth customer."

"Highness?"

"Escort this lady and myself to the treasure cave. Elliot has the keys, you see," he explained. "An' a good thing, too. B'cause I don't think I could manage th' intricacies of a lock by m'self, jus' now."

Arabella was incensed! So, Elliot had had the key all along, and might easily have let her into the room! He was a scoundrel, and no mistake. But then she reflected that the place *was* guarded, after all, and if anyone had caught her in there, snooping around with Elliot's key, it could have been awkward for both of them.

Collectors are an odd breed. Sometimes they get carried away; they become a little too focused, and Arabella would have been the first to admit it. Take the regent, for example.

Here he was, in the company of a beautiful . . . well, of a woman who embodied his ideal type, and all he could do was fawn over his antiquities, which, now that she saw them, weren't even that impressive. There were a few amphorae, a couple of busts on pedestals; nothing in comparison to the collection at the Naples Museum, and no sign of her statue, either. She took off the mask, in order to be certain she had not missed it through want of a clear visual field. But then Prinny pulled a cord, and the draperies covering what she had taken for the back wall drew apart, revealing another room. This appeared to have been hacked from living stone, though it could not have been, of course, existing as it did inside Carlton House in the center of London. It looked convincing nevertheless, and was roughly paved to resemble an actual cave.

"Welcome to the masturbatory," leered Prinny.

Here was beauty, indeed: the most magnificent statues, sculptures, and artifacts ever conceived by gifted artists with sex on their minds. For a few moments, Arabella forgot why she was there, and wandered through the ranks and rows of artworks, thinking each piece she saw more dazzling than the one before it, until finally, she came face-to-face with "her" bronze: the double-phallused Pan statue.

He was striding forward on cloven hooves, arms extended behind him with the backs of his hands forward and the fingers spread, as if he were pushing through tall grasses or low shrubs. Every visible muscle and sinew on the slim torso was bursting with virility, and from between his hairy haunches the two great, curving phalli, one thick, one thin, seemed to be leading him on to glory. Thankfully, the garish paint with which he had once been coated had worn off, but the glass paste eyes remained in their sockets, supplied with those unsettling square pupils characteristic of the genus *Capra*. The rest of the eye, which was all iris, was the color of marmalade. Another pair of horns sprouted from the head, curving gracefully back over the shoulders, and the face . . . nay, the entire figure, wore an expression of concupiscent joy.

Thy rod and thy staff shall comfort me, thought Arabella.

"George . . . you in here?"

It was the Duke of Clarence, one of the regent's many brothers. He appeared to be even more inebriated than Prinny was, for Arabella saw him pause unsteadily before a statue of the drunken Bacchus, preparing to address it as a kinsman. His mistake was, perhaps, understandable.

"I'm over here, Willy," said the regent. "What d'you want?"

"'S'not for me, you know. I's my boy. Osvaldo."

His *boy*? It was true, then! Osvaldo really was Clarence's bastard! Not only that; the duke actually *acknowledged* the connection! Good God, what a family! If one hadn't known them for royals, it would have been natural to mistake the duke and his reigning brother for a couple of muck shifters on a bender.

"What's *he* want, then?" Prinny asked.

"Says you've got a friend of his in here (*hic*). An' he'd like to know if he might come in, too."

Horrors! If Osvaldo were to address her by name in front of her enemy, the regent would recall the incident—perhaps regrettable, perhaps not—when she had called him a fat git from the depths of an unfriendly crowd, nearly inciting a riot. If he were to discover her true identity now, she would be executed, probably, for impersonating the sort of woman he found attractive. But Elliot had caught Arabella's panicked glance.

"That would be me, sir," he said quickly. "Have I your permission to go out to him? And shall I escort the duke out as well? His Grace seems to be having some difficulty in locating the door."

Clarence was indeed reeling about, and bumping his head repeatedly against the wall. There was a very real danger of his knocking over one or more of the pedestals and thereby smashing a number of irreplaceable objects.

"By all means," muttered the regent. "Get him out of here."

Elliot tucked a hand beneath the duke's elbow and steered him toward the exit. As they passed Arabella, Elliot murmured, "You're on your own, now," for he had seen the regent looking at her in a particular way.

Here, the reader might think, Well, Arabella is a courtesan, after all! This is what she *does*. Yes, but courtesans also have feelings. And the feelings she entertained toward the regent were not cordial. Besides, she held to the tenet that no matter how low her *fortunes* might sink, she would never lower *herself*. Degradation of that sort would destroy all the pleasure Arabella had ever taken in her profession, and she would have to give it up to become a laundress or something. Should my gentleman readers fail to grasp this perspective, I must ask that they simply take it on faith. The ladies, I know, will readily comprehend it.

Given the choice between having it off with the regent and obtaining her bronze—if she thought she could get him to give it her, in other words—Arabella would have found herself in an agonizing quandary. But the problem facing her now was simply how to get out of the treasure cave without yielding up her person, and without insulting the temptingly insultable ruler of the realm.

"Thank you, Your Majesty, for allowing me to see this," she said, turning from the statue. "I shall never forget it as long as I live."

She put her mask back on and made for the door. He followed her, smiling.

"'Tis a lewd, crude cave of wonders, madam, is it not?"

"Yes, indeed! But what a shame that it all has to be kept locked away like this! The whole world should see it!"

"I beg to differ, madam. The subject material is far too shocking to be put on display to . . . just *anybody*."

They were nearly out of the room now.

"That is what I meant," said Arabella sadly. "It's a shame that it is so, is it not?" And she stepped lightly over the threshold, into the corridor and out of danger, whilst the regent was still forming his response.

"I can't agree with you there," he said. "If salacious imagery were socially acceptable, it wouldn't be any fun."

He followed her past the gaming tables, where, as luck would have it, Charles was just sitting down to another game.

"Arabella!" he called to her. "I say, I'm a bit short of ready. Lots of coves in here owe me money, though. Would you lend me a fiver? Just till tomorrow?"

She scowled, shaking her head, and wouldn't the odious Osvaldo just *have* to pick that moment to intercede?

"Here, Beaumont; I'll stand you to a twenty, if you like. Miss Beaumont, I still have not discovered the whereabouts of your sister!"

The two names she had just been called buzzed around the regent's bleary brain like a pair of randy wasps: Beaumont . . . Arabella . . . Arabella . . . Beaumont.

One of the chief perils of this prince was that with his legendary pride and selfishness, his childish outbursts of weeping when things failed to go his way, his ruinously expensive bad taste and his drunken default state, there was a tendency to think him stupid. Because intelligent persons do not generally behave in this fashion. But what people often failed to realize was that all this self-absorbed, self-indulgent behavior was mere padding for an icy core, consisting of an essentially suspicious nature, a steely refusal to be taken advantage of, and the determination to be revenged upon his enemies. Even at his most soused, the regent was able to retain a watchful cunning that, as Mrs. Janks liked to put it, "would do a viper proud."

Now the two names by which his charming companion had been addressed continued to buzz: Miss Beaumont . . . Arabella . . . Miss Arabella Beaumont. He had it, at last. And then he turned toward her a look of sneering contempt.

" 'Tis a pity," he said in a voice that belied this sentiment. "I daresay I would not have slept with you, madam; no self-respecting man wants to go where dogs have been." He looked meaningfully at Charles, who had the decency to blush. "But we might at least have been friends, had you not insulted me so coarsely in the street last year."

From across the room, Cecil Elliot divined that something unpleasant was afoot, and unobtrusively rejoined them.

"Remove your mask!" snarled the regent. For truth to tell, though he'd connected Arabella with the shouted insult, he felt there was something more. If he could just . . . get his mind to focus.

She took it off.

"Oh, yes." It was all coming back to him now. "The murderess. Had a clever lawyer get you off. In more ways than one, I'll be bound!"

Arabella curtseyed. "Actually, they found the real murderer, Your Majesty."

"Ha! Some poor blighter unable to prove where he was on the night in question."

"Well, he actually confessed."

"People will say anything under torture. Guards, throw her out."

"Sir!" called Charles, who for a wonder was not in his cups. "Might I ask you to join me in a game of whist? I thought perhaps we could play for your entire Roman antiquities collection."

Quite on the spur of the moment, Charles had seen his

chance to do something helpful for somebody else, and so re-live the agreeable feeling of being adored and appreciated.

The regent turned to Elliot. "Who is this dog?" For al-though he'd been able to identify Charles with the incest scandal a moment ago, Prinny had already forgotten who he was, or wished it to appear that way for reasons of his own.

"Charles Beaumont, Majesty," Elliot replied, and then whispered in the royal ear: "Addicted to gaming. Always loses."

His information was woefully out of date for once.

"Does the fellow have anything worth staking, then?"

"No, sire, but his sister does."

The palace guard arrived, to usher Arabella out and away.

"Wait," said Prinny. "On second thought, leave her here a moment. . . . Madam, your brother wishes to play for high stakes, indeed. But he has no collateral, it seems, and I be-lieve that you do."

It took Arabella a few moments to find her voice, aston-ished as she was by her brother's sudden and highly unchar-acteristic act of selflessness. Nor did she stop to consider that Charles, now, had plenty of his own money to put up if he chose. But it is quite possible, reader, that the regent would still have insisted on shifting the risk to Arabella. In fact, I am almost certain that he would have.

"Ask what you will of me, sir," she said.

"Very well; you have a handsome barouche, with six mag-nificent horses. I'll have those, before witnesses. Also . . . your pretty little manor house, which I shall have gutted and re-fitted. And . . . if Beaumont loses, he is banished for life."

At last, Arabella found that she had reached the limit of what she was willing to sacrifice for the statue. She did not want to risk losing her home, even though it meant not hav-ing to see Charles again for a very long time. But to back out would be poor showmanship. Besides, she had not been given the opportunity to do so.

"Get her out of here, Elliot. And, madam, if you dare to gate crash one of my parties again, or to so much as set foot in this house, I shall have you disposed of. Quietly, efficiently, and permanently."

This was the closest Arabella had yet come to getting her bronze. She might actually achieve it at last. But it went deeply against the grain to meekly allow someone to insult her and to offer no reply.

"You need have no worries on *that* account!"

"Oh, I'm not worried. I'm the king, or as good as. You're a whore."

" . . . Or as good as," she replied as she was being led away, "and what I was going to say before you interrupted me, was that your house is the ugliest, most ostentatious monument to bad taste as ever was seen, and the sooner it is torn down the better!"

As they proceeded to Lustings in the hired carriage, Arabella thanked Elliot a thousand times for his intercession and assistance.

"Am I forgiven, then?"

"Oh, no! I am still angry about your shipboard behavior. But as I promised to give you a full hearing, you shall have a chance to exonerate yourself."

"Well, you see—"

"Not here. Wait until we reach Lustings, and are comfortable before a fire, with liquid encouragement close at hand."

The hour was late, or rather, early, and the servants were all fast asleep. It would have been most cruel to rouse anyone to build a fire at that hour. But such a dank chill permeated the downstairs apartments that there could be no question of holding a tête-à-tête there. So Arabella took Elliot up to her room, where Doyle, she knew, had lit a fire before retiring. The embers still glowed faintly in the grate, and the room was still warm.

"I hope you do not mind the informality," said Arabella, pouring out two generous glasses of brandy. "But this really is the most comfortable place in the house at the moment, and we shan't be disturbed here."

They sat before the embers, in Arabella's blue and gold armchairs, and Mr. Elliot told her the circumstances under which he had been obliged to leave her so suddenly. Originally, he had been bound for Naples as the Herculaneum collection's London escort. One attempt to steal it having been made already, it was Elliot's job to ensure that the valuable gift arrived safely at its intended destination.

"But I made rather a late start. The regent had a thousand little things that wanted doing, and I, apparently, was the only one who could do them to his satisfaction."

Elliot's face, turned toward Arabella, looked sculpted and beautifully noble in the pale light of early morning. His nose, particularly. "If you recall, Miss Beaumont, I was forever on deck, searching the sea with my spyglass."

"Yes; I had supposed you to be indulging an idle curiosity."

"That is what I wanted you to think. But I was looking for the *Sea Lion,* which carried the treasure, and I spotted her leaving at last, just as we were on the point of arriving. Apparently, she had made a late start, as well. So I had the captain signal the other ship, got my things together, and made my good-byes to you . . . I had to lie about who had signaled whom, for you'd have demanded an explanation had I told the truth, and the explanation at that time was not mine to give. Besides," he added with a wicked smile, "I knew that you were chasing the statue, and naturally I would not want to assist a competitor!"

"But how did you know I wanted the statue? I never told you so!"

"No; Charles did. But do not be vexed with me, Miss Beaumont; I found you so charming that I took precautions to secure your safety, in order to ensure your safe return, and have the chance of meeting up with you again."

"What do you mean?"

"I let it be known in certain circles that you were the regent's mistress."

The outer door creaked, faintly, and they both jumped as it began slowly to open. After a moment, a cat appeared, purring its approval at finding a bit of a fire and two warm and waiting laps.

"What a handsome animal," said Elliot, scratching Rooney behind the ears. "I must confess myself very partial to cats."

Arabella had known about the feline's continued tenancy from Mrs. Janks's letters, and was somewhat favorably disposed toward him, due to his reported interactions with Lady Ribbonhat. But she had informed the staff in no uncertain terms that the animal was to remain belowstairs at all times. Hence, she was on the point of throwing Rooney back out into the passage when she was checked by Elliot's words. Nor did she display any negative reaction when the cat sprang onto her lap and made itself at home there.

"I wish you could see what I am seeing," said Elliot with a smile. "'Cat and Courtesan, by Firelight.' The color of his fur complements your own hair most wonderfully! Is that why you got him?"

"No," said Arabella truthfully. "No. It was a complete coincidence."

The cock crowed from the top of the henhouse, and Elliot stood up, setting his glass on the mantel.

"Thank you for hearing me out, Miss Beaumont. I hope I am forgiven now?"

"Of course," she replied, rising, too, and placing her hands in his. "And as for the gallant services you performed on my behalf tonight, or, I should say, last night, I shall be forever in your debt."

"Is that so?" he asked, pulling her hands to his breast, so that the rest of her body was obliged to come, too. "An agreeable arrangement, indeed! This is one debt which I shall be most peremptory about collecting!"

She tilted her head slightly, so that Elliot could more easily reach her mouth and throat, and he inclined forward; was on the point of kissing her, in fact, when he evidently thought better of it and drew back.

"No," he said. "Not now. Not until I have more time to spend with you. The regent is expecting my return, and as we know, he is a most exacting prince."

"Do not you mean 'exasperating'?" grumbled Arabella.

"Yes. That, too."

Chapter 30

LETTING GO

There seemed little point now in going to bed, so Arabella changed her clothes and went downstairs, where she found Charles in the breakfast room, drinking brandy.

"You're up early," she observed.

"I haven't been to sleep."

"Where is my statue?"

Charles ran his fingers repeatedly through his hair, a habit with him when he was distraught, and she noticed how red his eyes were.

"Don't tell me you failed to win it!"

"Oh, I won it, all right! I won the whole bloody lot . . ."

"Thank goodness!"

" . . . In the *first* game. By the fifth, I had lost everything! Don't nag me; I am quite wretched enough!"

The long and short of it was, after losing everything, Charles had been expelled from Carlton House. His name had been struck from the guest list forever, and no less a personage than the regent's own social secretary had warned him against ever attempting to return.

"I don't mind *that* so much," said Charles, "for I was never in my life invited to a more hideous building! What I *do* mind is losing my knack! I failed to win so much as a far-thing after that first game! All my Italian winnings! Every-thing I have won since coming home! Gone! Finished! I shall never win again! And it's all your fault!"

"*My* fault?"

"Fortuna only works for the benefit of her owner. When I gambled for someone else I broke the charm."

"How do you know that?"

"Stands to reason: I'd never placed a bet for anyone else before. Then I did, and my luck evaporated! Do you see? It's because I did you a favor, Bell! I shall never do anybody a favor again, so long as I live!"

Belinda's fan lay on the floor where she had dropped it on coming in the previous evening. Arabella picked it up and began fanning herself, furiously, as she paced about the room.

"I have lost my house," she said to herself. "Lustings. I have lost Lustings." It was not registering, so she tried the next thing down. "My wonderful parchment ponies!" That she could comprehend. "A sad loss, indeed! Also a carriage. The regent did not specify *which* carriage, so I shall give him the least of those."

"He did, actually," said Charles.

"What?"

"The regent. He said he wanted the barouche."

"Oh, damn, damn! Well, he banished you for life, anyway, and that is some comfort. Of course, you will be free to come back after the regent dies, and his present mode of living cer-tainly augurs well for an early death. But I imagine I shall be free of you for at least another ten years."

"Bell . . ."

"Don't grumble, Toby; I can dispatch boxes of English co-mestibles to Marggrabowa, or wherever you will be staying, in the meantime, but perhaps you will not require it. Prussian food is reputed to be as bad as our own."

"If you will let me get a word in? Banishment was a condition pertaining to the first game only. And, as I said, I *won* that one."

"What? My one consolation is denied me, then? Bugger! To think that you should have lost everything *but* your right to remain in this country! It is *too* unfair!"

"Yes. Everything but that, *and* your blasted property!"

"What?"

"*I* am the one who suffers injustice from the fates, not you! You get everything you want, and I am left to make my way through life without Fortuna's blessing!"

"What are you saying, Charles?"

"Oh! So now it's 'Charles,' is it? Aye, you'll keep your house and your horses, and have your statue, too! Not to mention the rest of the bloody regent's bloody toss-off toys! They'll be delivered sometime this bloody afternoon."

"But . . . how . . . ?"

"Kendrick made me keep those things back after the first game. For all subsequent games, I had to put up my own collateral, and withdraw yours."

"Kendrick? Was *he* there?"

"What are you playing at?" growled Charles, pouring another drink. "You were talking to him!"

"But I never saw him, I tell you!"

"Arabella. *I* saw him bringing you punch!"

She blinked. "Do you mean, *he* was the rajah?"

"How could you not have known him?" Charles's mouth twisted in a sour grin. "But there, I am not surprised. You never have known him, have you?"

She simply gaped, for once at a loss.

"Kendrick had an invitation, too. Otherwise he would not have been there to look after your interests, because *you* never thought to invite him. I wish that he had not attended," said Charles, crossing to the sideboard for another bottle. "It would have served you right!"

Arabella sat down abruptly, for all the strength had gone out of her knees. Charles, with a rare display of decency, handed her a drink.

" 'S a shame," he said quietly. "The poor chap bends over backwards to see that you have everything you want. Yet for all the attention you pay him, he might just as well be dead."

By mid-morning, the snow had ceased to fall, and a watery winter sun shone out feebly through the leaden clouds as Reverend Kendrick dragged himself up his own front steps. He had paid an early call on the Bishop of Bramblehurst, and was now weary, as well as heartsick, for Kendrick, too, had forgone sleep following the revels at Carlton House.

His position was untenable. He saw that now. No matter what he said or did, Arabella would never think of him as he thought of her. He had forgone sleep, sacrificed solitary amusements, and devoted his heart and soul to procure for her the object that she currently prized above all others. She had never acknowledged it. Arabella shewed him less civility now than she had when they were children.

And following her indifference over the sword fight in which he might easily have lost his life, Kendrick's hopelessness had turned to a positive dislike of Arabella. The very sound of her voice made him ill, for a time. He had soon sorted that out, though, realizing that it was himself he disliked, the way he had acted toward her. Arabella was merely being Arabella, but Kendrick had lost his self-respect, and he simply could not go on. There was but one way out.

The rector sat down and began a letter to Belinda, thinking it would be kinder if her sister broke the news. Even now, he was thinking of Arabella; trying to spare her pain. He would post-date the missive, leaving instructions for its delivery after he was . . . gone. For if she should learn of the desperate act he contemplated, she might attempt to stop him. Or, worse yet, she might not.

*   *   *

The crates arrived at last, and Arabella knew a few hours of genuine joy, as she unwrapped, admired, and stroked the former contents of the royal masturbatory. Was there ever such beauty? Such life in mineral form? But in the end she was obliged to totter off early to bed, utterly exhausted from a lack of sleep and too much heartfelt excitement. And on the following day, she bid adieu to it all, when a team of specialists came to the house, to carefully pack up the artifacts once again. Arabella observed from her window as the crates were loaded onto carts, pressing a handkerchief to her face to staunch the tears. Her heart began to beat wildly as she watched the carts pass down the drive; she nearly ran out and stopped them. But in the end, she controlled her impulse, and allowed the precious cargo to proceed back to Naples, where Prince Palmadessola waited to receive it.

She obtained some pious satisfaction from having included the entire masturbatory collection, including pieces that had been in England for more than a century. Not all of it had come from Herculaneum, but it was all Italian, and Arabella had wanted to do the right thing.

Snow had started to fall again. Rooney, who had been gazing at it out one of the other windows, looked round when he heard Arabella sniffling, and leapt to the floor, that he might rub himself against her ankles. She scooped him up and sat down at her desk, simultaneously stroking his fur and composing a letter to Lady Ribbonhat:

> *Dearest Madam,*
> *Thank you so much for the gift of this*
> *wonderful cat, who makes himself more useful and*
> *agreeable with every day that passes. I must*
> *confess I have grown quite attached to Rooney, as*
> *we call him, and he has grown quite inordinately*

fond of us! How you were ever able to part with
him is beyond my comprehension, but I am very
glad that you managed to find a way to do so.

Thank you, also, for sending along a ream of
your personal stationery, which, you may have
noticed, I have used to write you this letter. The
duke keeps your family's seal in my library desk,
for any chance correspondence he happens to write
while staying here, so I have everything ready to
hand. What fun I shall have, writing to the
various people you know, and pretending to
be you!

"Hello!" Belinda put her head round the open door, setting off, as she did so, the sweet tintinnabulation of little
bells. Glancing swiftly up, she was amazed to see one of the
ancient Roman, poly-phallused ringers looking for all the
world as though it had never hung anywhere else.

"Bell! You pledged to return everything!"

"I also promised Mr. Soane that he should have his marbles," said Arabella. "And I *had* to keep *something* for myself, Bunny. With over two dozen *tintinnabula* in the
collection, I scarcely think that one will be missed. What may
I do for you?"

"Well," said Belinda. "I was only looking in to see if I might
cheer you up, but you don't appear to require my help."

"Oh, but I *do*, though!" cried Arabella, rising to draw her
into the room. "I am very much in the doldrums today,
thinking of all the trouble I took over nothing! The truth is, I
am not a very good sleuth, Bunny. Everything had to be explained to me by people who had known what was happening all along."

"Only because the thieves had a head start," said Belinda.

"I am certain that you would have found the statue, right enough, had we already been in Italy when it first went missing. I don't know why you are being so hard on yourself; you went in search of your bronze, and you found it! Despite the fact that the whole affair was wrapped up in politics, you *found* it. You won!"

"Yes," said Arabella. "Yes, I did, didn't I?"

"And it was very good of you to go and see about the smuggler's widow."

"Well, I didn't. When I went out to the house to give her some money, I found her in the midst of an enormous celebration. It seems the entire community had hated her husband, and now they were helping her enjoy her new freedom. She didn't require any help, as far as I could see."

"But you made an attempt," said her sister, "and that was a kindly gesture. Now, come and see how I have been spending the morning."

Accordingly, Belinda led the way to the breakfast room table, where, in an enormous bowl of Venetian glass, she had re-created the ruins of an ancient Pompeian garden, in miniature.

"Look!" she said, handing Arabella a tiny figure. "I have made the Pan statue in modeling clay!"

Arabella smiled. "Oh, Bunny, this is exquisite!"

"It makes a nice souvenir of our trip, since we were never able to paint any pictures. This is even better, I think. Look at the tiny cypresses!"

"Won't they outgrow the bowl?"

"Eventually. But cypresses grow very slowly. Do you know what I think?" she asked, turning to Arabella. "I think that for a foreigner who didn't speak the language, you did a jolly good job of sleuthing! In fact . . . you were superb!"

"Was I?"

"Oh! but-a yes!" cried Belinda, kissing her fingertips in the Italian manner.

"Even though I was not able to solve the mystery using my brains?"

"What does that matter? You got your statue in the end, restored it to the rightful owner, ate delicious food, rode out a scandal, experienced the past in a way very few people ever have, saw beautiful things, and nearly got yourself killed! I would call that a very grand adventure indeed!"

"Thank you, Bunny!" said Arabella, embracing her. "You are better than a tonic! . . . And what of you?"

"Well," she said softly. "I had an adventure, too. I fell in love with an old man, who turned into a handsome prince, who turned out to be not so much in love with me as I thought he was."

"And you're bearing up remarkably well!" said Arabella, putting her arm round Belinda's shoulders. "Now we can each of us boast of a great, lost love in our past, which is bound to strengthen our characters! Look at the snow! Let us go out of doors to admire it firsthand. I suddenly feel like ruminating on the successful conclusion of our great adventure, now that I at last know everything!"

But Arabella did *not* know everything, even then. For Belinda had a letter secreted in the bodice of her gown, and took great care that it should not crackle when she moved. Should you like to hear what it said? Some of you would, I know. And the rest of you, those who believe that mush belongs upon the breakfast table inside a bowl, rather than upon the pages of a letter inside a young lady's gown, may disregard this next part. Please feel free to proceed into the garden with the Beaumont sisters. The rest of us will meet you out there.

My dearest Belinda,

I cannot blame you if you destroy this letter without reading it, but I hope—I pray—that you will not do that until you are apprised of my feelings. I have treated you unforgivably, I know. I am a dog! A villain! A monster! But I hope you will believe me when I tell you that I thought I was doing what was right for both of us. I felt certain of it, right up to the day you left. And then my carefully built card house came crashing down upon my head! You are gone! Gone from me! How shall I bear this? For I am certain you will have guessed by now, my darling, that I have fallen in love with you.

We have, true enough, many obstacles in our way. I am a married man, a father, a prince, and a Catholic. A vast ocean lies between our countries. But do you know what I am doing? Do you? In my mind I am standing just now upon one of those little tables out on the terrace at the villa, and I can see your darling head, far across the water, shining above all these problems. One day, cara mia, we shall be together. I feel this with my heart, and I believe it, in my soul.

I hope that you will write to me now and then, so that I may keep your letters in a secret place and from them draw the strength of your love, when I am close to despair. I say that without even knowing whether your feelings have survived my brutal, inexcusable behavior. But love has made me an optimist: I feel that you must love me

*again, if I prostrate myself before you and beseech
your forgiveness. And I do. Please, Belinda, my
darling, my life! Can you forgive me?*

Yours <u>alone</u>,
Detto

*P.S. I still have those bed socks which you
knitted for me. I never wear them, because I never
want to wear them out: They are the only things
of yours which I have, hence they are very
precious. Besides, they look like penises. How
would I ever explain them to my wife?*

So very touching. All right, now let us join the others, for I want to tell you about a thought that is going round and round inside Belinda's head just now, like a song, while she is speaking and doing other things. It is not the least bit irritating, this thought, and were it a song indeed, one should be able to listen to it all day and never tire of it. Not if one were Belinda, anyway. Here it is, just as she conceived it:

"*Yours <u>alone</u>!*" He has underscored 'alone'!"

The sisters sat opposite one another in the pergola, appropriately attired, breathing in the scents of snow and the slumbering garden. Cara the greyhound had accompanied them, wearing the bulky yellow shell that Belinda had crocheted for her. When Arabella glanced down at the long-nosed creature with the round, yellow body, the wind blowing her ears forward into stiff points, she could not help laughing.

"Cara looks like an anemic armadillo!"

"I do not know what that is, but you may laugh all you like," said Belinda calmly. "She is warm and insulated, which is all that matters."

"Do you know, I was instructed not to tell you this, Bunny, but I believe that I shall, anyway. Cara was not a gift from Charles, after all."

"I know," she said, straightening with pride. "My prince gave her to me."

Arabella was astounded. "How did you guess?" she asked.

"Because of her name. 'Cara' was what he used to call *me*. Now, whenever I address my pet as 'Beloved,' I am really speaking to *him*."

"Bunny, dearest, this man, formerly known as Bergamini, may be a prince, and patron of an important museum. He may be risking his life for his country, which is very brave and noble of him, and we both know that he possesses an exquisite sense of aesthetics. But insofar as you, personally, are concerned, he is nothing but a cad."

"That is your opinion," said Belinda. "It is not mine."

"Hmm. In short, I suppose I dislike this . . . this 'Prince Palma-desolate' in much the same way that *you* dislike the late Oliver Wedge."

"No," said Belinda, wearing her serenity like a halo. "The prince has never tried to kill me. And he is still alive. It is not the same at all."

Arabella was silent for so long that Belinda supposed her to be sulking.

"Do you know," she said brightly, "this spot puts me in mind of the meditation grove at the Villa Belvedere. Do you remember? The vista from here is completely different, though, of course."

Arabella made no reply.

"I am sorry that you were unable to keep your statue, Bell. But you have made a noble, selfless gesture in returning it to Professor Bergamini. I mean, to Detto—to Prince Palmadessola. He will know how to make it available to at least some of the public, until the rest of the public becomes sophisticated enough to look at art without feeling shocked. At least *you* got to see it, and we all enjoyed a splendid holiday."

Arabella's eyes were dreamy. Her thoughts seemed fixed elsewhere.

"Bell."

"Hmmm? Sorry, dear. I'm just . . ."

"Are you fretting about the money you lost on the statue?"

"No, not really."

"Then why are you so unfocused?"

"Perhaps it is because I am engaged to go riding with Mr. Elliot tomorrow."

"Oh! I am glad! Mr. Elliot is a nice man. At what time do you expect him?"

"He keeps a very busy schedule, so we shall need to make an early start. He is coming over tonight, in fact, at about eleven."

"O-ho!" said Belinda. "*Now* I perceive why you have been so inattentive! That is quite . . . Bell . . . ?"

But Arabella had drifted off again. The gray-green eyes rested on a spot just past Belinda's right ear, and Belinda had a sudden feeling that Bell was looking at someone who was staring at them, from behind.

"Do you know, Bunny," said Arabella. "I believe you were right, after all."

Belinda half-turned, expecting to see the gardener, or Mrs. Janks with the tea tray, or almost anyone at all but whom she in fact did see: the great god Pan emerging from the shrubbery, all hard and excited.

From where she was sitting, Belinda could almost imagine herself about to be ravished.